A Dangerous Lie

by

Ellen Shapiro

INDIES UNITED PUBLISHING HOUSE, LLC

Paperback: 978-1-64456-764-7
Kindle: 978-1-64456-765-4
ePub: 978-1-64456-766-1

Library of Congress Control Number: 2024918740

INDIES UNITED PUBLISHING HOUSE, LLC
P.O. BOX 3071
QUINCY, IL 62305-3071

Other Novels by Ellen Shapiro

TRACEY MARKS MYSTERY SERIES

Looking for Laura

Secrets Can Kill

Missing or Dead

Memory of Murder

MADDIE LANDON MYSTERY SERIES

Buried in the Attic

Murder on Drake Street

In loving memory of my brother, Arthur Shapiro.

CHAPTER 1

The sign on my office door read *Maddie Landon, Private Investigator*. I was just shutting down my computer, getting ready to leave for the day, when I heard the door open and a voice shouting, "Maddie, are you here?" And then footsteps moving quickly toward me.

I would have known that voice anywhere, but I was totally surprised to see her standing in my office. Samantha looked exactly the same, except her wavy shoulder-length brown hair now had streaks of green instead of purple. Her seventeen-year-old face was sprinkled with freckles around her small nose.

"Maddie, you have to help him. He didn't rape her. I know he didn't."

"*Whoa*, slow down." I hadn't seen Samantha since I found her biological parents more than a year ago. It was complicated to say the least. The last time I saw Sam, the family was in therapy trying to get their lives back together.

"Sit and start from the beginning."

"You remember I go to the Kinley Private school here in Manhattan. Well, Jason also goes to Kinley except he's there on a scholarship. I know he would never rape anyone."

"Sam, you have to calm down and tell me what happened slowly."

"This girl in my school, Mia Franklin was raped, and she accused Jason. I don't know why she would say that but she's lying. I know she's lying. Jason is my best friend and he would never hurt anyone."

"Where is Jason now?"

"He's home. His mother borrowed money to pay his bail."

"Does he have a lawyer?"

"Yes, but he's a lawyer you don't have to pay."

"You mean a public defender. How old is Jason?"

"Seventeen."

"And how old is the girl he allegedly raped?"

"I'm not sure. None of this matters since he didn't do it."

"Sam, it's not that simple. I wish it were. First, even if I wanted to take the case, I can't do it without his parents' consent."

"It's only his mother and she doesn't have any money. I could pay you. I could help you with the investigation and whatever money I earn you can keep."

"That would be nice, but unfortunately you can't be involved. You might compromise the case and it could be dangerous."

"I don't care."

"You may not, but I do, and your parents might have something to say about it. How are things at home?"

"Okay."

"How are you getting along with your father?"

"I'd rather not talk about it," she said, but I could tell by her clenched jaw she wasn't telling me the truth. When Sam found out what her father had done, she was so angry she didn't want to live in the same house with him. Who could blame her. When Sam's birth mother decided to give

Sam up for adoption, Sam's father deceptively adopted Sam without her birth mother's knowledge. It all came out eventually, the father's affair with Sam's birth mother and Sam learning that all these years later she was living with her natural father. Unfortunately for Sam, I also learned that her birth mother was murdered a few months after Sam was born.

"Listen, Sam. Everything is going to be fine. Have Jason's mother call me. Will you do that?"

"I gotta go."

Typical Sam. When Sam first came to me to search for her biological parents, I wasn't prepared to deal with a teenager as a client. I had no experience with teenagers and Sam was like a bull in a china shop. She never said hello or goodbye, whether on the phone or in person. But over time she grew on me. Maybe I just got used to her abruptness or perhaps it was because we were both adopted. In spite of the fact that Sam could be a pain in the neck, there was something very endearing about her that I couldn't ignore.

When she left my office, I was curious about this boy Jason and why the police arrested him. What evidence did the police have? Right now there wasn't anything I could do until I heard from Jason's mother.

I quickly locked up my office since I was running late for my therapy session with Dr. Goldberg.

CHAPTER 2

Sitting in my therapist's waiting room, the walls felt as if they were closing in on me. I recently met my biological father and I would be lying if I said it was a tearful reunion. I never had any intentions of looking for my birth parents. Why would I? For thirty-seven years I was sure they never wanted me.

"Maddie, come in."

Dr. Goldberg reminds me of someone's grandmother. She is short with gray hair and her clothes are matronly looking. Her calming voice puts me at ease and the office always smells of lilacs. I wonder if she sprays it with air freshener.

I sat down in my usual spot, a gray couch opposite Dr. Goldberg who sits in a low back beige upholstered chair. Between us is a small coffee table with a box of tissues on it. Looking at the box I wonder how many patients have cried while spilling out their life story.

"It's been a while since we last met," Dr. Goldberg said. "What's going on?"

"Now that I finally met my birth father, I don't know how I feel," I said, my leg shaking.

"That's not unusual. You never knew him. Besides the fact that he's your biological father, you have no emotional connection to him. If you choose to have a relationship, it's going to take time."

"I wish I never read the letter my parents left me."

"Were you doing it for them or for yourself?"

"Of course it was for them. I loved them and that was their wishes, not mine," I said, a little too forcefully.

"Do you think there might have been some part of you that wanted to know why your birth parents gave you up for adoption, and the letter was just the impetus to seek them out?"

"Why would I. They abandoned me. For all I know, they were junkies."

"Maybe that's what you needed to believe. Sometimes we tell ourselves all sorts of things to keep from being hurt. Is it possible when you read that letter it gave you the freedom to do what you always wanted, to search for your biological parents?"

"I never looked at it that way."

"Why don't you tell me what it was like meeting your birth father?"

"We met in the hotel lobby where he and his wife Jennifer were staying. I was relieved she wasn't with him when I got there."

"Do you know why she wasn't with your father?"

"He thought I'd be more comfortable if it was just the two of us since it was our first time meeting."

"It sounds like he was taking your feelings into account."

"I guess." I didn't say anything for a while. I finally said, "We went into the hotel lounge and talked."

"Can you tell me about your conversation?"

"He told me about his life growing up in Philadelphia and his relationship with my biological mother."

"How did that make you feel?"

"I was a little uncomfortable hearing him talk about her. When I had called him out of the blue, he was angry that he never knew what happened to Lydia, my mother, and that he had no say in my adoption. It was difficult listening as he was telling me how he felt not knowing of my existence."

"That must have been hard for you to hear."

"I'd rather not talk about it now."

"We can talk about something else, but at some point, you need to confront those feelings. Did you tell him anything about yourself?"

"Just what I do as a private investigator and the kind of cases I get involved in."

"So nothing personal?"

"Can we change the subject?"

"How are things going with Jesse?"

"What do you mean?"

"Have you made any decision about moving in with him?"

"It weighs on my mind but that's as far as it goes."

"You can use fear as a crutch but that won't help you move forward. You have to decide what's more important, your relationship or holding on to the fear. It's that simple. There is no in between."

I was glad when the session finally ended. My head felt as if it was going to explode. I knew Dr. Goldberg was right, but I knew from my past that at any moment you can lose everything.

I parked my car in the garage and took the elevator up to my apartment, my home on the Upper West Side of Manhattan for the past thirteen years. The Upper West Side is an affluent, primarily residential area bordered by Central Park and Riverside Park. It is known for Lincoln Center and its wonderful museums, including the Metropolitan Museum of Art.

After changing into my boxer shorts and an oversized T-shirt, I opened my refrigerator in search of something to eat for dinner. I pulled out some leftovers and made a salad. Thankfully, the bottle of Cabernet Sauvignon on the counter was still half full. As I was pouring myself a glass, I heard my phone ringing from inside my backpack.

"Hey, you. I was just about to take a sip of my wine," I said to Jesse.

"Far be it for me to stand between a lady and her wine."

"Cute. You definitely know me."

Jesse is also a private investigator. I have my own firm and Jesse works for two criminal attorneys in Connecticut.

"Are you going crazy without a case to keep you busy?"

"Actually, for the moment it's nice, though I'm not sure how long that will last. You know how I thrive on the excitement when I'm involved in an investigation. There is a possibility I might have something. It's a wait-and-see situation," I said.

"If we got married, I'd have to take you in sickness and in health," Jesse said, chuckling.

"Good to know."

"Do you want to tell me about it?"

"There's not much to tell at the moment. Samantha made a surprise visit to my office, all upset about a friend of hers from school that was accused of raping a girl. She wants me to help him since she's convinced he didn't do it. He's there on a scholarship and according to Sam, the mother has no money."

"Do you plan on taking the case if the mother contacts you?"

"I haven't made any decisions."

"It could be interesting."

"We'll see."

"I was thinking you could drive up to my place this weekend?" Jesse lives in Chester, Connecticut, a small rural town on the Connecticut River with lots of charm and cute little shops and restaurants. We normally take turns on the weekends, but with the weather being fairly warm for September, it would be nice to take advantage of Jesse's outdoor grill and patio.

"If you're still at work when I get there, you can find me out back relaxing with a glass of your finest wine. On second thought, maybe I should stop at the wine store in town," I said.

"Wiseass. Sleep tight."

"And you do the same."

The nightmare is always the same. I'm driving in the car with my parents. It's late at night and it's raining. My father told me we're going on a surprise trip. I was excited. I could hear my parents in the front seat singing and laughing. And then there's a horrible crashing sound, the car tumbling and flipping over. I'm being thrown from side to side, hitting my head against the window, the roof, and the door of the car. I'm yelling for my parents but they don't answer me. I'm trapped. I can't get out. I'm screaming but no one hears me. And then I black out.

I bolt up. I'm drenched and my heart is racing. I run to the bathroom and rip off my T-shirt, splashing water all over me. Eventually I drift off but sleep fitfully for the rest of the night until the alarm wakes me.

CHAPTER 3

In the morning, I had trouble getting out of bed, but I pushed myself to go for my usual three-mile run in the park, which is only a few blocks from where I live. I noticed the playground was empty. The nannies and their charges usually come around late morning. In the early hours, the runners take over the park.

On the way back, I stopped to pick up fresh bagels and two coffees, one for my doorman Louis. I whiffed in the smell of the freshly baked bagels.

"Here you go," I said to Louis, handing him a coffee and a bagel as I approached my building.

"Why thank you, Miss Maddie. It's nice to have a fresh cup first thing in the morning."

"I know you're not crazy about the coffee that's in the office."

"Let's keep that our little secret," he said, winking at me.

Louis has been my doorman since I moved into the building. It's comforting to know that I have someone close by who cares about me. I feel the same way. He laughs when I tell him he can never leave. Though he's getting up there in age, I keep my fingers crossed he never retires.

Walking into my apartment, I placed my keys down on an oak side table my mother and I bought at an estate sale when I was ten years old. A lot of my furnishings come from the house where I grew up in Queens, one of the five boroughs of Manhattan. I always get a warm feeling knowing I'm surrounded by the antiques my mother loved.

After shedding my running clothes, I showered and dressed in my standard wardrobe: jeans, a T-shirt, and short black boots and had my usual breakfast, a bowl of cheerios and milk.

I walked the fifteen blocks to my office, which is located on the first floor of a brownstone. There are three offices on the first floor: mine, Larry Banks, a criminal attorney, and my Cousin Will, who has an insurance agency. There are three apartments on the second floor, all occupied.

I picked up the phone and called my friend Annie.

"Do you want to get a drink later," I said, before she even had a chance to say hello.

"Everything okay?"

"Yeah. I'll explain later."

"I'll meet you at The Dead Poet at 6:00 p.m."

Annie and I met in the eighth grade, not too long after my adoptive parents were killed. As a child, I shied away from making friends, but Annie eventually wore me down. It was Annie who suggested I become a private investigator after I quit the police force more than five years ago.

I was going through a rough time back then. I knew I had no future with the New York City Police Department. It was too much of an old-boy network and after my partner quit, I was having a hard time adjusting to the office politics. I liked being a police officer. It was a tough decision to leave, but I knew it was the right one for me.

When you first walk into my office, there's a reception area, but I've never had a receptionist. At first I couldn't afford one, then I realized I liked being by myself with no one I had to interact with. The other room is my office where I have my father's inlaid mahogany desk, a comfortable office chair, and two black vinyl chairs with backs for clients to sit. Since nothing was going on at the moment, I forced myself to take on the tedious chore of administrative paperwork, which included paying my monthly bills.

At 5:30 p.m., I packed up and walked over to The Dead Poet, an Irish bar on Amsterdam Avenue on the Upper West Side. When I walked in, I was greeted by the hostess, Maggie.

"Where's Annie?" Maggie said.

"She should be here any minute." Needless to say, Annie and I are regulars. Maggie sat me at a table for two. The place is a celebration of poets and writers, lined with portraits on the mahogany-paneled walls. The bar is frequented by college students, Upper West Side locals, musicians and professionals alike.

Annie leaned over and gave me a kiss on my cheek before she sat down. I'm about 5'8" and Annie is almost six inches shorter than me, with short, curly brown hair, a boyish figure, and a smile that lights up a room. Annie is everything I'm not: outgoing, trusting, and an optimist.

"I can't wait till it gets cooler. I've had enough of summer," Annie said.

"And I thought I was the pessimist in the group."

"You are, but hot is hot. I could use a nice cool margarita."

"What's wrong?" I said when I saw a slight frown on Annie's face.

"It seems that all Doug and I do lately is argue. He wants us to start trying again and I'm not sure this is the right time."

About two years ago, Annie was pregnant but lost the baby in an automobile accident. It was a rough time for both her and Doug. Though Annie doesn't like to talk about it, I know it still weighs on her.

The waitress came over and we ordered drinks and a few appetizers.

"I thought that's what you wanted, too."

"I'm not sure what I want. First, it's lousy timing. The practice is building, and I don't want to leave Matt in the lurch." Annie is a matrimonial attorney and Matt is her partner.

"You can still work up until the time you're ready to give birth."

"But then what? I know I won't want to leave the baby for the first few months. We would have to hire an associate and I'm not sure the practice can afford it."

"You don't know how long it's going to take before you get pregnant and then it's nine months after that. By that time, you'll be ready to take on an associate. I can tell there's something else bothering you."

"I'm not sure I can go through it again. I'm petrified I'll lose the baby."

"But it was the automobile accident that caused the miscarriage. It wasn't your body that rejected the baby."

"I know. It might not be logical but that's how I feel."

"Who am I to give advice? I can't even commit to a relationship with someone I'm crazy about. It's just that I want you and Doug to be happy, and I think if you don't try, you'll regret it."

"I will take your advice under consideration. Now what is it you're dying to tell me?"

"Samantha showed up at my office today."

"She did? Is she okay?"

"Her friend Jason is a student at Sam's school and was accused of raping a girl who attends the same school. Apparently, he's there on a scholarship because the mother can't afford the tuition. You should have seen her. She was Sam at her best."

"You gotta love her. So, what's her plan?"

"What do you think? She's already involved in the case when the mother hasn't even contacted me."

"How well does she know this boy?"

"According to Sam, they're best friends, and she was so adamant that he didn't rape this girl. All I can do is wait to see if the mother contacts me."

"If Sam has anything to say, it won't be long before the mother calls. What will you do at that point?"

"At this moment, I don't know. I think I would need to hear from both the mother and the boy before I make any decisions."

"And if she can't pay you, would you take the case pro bono?"

"I need more information before I can make that determination."

"Have you spoken to your birth father lately?" Annie said.

"He called me a few days ago. He'd like me to come out to California so I can meet my stepbrothers."

"What did you tell him?"

"I didn't know what to say. I told him I'd think about it. He sounded disappointed. Maybe there's something seriously wrong with me. After all this time, I finally got to meet my birth father, so why did I blow him off?"

"You didn't exactly blow him off. I think you're too hard on yourself. What did you expect? You would meet this person who has never been in your life and have these warm and fuzzy feelings toward him? If you did, then I would think there's something wrong with you. You'll figure it out."

"It's just that I've been in therapy for almost a year now and I'm still no closer to committing to Jesse. Most people don't have a problem with marriage or living with someone. Why can't I be more normal?"

"That doesn't mean they're necessarily happier than you. Who knows the reasons why people do what they do. I'm crazy about you."

"You don't count."

"Thanks a lot," Annie said, grinning. "I think I better get home. I still have to prepare for court in the morning. My client's almost ex-husband thinks he can get away without paying any alimony or child support. What a sleazebag. I'm gonna wipe the court with this guy."

"I'm glad I'm not up against you," I laughed.

We shared a cab going home, stopping first at Annie's apartment building. I hated that Annie was hurting and that

I couldn't do anything to make it better. It was usually me who needed Annie's support, not the other way around.

CHAPTER 4

Two days later, I was sitting at my desk working on a locate search. The attorney was in a bind. His client's trial was coming up and his star witness was nowhere to be found. My phone rang.

"Is this Ms. Landon?"

"Yes. How can I help you?"

"My name is Nina Demsky. My son Jason is in terrible trouble. Can I see you? It's very urgent."

"Ms. Demsky, please call me Maddie. When can you come in?"

"I clean houses every day so it's not easy finding the time, but for my son, I'll come whenever you say."

"Where do you live?"

"In Queens. I can take the train. It's no problem."

"Can you come in around 4:00 p.m. today?"

"Yes, I can manage that. Thank you."

"Do you have my address?"

"Jason's friend Samantha gave it to me."

"Good. I'll see you then."

Around 4:00 p.m., I heard a knock at the door. I quickly got up and greeted Ms. Demsky. She looked younger than I expected, maybe in her mid-thirties. Nina was dressed in jeans, a blue button-down cotton shirt, and beige sandals. Her blonde, straight hair was cut to her chin, just like mine, except my hair was light brown. When she spoke, she had a slight accent. I led Nina into my office.

"Please sit. Can I get you any coffee or tea?"

"No, thank you. I'm very nervous. I haven't been sleeping well since Jason was arrested."

"Why don't you tell me about yourself?" I said, thinking it might calm her before I started asking questions about her son.

"I came here from Poland almost twenty years ago. When I first arrived, I stayed with some Polish friends of my parents. I learned English and began cleaning houses. It wasn't easy. At first, I only had a few jobs, but thankfully through word of mouth, I started to get more houses to clean."

"Are you married?"

"No. Jason's father was never in the picture and I have no idea where he is. I raised my son by myself. It's been difficult. Jason is a very bright boy and I was fortunate that he was able to attend private school on a scholarship. Now all his hard work was for nothing," she said, practically in tears. "He won't be able to go back to that school and all his future dreams are gone. All because a girl lied and accused him of raping her. My boy would never do such a horrible act."

"Why do you think she accused him?"

"I have no idea." Her hands twisted feverishly.

"How long ago did the rape occur?"

"I'm not sure, maybe six weeks ago. Jason's lawyer told me the police investigated and they had enough to charge him. I don't understand how they could arrest him."

"What did the lawyer tell you?"

"There was a camera outside the girl's house that saw Jason going inside with Mia and then leaving a little while later. And the police said no one else had been there that night. I don't care what the police said, Jason didn't do it."

I doubt the police would have arrested him on that alone, I thought to myself.

"Was there anything else?" Nina looked down. "Did something else happen?"

"It was really nothing, but he has a juvenile record. When he was thirteen, Jason got into a fight with a kid in our neighborhood and broke the boy's nose. It wasn't Jason's fault. He was provoked. I think the police know about what happened."

I wondered if they were able to get Jason's juvenile record unsealed.

"Do you know what the fight was about?"

"He said the kid was making fun of him, but he wouldn't tell me why."

"Is there any other violence in his past?"

"Of course not. Jason's a good boy."

Every parent thinks their kid walks on water.

"Where is Jason now?"

"He's home. Fortunately, an old friend was kind enough to lend me the money to pay for Jason's bail, otherwise I don't know what would have happened to my son."

"Can you give me the name of his public defender?"

"Yes. I have it here." She opened up her bag and gave me the piece of paper with his name and number on it.

"Samantha says you're the best, but I know you must charge a lot of money. I can pay you a little each week from my cleaning jobs. I know it's not much, but I promise I'll pay you back every cent I owe you."

"Why don't I do this. Let me speak with Jason first and then we'll talk."

"Thank you. I can't tell you how much this means to me."

"Please don't thank me yet. Why don't I come by tomorrow, say around 5:00 p.m.?"

"I have a few cleaning jobs on Thursdays, but I'll see if I can switch some of them around. I think Jason would be more comfortable if I was home when you came."

"Call me if there's a problem."

After Nina Demsky left, I picked up the phone and dialed Paul Greer's number, Jason's public defender. Hopefully, he could fill me in on what the police had on Jason. I left a message on his voicemail. It still wasn't clear to me why they arrested him. There had to have been more to the story than what Ms. Demsky told me. About an hour later, my phone rang.

"I'm trying to get in touch with Maddie Landon. This is Paul Greer."

"Mr. Greer, thank you for returning my call. I'm a private investigator and former police detective with the New York City Police Department. I was calling about your client, Jason Demsky."

"How can I help you?"

"Jason Demsky's mother came to see me."

"I'm surprised she could afford a private investigator."

"I was referred by a good friend of the family and if you don't mind, I'd like to talk with Jason." Even though I planned on talking with him whether Paul Greer agreed or not, I thought I would give him the courtesy of a call so as not to ruffle his feathers.

"Any help I can get is fine with me."

"Can you tell me what the charge is?"

"Rape in the first degree, which is a B felony. He's looking at five to twenty-five years. Unfortunately, when it's forceable rape, age doesn't come into play."

I swallowed hard.

"Was there any forensic evidence found?"

"No."

"Can you tell me what evidence they have on him?"

"The most damning is that he was caught on camera going in and out of her house on the night she said she was raped. No one else was seen going in or out that night. Also, she called a friend right after it happened and said that Jason Demsky had raped her."

"I heard he had a juvenile record. Do you know if the police found out about it?"

"They did. And somehow, they were able to get it unsealed."

"Was there anything else?"

"Jason was overheard by several students arguing with Mia Franklin about a week or two before she was raped."

"Do you know what the argument was about?"

"I don't."

"But with no forensic evidence, I'm still unclear why he was arrested."

"I guess they thought they had enough circumstantial evidence. Also, the victim's parents are very wealthy and maybe had a lot of influence. That could have been a factor."

"Was there a rape kit done?"

"There was. They found slight bruising around her genitalia, but since she didn't go to the police until a few days after it happened, all the DNA was washed away. Also, the maid had washed the sheets from her bed."

"Do you know why she waited a few days to report the rape?"

"I have no idea. It wasn't in the police report."

"That's too bad. Were there any drugs or alcohol found in her system?"

"If there were, they didn't show up in the toxicology report. Too much time had gone by."

"What was your take on Jason?" I asked.

"He didn't strike me as someone who would force himself on a girl, but as we know, shit happens."

"Interesting. Okay, I appreciate the information. I'll be in touch."

Maybe from watching too many Law & Order episodes and from my own experience in law enforcement, I'm a little leery of public defenders. They seem to have a reputation for being overworked, and therefore can't devote too much time to any one client. I hadn't met Jason Demsky, but I wasn't ecstatic that his future might depend on an overworked lawyer.

CHAPTER 5

The following day, I drove to Queens. Nina and Jason live in an apartment building off of Queens Boulevard on Austin Street in Forest Hills. Austin Street is about a mile long, with neighborhood shops ranging from big box stores to smaller shops. At some point, the street becomes residential with six-story brick buildings that were probably built in the fifties.

Whenever I'm in this area, I can't help but remember the garden apartment I grew up in not far from here. I teared up thinking about my parents, knowing how much they loved me. I can still visualize my father and me playing catch with the baseball mitt he bought me. That mitt was the best present I ever got. My mother gave up on buying me dolls when I chopped the head off the last one she bought me. Though I have wonderful memories of that apartment, unfortunately it also comes with too much pain.

I checked the building directory for the name Demsky and rang the bell. I was buzzed in and took the stairs up to the fourth floor. I'm not a fan of small spaces, especially elevators when they can get stuck at the most inopportune times. Ever since the night my parents died and I was trapped in the back seat, I fear I'll be stuck with no way out.

"Over here," I heard Nina Demsky say as she ushered me into her apartment. The living room was large. Though the furniture was worn in spots, the place was spotless. I'm pretty sure new furniture was not a high priority.

"Please sit."

"Where's Jason?"

"He's in his room, probably playing video games on his computer. I can't blame him. He can't go back to his school. I'm so worried for him."

"Would you mind if I speak to Jason alone? Sometimes teenagers will open up more if a parent isn't in the room with them."

"If you think that's better. I'll just let him know you're here."

I remember the first time I questioned someone when I was a rookie on the police force. I was a bundle of nerves, hoping no one would notice, especially my partner. Even though I'm a more skilled interviewer now, questioning a teenager is always a challenge.

"Jason," she said, as she knocked on his bedroom door, "Ms. Landon is here to see you." A moment later, the door opened.

"Hi, Jason. I'm Maddie. I'm a private investigator and a friend of Sam's." His room looked like a typical teenager's. Posters of famous sports people hung on the walls. Where the living room was immaculate, his room was a mess.

"I gather you're into sports," I said, looking all around.

"I guess." The way Jason said it, I got the impression I was the last person he wanted to talk with. Jason was a skinny kid, all arms and legs, probably going through a growth spurt. His light brown hair was falling in his eyes.

"Do you mind if I sit down?" Jason shrugged his shoulders, so I took that as a yes and pulled up a chair that was against the wall. Jason sat at his desk.

"Why don't we talk about Mia Franklin."

"I don't understand why she would accuse me of raping her. I would never do that to her or any girl. I liked Mia."

"Tell me what happened?" Though at first Jason appeared aloof, his hands were now clenched at his sides and his face was turning red.

"Mia and I were at a friend's house studying and then I walked her home. She asked me if I wanted to come up."

"Did she say why?"

"No. Though I thought it could be about math since she wasn't doing well in that subject."

"What time did you get to her place?"

"It was around 8:30 p.m."

"Was anyone home?"

"No. Her parents were out. She told me they weren't going to be home till late since they were seeing a Broadway play and then getting something to eat afterward."

"What were you doing during that time?"

"Just talking. Nothing else, I swear. When I left, Mia was fine."

"Can you think of any reason why she would accuse you?"

"I can't. I don't understand any of this. I thought we were friends. Doesn't she understand what she's done to me?" Jason started pacing and became more animated. "My scholarship has been taken away. I had plans of becoming a doctor. Now all that's gone. My mother will have to clean houses for the rest of her life," Jason said, raising his voice.

Though Jason had every right to be angry, could his temper have gotten him in trouble that night?

"You can't think like that. You don't know what's going to happen in the future."

Jason looked at me but didn't say anything.

"I was told that you had an argument with Mia at school. What was that about?"

"It was nothing."

"I have to know if I'm going to help you."

"I asked her out and she said no. When I asked her why, she wouldn't give me a reason. I probably shouldn't have insisted, since that's when she got angry and walked away."

"That must have hurt."

"Maybe, but I didn't rape her."

Jason looked like he was on the verge of crying but was trying to hold back the tears.

"If she was angry at you, why would she invite you up to her place?"

"That was a week before and I had already apologized."

"Do you know if she was having problems with any other kids in the school?"

"I have no idea."

"Can you tell me who her friends are?"

"She hangs out with Sandra Carlson and Tiffany Blake."

"What about any boys?"

"Maybe Sandra or Tiffany would know."

"Can you tell me the name of the person whose house you guys were studying at?"

"His name is Robert Dean."

"Anything else you want to tell me?"

"I didn't rape Mia."

It was like pulling teeth getting any answers out of Jason. I doubt if he was telling me everything. I just didn't know what he wasn't telling me.

"Is there a friend of yours I can talk with besides Sam?"

"Why do you have to talk with anyone else?"

"It's my job to speak with everyone connected to the case."

"Maybe I need to call him first."

"That's not how it works. I need his name. I'm just going to ask him a few questions." He seemed hesitant but finally told me his name was Marshal Berger. Was there a reason he didn't want me to talk with his friend?

"Thanks. We'll talk again soon. Try not to worry."

When I walked back into the living room, Nina Demsky was sitting on the couch thumbing through a magazine quickly. When she saw me, she stood up, the magazine dropping to the floor. Rushing up to me, she asked how Jason was doing as she rocked back and forth.

"Understandably, he's angry and upset."

"I worry he's going to hurt himself," she said, her eyes watering.

"Is there a reason you're concerned?"

"He just sits in his room and plays on his computer all day. He barely eats."

"Is there anyone he can talk to?"

"You mean like a therapist?"

"There are places that work on a sliding scale depending on your salary."

Ms. Demsky had a weird look on her face. It dawned on me that most of her clients probably pay her in cash.

"I know someone who might be able to help. Maybe she'll have some ideas. Let's sit." I took out my standard contract, leaving out the retainer amount.

"Don't I have to give you any money now?"

"We'll figure that out later."

"I don't know how I'll ever repay you."

"For now, just take care of your son."

When I came to see Jason, I had my doubts about whether I wanted to sign on for this case. It would be taking up a lot of my time with no money coming in except for some small jobs from other clients. I thought about what Nina Demsky went through, first coming to this country all by herself and how hard she had to work to give her son a good life. What would it do to her and Jason if he was found guilty? It was Nina's words that made my decision for me.

On the drive back, I thought about my conversation with Jason. It was too early in my investigation to rule him out, but there was a part of me that believed him. From my experience, I know that people hold things back, especially teenagers. Maybe he doesn't trust me. The only way to find out what happened was to begin by questioning the two girls who are friends with Mia Franklin.

CHAPTER 6

I was tired by the time I got home. I poured myself a glass of wine and sat in my favorite chair in the living room. It was an overstuffed blue and gray tweed wingback that my father sat in reading the newspaper when he got home from teaching every day.

Sitting in his chair, I remembered all the times when I was a little girl jumping up on my father's lap and snuggling against him as he read the newspaper. He would push the paper aside and stroke my hair. I can still feel his presence as I sipped my wine.

I went with my usual dinner when I had nothing in the house to eat—a peanut butter sandwich. I changed and brought my sandwich and a stack of potato chips to bed with me, along with my wine. In my world, wine goes with everything. I turned on the television in time to see the end of Wheel of Fortune. Though I rarely figured out the puzzles, I liked rooting for the contestants to solve the bonus round.

***

I was up early the next morning and headed to the gym, where I did my usual routine, working out with weights and finishing up with abs. The morning gym crowd are mostly men and women who have jobs they have to get to by 9:00 a.m. or a business they have to run. Early morning suited me. Everyone was there to work out and not to socialize.

When I got back, it was after 8:00 a.m. I showered and debated whether to ask Sam to meet me after school to point out Mia's friends. I wasn't happy about getting her involved, but from the description Jason gave me of Sandra and Tiffany, there was a chance I wouldn't be able to recognize them, so I thought I would take a wait-and-see approach.

I packed my overnight bag since I was leaving straight from the school to head up to Jesse's place.

I arrived early and found a parking spot a few blocks away. The school was on the Upper East Side of Manhattan. I waited outside about thirty feet from the school's front door, hoping to talk with either Sandra or Tiffany. Unfortunately, there was a mob of kids that came out all at once. There wasn't any way I would be able to spot these two girls. I saw Samantha's hand shoot up and wave to me as she exited the school. She quickly came over.

"What are you doing here?" Sam said, all excited.

"Listen, Sam, do you think you can point out Mia's friends, Sandra Carlson and Tiffany Blake, without drawing any attention?"

"Do you want to talk to them?"

"Sam, if you want to help, tell me when you see either or both of the girls."

"I bet they know what really happened. I can probably get them to talk."

"No, you're going to stay out of it. Do you understand? You could jeopardize the investigation and

Jason could wind up going to prison." I thought that might scare her.

"There's Sandra, the one with the brown hair in a ponytail, with a black backpack."

"Shush, not so loud. What about Tiffany? Do you see her?"

"Not yet. Wait, there she is. She's the skinny girl with reddish spiky short hair that she dyes."

"I see her. Who's the woman with her?"

"I'm pretty sure that's her mother. Are you positive you don't need any help? Kids don't like talking to grownups." I knew what Sam said was true.

"If I have any problems, I'll call you and we'll figure it out together." I was hoping that would satisfy Sam, at least for now.

Sam left abruptly and I noticed she joined up with a group of kids that were hanging around outside the school. I kept my eye on Sandra Carlson as she was walking by herself down Madison Avenue, following at a distance, wanting to make sure no one else was going to join her. She stopped in a café. I saw her pointing to something in the glass case to the guy behind the counter. She then sat down at a small round marble table for two, a perfect time to join her.

"Excuse me, is this seat taken?" Sandra barely looked up. She was too busy scrolling on her phone and eating her croissant. I sat down before she had a chance to say no.

"Sandra, my name's Maddie." She looked up quickly.

"How do you know my name? Were you following me?" she said, in a suspicious manner.

"I'm a private investigator looking into the rape allegation of Mia Franklin."

"Wow! Really? I never met a private investigator before. Do you have anything to prove you're a PI? You can't be too careful." I showed her my laminated card.

"That is so cool."

"I want to talk to you about Jason and Mia."

"I don't know if I should be talking with you." Her eyes looking all around.

"There's no reason why you can't. I'm interviewing people close to both of them. Why don't we talk about Jason. Do you know him?"

"We go to the same school. I think he's a senior."

"I heard that Jason and Mia got into an argument. Do you know what that was about?"

"I didn't hear it myself, but Mia said that Jason asked her out and he refused to take no for an answer."

"Do you know why she wouldn't go out with him?"

"She said he was kind of a geek." Sandra kept pulling at a strand of hair that never made it into her ponytail.

"But I got the impression they were friends."

"To tell you the truth, I think Mia is using Jason to help with her studies. I don't think he realizes it. Are you sure I can talk with you?"

"I am. I only have a few more questions. I heard she told a friend right after she was raped that it was Jason. Was that you?"

"No. Mia wasn't lying, if that's what you're getting at."

"I'm not saying she was lying. If you're her best friend, why didn't she tell you?"

She glared at me. I gather she didn't like what I had just inferred.

"Do you know why she waited to report the rape?" I said.

"I don't want to answer any more of your questions."

"Why? Is there something you're hiding? Because if there is, I'll find out. So, if you have anything else you want to tell me, now's the time."

"No. Now please go away."

I didn't think pressuring Sandra anymore would get her to open up. I thought I would leave it for now in case I wanted to follow up at a later date.

"Well, thank you, Sandra. By the way," I said as I was getting up. "How old is Mia?"

"Sixteen."

"Thanks again."

One thing I was pretty sure of, kids are loyal to their friends and would lie for each other.

CHAPTER 7

After leaving Sandra Carlson, I walked back to my car. Before heading to Connecticut, I emailed my source who obtains cell phone records and requested the two most recent statements for Mia's cell phone. Teenagers love to talk and text on their phone. Maybe I could find out who she was in contact with before and after the rape.

I then put in a call to Dr. Goldberg. She might know a place where Jason could get therapy for a minimal charge. I left a message on her voicemail.

I didn't get up to Jesse's until almost 7:00 p.m. His car was parked in the driveway. I grabbed my overnight bag and walked toward the back of the house where Jesse was sitting and drinking a beer on the patio. The back of his house is surrounded by woods with no other houses close by. Jesse lives in a small brick house with a loft area where he has a bedroom, office, and a bathroom. About two years ago, he remodeled the kitchen, installing all new stainless-steel appliances and a wood floor. The wood cabinets are white and above the sink are black and white subway tiles. In the corner, he has what looks like a small ladder with plants on each of the rungs. The living room has a fireplace where, during the winter, we enjoy sitting on a blanket with our wine and letting nature take its course.

"Did you know that drinking alone is the first sign of alcohol abuse?" I said as I approached him. He got up and I walked into his arms. Jesse is a good five inches taller than me. His very dark brown piercing eyes can be incredibly alluring.

"You feel good," I said, wrapped in his muscular arms.

"Are you starving?" he said.

"I am, but I'm not opposed to waiting."

By the time I took a quick shower, Jesse was out on the patio grilling. I remember the first time we met. Jesse was on a case that brought him to New York. We both happened to be at a Barnes and Noble on the Upper West Side looking at mystery novels. I glanced at him, noticing his dark, piercing eyes. He smiled at me. Though I tend to keep to myself, when he asked me if I had any suggestions, I told him I was a big fan of the Michael Connelly books. And here we are a year and a half later.

"Yum, ribs. They smell amazing." Jesse had a bottle of wine on the table, which I immediately filled my glass with. The back patio lights were turned on.

"Are you sure you want to be associated with a possible alcoholic," Jesse said, grinning.

"Absolutely. If anyone in this duo has leanings toward alcoholism, it would definitely be me. I hate to admit this, but last night I had a peanut butter sandwich with wine. How's that for gross?"

"I guess I'll have to keep a close eye on you," Jesse said playfully.

When my phone rang, I noticed it was Dr. Goldberg. I signaled to Jesse that I had to take the call.

"Dr. Goldberg, thank you for calling me back." I went on to explain the situation with Jason. She said she'd make a few calls and get back to me on Monday.

As we were eating, I told Jesse about my new case and the reason for the call from Dr. Goldberg.

"So, what do you think?" I said when I was finished talking.

"It's way too early to make any assumptions. You said there was a camera that caught him going in and out of her house. Is there any other way to get into the house where someone wouldn't be noticed?"

"I don't know. But wouldn't the cops have checked it out?"

"From what you've said, the fact that she accused him, and he was caught on a camera around the time she said she was raped, they most likely didn't bother looking any further. From that point on, they probably focused their investigation on him."

"I knew I kept you around for a reason."

"And I thought it was for my good looks and my stud body."

"That too."

"I'm interested in why you decided to take the case?"

"I'm not exactly sure. I think it was a combination of Jason's situation, his mother who has struggled to give her son a good life, and my own curiosity that couldn't resist."

"Maybe you're just getting soft. How is Sam doing?"

"Hard to tell. She keeps her feelings close to the vest. I know she's dying to get involved. It's going to be hard keeping her in check."

"Sounds like someone else I know," Jesse said, feigning a hurt arm when I lightly punched his shoulder.

We polished off most of the bottle of wine and were fast asleep by 11:30 p.m.

***

The rest of the weekend went by quickly. We spent the better part of it outdoors hiking at Cockaponset State Forest, the second-largest forest in Connecticut. Pattaconk Lake is located in the state forest. As we walked by the lake, I noticed there were people taking advantage of the warm weather and swimming in the lake. Jesse had packed a picnic basket filled with wine, cheese, French bread, and brownies, which we gorged on after hiking for a few hours. Before I met Jesse, the closest I got to hiking boots was passing a sports shop in the middle of Manhattan.

***

Monday morning, before I pulled out of Jesse's driveway, he leaned into my car and kissed me hard on the lips. Every time I leave Jesse, I have this nagging feeling in the back of my mind that he might decide he no longer wants to wait until I'm ready to move in together. He's been patient till now, but when will his patience run out? I realize that all the talking in therapy might not assuage my fear of commitment. I would have to take a leap of faith and just plunge in, but not today.

I blocked those thoughts from my mind and instead went to where I was more comfortable, thinking about the case. Going on the assumption that Jason Demsky didn't rape Mia Franklin, then why would she accuse him? It didn't make sense unless there was something else going on. I needed to speak with Mia's friend, Tiffany Blake. Since Mia didn't call Sandra right after she was raped, I was pretty sure it was Tiffany.

My phone rang as I was exiting the Taconic Parkway.

"Hello."

"Maddie, it's Dr. Goldberg. I have the name of someone who would be willing to talk to your client, and there would only be a minimal fee. I'll text you the name and telephone number."

"Thank you so much."

I called Ms. Demsky and left a message with the contact information Dr. Goldberg gave me. Hopefully, she'd follow up since Jason really needed to talk with someone he could feel safe with.

I was sitting at my office desk with my computer open when my phone rang. It was Nina Demsky thanking me for the information on the therapist.

"You're welcome. I have a question. Does Jason date?"

"I think he hangs out with girls but he never mentioned anyone in particular that he went out with. Why?"

"I was just wondering. Thank you. I'll be in touch."

I was curious why Jason would insist that Mia go out with him in front of his fellow classmates. That seemed odd to me. Though Jason didn't strike me as being an aggressive kid, I've learned that anyone at any time can act out of character when pushed to their limits.

CHAPTER 8

I opened up my emails and saw I had an attachment from my source with the cell phone records I had requested on Mia Franklin. I quickly printed it out and started sifting through the numbers. Mia certainly spent a lot of time on the phone. There were a few numbers that she seemed to call or text more frequently. I jotted them down and looked them up. Two of them belonged to her friends, Sandra Carlson and Tiffany Blake, the third was to a Logan Kelly who she called at all hours. Maybe a boyfriend? There was one other number that was called a few times. It belonged to someone named Ben Bradley. I didn't think these kids would be in any of my databases and I was reluctant to ask Samantha if she knew them.

I thought I would take a crack at Logan Kelly. If he was her boyfriend, Mia might have confided in him. I was deep in thought when my phone rang.

"Did you talk to Sandra?" Samantha said eagerly.

"Sam, we went over this. I can't tell you anything. If anyone found out, it would taint the investigation. But there is a way you can help Jason."

"How?" She jumped on what I said.

"Do you know who Logan Kelly and Ben Bradley are?"

"Is that it?" she said, sounding disappointed.

"No. I need you to tell me everything you know about Jason. Look, you're frustrated, I get it, but I can't talk to you about the case. There are other ways to be involved that are really important." This should stop her badgering me. Fingers crossed.

"Are you calling from school?" I asked her.

"I have a free period."

"How about I meet you after school?"

"Where?"

"You pick the place."

Before hanging up, she mentioned the name of a coffee shop a few blocks from her school. I had questions for Sam. I knew next to nothing about Jason or Mia, and I was hoping she could fill me in on some of the blanks.

Sam was outside the coffee shop waiting for me. She was wearing her school uniform, a blue pleated skirt that ended right above her knees and a gold-colored blouse.

"Let's go inside," I said.

We got a booth in the back. Every time I look into Sam's big, green eyes, I'm reminded of her birth mother and how she was tragically murdered shortly after Sam's birth.

"So, what can I get you gals?" the waitress said.

"I'll have a coffee and a buttered toasted bagel."

"And you, young lady?"

"I'll have the same, except I want cream cheese on my bagel."

"Two coffees coming right up," the waitress said as she walked off.

"Are you allowed to drink coffee?" I said.

"Duh! I'm seventeen. Do you know children in other countries grow up drinking coffee?"

I didn't know if Samantha was right, so I decided not to argue the point.

"How is your mom?" I asked.

"I don't want to talk about my parents. I thought I was here to talk about Jason."

"You're right." I didn't want to get into a pissing match with Sam. "Let's start over. When did you and Jason become friends?"

The waitress brought our coffee and bagels and left.

"We started hanging out when we were in ninth grade," Sam said, diving right into her bagel.

"What did he tell you happened that night?"

"He said he was at a friend's house with Mia and then he walked her home."

"Were they dating?"

"No. They were just friends."

I was thinking maybe Jason wanted to be more than friends. Maybe he came on to her and she rejected him. I couldn't get a read on Sam's face. Was she holding back or telling me the truth?

"I get the feeling you don't like Mia."

"I think she's a snob and totally spoiled. Her family is super rich and she thinks she's better than everyone else. Her father is some big shot at a hedge fund."

I was impressed that Sam even knew the words hedge fund. I don't even know what a hedge fund is.

"Jason is as straight lace as it comes. He goes to school, studies, and works at a grocery store at night close to where he lives."

"I heard he asked Mia out."

Sam averted her eyes.

"Sam, I need the truth."

"Jason told me he did it on a dare."

"What does that mean?"

"The guys egged him on to ask Mia out."

"Why?"

"Because they're idiots and Jason is an easy target. He thinks if he does what they say, he'll fit in."

"Was Mia in on it?"

"I don't know. If I knew what they were up to in advance, I would have talked him out of it. He felt humiliated."

I thought that was interesting.

"Do you know a boy named Logan Kelly?"

"I think he's dating Mia or maybe they just hang out. Not sure."

"What do you know about him?"

"He's one of the popular boys. Thinks he's God's gift to women. A real jock."

I guess things haven't changed that much since I went to school. I was not one of the popular kids. I was the one kids picked on, but I ignored most of them and the ones who didn't like being ignored tried to pick fights with me. That didn't work out so well for them. I had a mean left hook. They never even saw it coming.

"Do you think it was Logan who raped Mia?" Sam asked.

"No, I don't." I had no clue, but I didn't want Sam to even think for a moment that Logan Kelly could have had any part in what happened to Mia.

"Do you know someone named Ben Bradley?"

"I think he used to go to my school. He may have been a couple of years ahead of me."

"Have you heard any talk around school about what happened to Mia?"

"They all think it's Jason. I know they talk behind my back but I don't care."

No wonder I liked Sam. We were definitely two peas in a pod.

"I want to help. I know you think I'm going to screw things up but I won't. I see these kids every day. Maybe I can find out stuff you can't."

"You are helping me. Answering my questions is providing me with information I couldn't get from anywhere else." Sam had a frown on her face.

"I don't want to just answer your questions, I want to get involved. Jason is my best friend. If anything happens to him, I'll hate myself if I didn't do anything to help him." She got up in a huff and left.

I couldn't fault Sam for the way she felt. I was just afraid of what would happen to her if she talked to the wrong person.

CHAPTER 9

I started walking crosstown toward my apartment. I was getting a clearer picture of Mia Franklin. Though I shouldn't make any judgments about someone I never met, I got the impression from Sam that Mia was an entitled kid. She was the kind of girl you hated in school if you were not part of the in-crowd. I wanted to talk to her but I knew that would be a long shot. Even if I was able to get her alone, she would have no reason to speak with me once she knew I was working for Jason.

When I reached Park Avenue, I thought I would take a detour and make a surprise visit to Jason's friend Marshal Berger. Marshal lived in a high-end building on Park Avenue. I was stopped by a doorman.

"Hi, I'm here to see Marshal Berger."

"May I ask who's calling?"

"Tell him my name is Maddie Landon and I'm a friend of Jason Demsky."

He picked up the desk phone and heard him talking to someone. The next thing I knew, he told me to go up to apartment 7E. *Do I dare take the elevator?* Since I figured this building would have its elevators checked all the time, I entered and pressed the seventh-floor button, holding my breath. It took off with no problems. I stepped out and looked for apartment E.

The door opened to a slender-built teenager, with curly brown hair and a nose that had a slight hook but did not detract from his good looks.

"Come in."

"I was in the neighborhood so I thought I'd take a chance that you were home. I'm a private investigator hired by Jason's mother. Are your parents home?"

"No, they're out."

Marshal was very polite and asked if I would like to sit in the living room. I looked around as he led me into a room that was probably larger than my entire apartment. All the furniture was upholstered in white. The artwork on the walls was probably worth thousands. I sat down hoping I didn't have anything on the seat of my jeans that would leave a mark on their white couch. On the wall opposite the couch was a landscape of the ocean, with small children playing in the sand. The sky had shades of blue with clouds overhanging.

"Did Jason tell you that I'm investigating the rape allegation?"

"Yes, and I want to help Jason in any way I can."

"Good. How long have you been friends?"

"I've known Jason since we were in the seventh grade."

"Are you a senior now?"

"Yes. I can tell you that Jason had nothing to do with what happened to Mia Franklin."

"How can you be so sure?"

"I know Jason."

"Unfortunately, that wouldn't be good enough if his case went to trial. Did he tell you he was with Mia Franklin on the night she was raped?"

"Yes, but he said nothing happened; they just talked."

"I'd like to believe Jason, but the outside camera shows that no one else entered her house until her parents came home."

"Maybe she made the whole thing up."

"Why would she do that?"

"I don't know. From what Jason has told me about her, she thinks she's better than everyone else."

"But making up a story that you were raped is very serious."

"All I can say is that I believe what Jason told me."

"Changing the topic, I was informed that Jason asked Mia out on a dare. Do you know why he would go along with it?"

"These jerks have always tried to humiliate him. Jason just wanted to fit in. He was an easy target. They think they're better than him because his mother cleans houses for a living, yet he's probably smarter than all of them. I guess he thought if he did ask Mia out, maybe they would finally accept him. I told him not to go along with it; he would never be part of their stupid group."

"You seem to know him pretty well."

"When Jason first came to the school, we were partners on a biology project, so I got to know him. Did you know that he tutors kids for free, or he did tutor kids, but since the rape charge, none of the students want his help. It's probably their parents that don't want their kid around Jason."

"I didn't know that. Doesn't it seem a little odd that Mia would befriend Jason?"

"I'm pretty sure Mia has been using him to help with her studies. She's not very bright. She's just a spoiled rich kid."

"Would you happen to know Logan Kelly or Ben Bradley?"

"Logan goes to our school. He's a junior. I think Mia and Logan are seeing each other but I'm not sure. Maybe Bradley graduated a few years earlier."

"Do you know where Logan lives?"

"Yeah, I went to one of his parties at his house in Bronxville."

"Here's my card. Text me his address. If you think of anything else, please contact me."

I decided not to trust my luck again and took the stairs down. I liked Marshal. He seemed very mature for his age. It's hard to figure out why one person befriends another person. Annie and I are complete opposites. It seems as if Jason and Marshal are very different. Maybe that's what drew them together. Did I learn anything from Marshal? I thought his take on Mia's relationship with Jason was interesting, similar to what Sam told me. If Mia was using him, would she have qualms about accusing him of rape? It's a stretch. Without questioning Mia, I had no clue whether she was making it all up. And if she was, why?

CHAPTER 10

My phone rang as I was walking home. It was my birth father, Harris Tyler. I let it go to voicemail since I knew why he was calling. He wanted me to come out to California and meet his sons. I decided to take the coward's way out and deal with it at another time. The thought of this whole new family was more than I bargained for. I didn't need complications. All those nights that I lay in bed crying, wondering why my birth parents gave me up for adoption, and thinking the worst. Those thoughts still haunt me.

* * *

The following afternoon, I drove up to the Bronxville Train Station waiting to catch Logan Kelly exiting the train. Bronxville is just north of Manhattan in Westchester County. I had a pretty good description of him from Marshal Berger. It was almost 5:00 p.m. when I spotted Logan exiting the train. He was a good-looking kid with blonde hair and a muscular build. He was around 5'7" but he was still young and would probably have a growth spurt in the next couple of years. I caught up to him.

"Logan?"

"Yeah! Who are you?"

"My name's Maddie Landon and I'm investigating the alleged rape of Mia Franklin." I didn't say who I was working for and I was hoping he wouldn't ask.

"I already spoke to the police."

"I just had a few follow-up questions. I'll be quick. Did Mia tell you what happened?"

"Yeah. I'd like to kill him for what he did to her. She's a basket case."

"Are you and Mia dating?"

"Why is that your business?"

"It's just a simple question."

"It's loose. We date but we see other people."

"Was she seeing Jason?"

"She doesn't tell me who she dates, but I doubt it."

"Why is that?"

"You'd have to ask Mia."

"I'm surprised you wouldn't care that she dates other people. Aren't you the least bit jealous?"

"I don't remember seeing your badge."

"I'm a private investigator," I said, showing him my PI license.

"What are you doing? Trying to trick me?"

"Not at all. I'm just trying to find out what happened."

"I know what happened," he said. "I'm not answering any more of your questions." He got into his car and left. These kids are a pain in the ass. They think they can do whatever they please with no consequences.

I picked up my phone and dialed Jason's public defender, Paul Greer. After four rings, it went to voicemail. I had questions for him that I wanted answers to.

"Mr. Greer, it's Maddie Landon. Can you please call me back when you get this message."

I wanted to make one more stop before heading home. I decided to pay a visit to Robert Dean, the young man whose apartment Jason said he and Mia were studying at the night Mia was allegedly raped. Robert Dean lived on the Upper West Side on Columbus Avenue.

When I arrived at his building, the concierge asked me my name and who I was there to see. I heard him relay my message to whoever was on the other end of the line.

"You can go up. It's apartment 14G."

"Thanks," I said as I walked to the elevator. I debated whether to take the stairs but the thought of fourteen flights did not appeal to me. I decided to take my chances that the elevator wasn't going to break down. My phone buzzed just as the elevator doors closed.

"Hello."

"Ms. Landon?" I recognized Paul Greer's voice.

"Mr. Greer. Would it be possible to call you back in about thirty minutes?"

"Yes. That's fine."

"Thank you."

I meandered through the halls till I came to Robert Dean's apartment. Expecting to see a teenager at the door, I was confronted by a woman, probably in her forties, with a body that was likely sculpted from serious weight training. She was wearing a white T-shirt and tight jeans. Her dark brown wavy hair was down past her shoulders. Her lips looked like they had one too many injections.

"I'm very sorry to bother you at this hour but I was hoping to speak with your son Robert."

"And who are you?" she said with an attitude.

"Maddie Landon, I'm investigating the alleged rape of Mia Franklin."

"And what has this got to do with my son?" she said, as we were standing in the foyer on a hand-braided runner that may have cost more than all my furniture and rugs combined.

"I was informed that Mia and Jason were here that night."

"And who told you that?"

"Jason Demsky. I just need to ask your son a few questions."

"Mom, let her in. It's alright." Robert was standing behind me. He was a tall, skinny kid who had the unfortunate luck of being cursed with teenage acne.

"Well, don't be long. Dinner is almost ready," she said, not happy that I was talking to her son.

While following Robert to his room, I noticed all the beautiful oriental rugs on the gleaming wide-planked hardwood floors. Robert's room was filled with all sorts of electronic equipment. When I was a kid, I played with an erector set building skyscrapers. In the nineties, if there were computers, I didn't have one.

"Do the kids call you Robert or Bobby?" I said. Robert motioned me to sit on his bed while he sat at his desk.

"Everyone calls me Robbie."

"I'm Maddie and I'd like to ask you some questions about the night Jason and Mia were here studying."

"Are you with the police?" he asked.

"Actually, I'm a private investigator," I said, showing him my card.

"Did Jason hire you?"

"Jason's mother did. She's very concerned about her son."

"I don't know what happened. I can't help you." Robbie was fidgeting with his hands.

"That's okay. Can you tell me what time Mia and Jason arrived here and what time they left that day?"

"I'm not exactly sure. Maybe from six to eight."

"Did you notice any tension or problems between the two of them?"

"Not that I remember. Everything seemed fine."

"Do you guys usually study together?"

"It's normally just Jason and me, but Jason called me and asked if Mia could study with us."

"Did he give you any reason?"

"I don't think I asked."

"Weren't you curious at all? Or maybe you liked the fact a pretty girl like Mia was going to be studying with you."

He stammered for a moment. "I guess," he said, his face turning red.

"Were you there when Jason asked Mia out and she told him no?"

"I heard about it. I was surprised since I didn't think Jason was interested in Mia."

"Why did you get that impression?"

"Just from the times we've talked about girls. Maybe I'm wrong."

"What about Mia, does she date?"

"You'd have to ask her. I don't really know her that well."

"What else can you tell me about Jason?"

"Like what?"

"You tell me."

"I know that Jason is very studious and kind of keeps to himself."

"Why do you think Mia wanted to study with Jason?"

"My best guess is she knew Jason was willing to help her."

"Robbie, I've spoken to a few people who know both Mia and Jason, and it appears no one has any answers as to why Jason would rape Mia or why Mia would accuse Jason. If you know something, you need to speak up now. If I find out you haven't told me the truth, you could be in trouble for withholding information." It wasn't true but I was tired of these kids dicking me around. Robbie's eyes opened wide.

"I don't want to get anyone in trouble."

"I promise you won't."

"I like Jason, but I get the feeling he's very secretive."

"In what way?"

"Don't get me wrong. I like hanging out with him, but there are times when he seems distant. Like I don't know what's going on with him."

"Did you ever ask him about it?"

"No."

"Can you take a guess what he might be hiding?"

"I really don't know. I'm sorry. Can I ask you a question?"

"Of course."

"What's going to happen to Jason?"

"I'm not sure. But he can use a friend right now. If you think of anything else, please contact me."

CHAPTER 11

Walking down the fourteen flights, I had a chance to think about what Robbie told me. I was baffled. Did Jason have something to hide? Was Mia using Jason? Though Jason was very bright, it seemed as if he was also naïve, or maybe he was playing along. He could have liked the fact that Mia wanted his help. But why would she accuse Jason? Nothing made any sense.

I was walking to my car when I realized I had forgotten to call Paul Greer back. I quickly dialed his number.

"Mr. Greer, it's Maddie Landon," I said when he answered. "If you don't mind, I have a few questions."

"Go ahead," he said. I could hear in his voice that he seemed distracted.

"When Jason was pulled in for questioning, did he have any scratches on his arms?"

"I can check but I don't think so."

"Don't you think that's odd? I can't imagine Mia didn't fight back."

"Don't forget, Mia didn't report the rape for a few days. If there were any scratches, they may have healed. And I guess the police didn't think it made a difference. They already had their suspect."

I doubted the scratches would have healed that quickly.

"Did you happen to check around the back of Mia's house?"

"For what? The only camera was in the front."

"Well, maybe the person came in through a back door."

"I guess it's possible."

"Thank you. I appreciate your time." I was being nice, but underneath I was trying to keep my anger in check. It didn't seem as if Mr. Greer was doing much to help his client.

"Oh, one other thing. Do you know Mia's parents' names?"

"Hold on a second."

A minute later, I heard Mr. Greer's voice. "Stephen and Melissa Franklin."

"Thank you."

"Let me know what you find out."

"Sure." I wanted to tell him to get off his ass and do his job but kept that to myself.

It was a long day and I was glad to be home. I was fixing myself something to eat when I saw Annie was calling.

"I was just about to bite into my delicious egg sandwich," I said to Annie.

"You really need to keep your refrigerator stocked. I don't want to find you dead on your kitchen floor from starvation with rats nipping at your body."

"Thanks for the lovely visual. So how did it go in court?" I asked.

"After revealing to the judge bank accounts my client's husband had no idea we knew about, he awarded my client a sizable settlement. I love when that happens. Unfortunately, too often the woman gets the shaft. Men seem to find all sorts of ways to hide their money so their spouse can't get hold of it."

"You are a tiger."

"I am. Anything new on the case?"

"Nothing that makes any sense so far. Though the police were hell-bent on arresting Jason, from what I've learned so far, some things don't add up. Jason was at a friend's house studying. The victim, Mia, was there as well. It was dark when they left, so he walked her home, and according to Jason, she asked him to come in. The street camera shows him going in the front door and then leaving approximately forty minutes later. He doesn't deny any of this. She apparently called her friend that night and told her that Jason had raped her. She doesn't report the rape until a few days later. At that point, all DNA is gone. The only thing they could say for sure was that there was some minor bruising on her genitalia area. I was told that the maid washed her sheets from that night."

"What else do they have on him?"

"He was seen arguing with her approximately two weeks or thereabouts before the alleged rape."

"What was that about?"

"It turns out some guys dared Jason to ask her out, and when she refused, there were some words. From what his friends Marshal and Sam said, Jason went along with it because he wanted to fit in."

"Teenagers can be so stupid. But why were they studying together if they had an argument?"

"Jason said he apologized to her. From what I was told, it appears Mia was using Jason to help with her studies."

"Anything more?"

"Yeah. He has a juvenile record that somehow the police were able to unseal. He had broken a kid's nose during a fight. His mother said the kid provoked him, but Jason wouldn't tell her what was said."

"What are you thinking?"

"I don't see a motive, unless he was really angry that she had rejected him. Maybe when he was at her place they got into it again and he lost it. Though the cameras caught only Jason going in and leaving, something doesn't feel right. I would like to know why the maid washed the sheets."

"Maybe Mia had no intentions of reporting the rape?"

"But why?"

"I guess that's what you have to figure out."

"Thanks a lot. How are you doing?" I asked.

"I'm not sure how to answer that."

"Is that the lawyer in you talking?"

"You got me. I'll talk to you tomorrow."

I knew Annie well enough to know she was avoiding the subject of her and Doug.

CHAPTER 12

In the morning I decided to take my car to the office since I thought I might need it later in the day. Getting around in the city with a car is usually too much of a hassle. It's almost impossible to find parking spots and the traffic is a nightmare. It's easier to walk or Uber around.

Sitting at my office desk, I turned on my computer and did an in-depth database search on Stephen Franklin, Mia's father. I knew they lived somewhere on the east side. The address listed for him was in the East 80's off of Madison Avenue. Mr. Franklin worked for a hedge fund company called Washington Securities. The brownstone he and his wife owned was valued at six and a half million dollars. I was never big on fantasizing, but I was curious what it would feel like to be able to afford a house worth that much.

Getting back to reality, I thought now would be a good time to check out the place. Hopefully, no one was at home. I drove to the Franklins' address, and found a parking spot on the opposite end of their block.

The Franklins' brownstone was the last one at the end of the street. I spotted the outside camera, which was angled right at their house. I walked around it so I wouldn't be caught on camera. There was a gate that led to the side of the house. It was locked, but nothing I couldn't climb over. That's when I heard someone calling, "Who's there?"

It was an elderly, heavyset woman standing on the top step of their brownstone.

"Can I help you?"

"I hope so," I said, as I walked up the steps to speak with this woman. "My name's Maddie Landon. I'm investigating the alleged rape of Mia Franklin. Are you a relative?"

"Oh no, though I've been with the family for many years. I'm Mia's nanny. Well, I was, but mostly I take care of the house now. Poor Mia. She's not quite herself."

"Do you live here?"

"I did, but not since Mia was thirteen."

"Can we step inside?"

"I really don't think I should be talking with you. The Franklins would be very upset if they knew."

"This conversation is just between us."

"Please be quick," she said, as she closed the front door behind us. I was now standing in a large foyer with beautiful black and white marbled flooring.

"I was told she didn't tell her parents that she was raped until a few days after it happened."

"That's not exactly true. Miss Mia never told her mother. It was the school headmaster that called Mrs. Franklin."

My interest was piqued. "Do you happen to know the name of that person?"

"No. I'm sorry."

"Did Mia ask you to wash the sheets?"

"Why yes. It was before we knew what had happened. The sheets were balled up on the floor and Mia asked me to put them in the wash. I thought it was a little odd that she had changed her own sheets. I love Mia but she's spoiled and has never changed her own sheets in her entire life." I thought that was very interesting.

"Do you know if Mia has a boyfriend?"

"Please, I don't want to answer any more questions."

"Would you mind if I take a quick look in Mia's room?"

"Yes. Mrs. Franklin would be very angry if she found out. I think you better leave now. Mrs. Franklin might be back at any moment."

I thought I shouldn't push my luck. "I appreciate you talking with me. I'm sorry I didn't get your name."

"It's Mrs. Gomez. Please, I don't want any trouble."

"I promise nobody will know we spoke."

After speaking to Mrs. Gomez, I decided to wait around a while. I was hoping she would leave the house at some point so I could take a look around. Though I realized I was probably caught on the camera, I was betting on the fact that nobody normally checks it.

Standing outside where I wouldn't be seen, I was very curious about who reported the rape to the headmaster. The only two people who originally knew about the rape were Mia's friends: Tiffany Blake and Sandra Carlson. Did one of them report it? But I was more curious why Mia didn't tell her parents she was raped.

Thirty minutes later, I was about to leave when Mrs. Gomez came out of the house with a shopping cart. I waited till I saw her walk toward the end of the block and turn the corner. Before jumping the gate, I scanned the area to make sure no one was looking in my direction. Walking quickly to the back of the house, I didn't notice any cameras. There was a back door that led to a basement. The lock didn't appear to be new. If someone did come through this door, either they jimmied the lock or they were let in.

I glanced around for a few moments, but there was nothing unusual that caught my eye. Could someone have come in through the back door without being caught on the camera? I quickly jumped the gate and walked in the direction of my car. Though I can understand why Mia would want to take the sheets off her bed, what would be the reason she would want Mrs. Gomez to wash them? Jason's DNA could have been all over them. Unless it was someone else's DNA on the sheets that she didn't want anyone to know about. Again, why?

CHAPTER 13

Instead of going straight back to the office, I thought as long as I was there, I'd canvass the area. Maybe somebody saw something suspicious that night.

After knocking on several doors with no luck, I was just about to give up when I was rewarded on my last attempt.

"May I help you?" A man, maybe in his late sixties, bald with a slight paunch, was standing at the door. I heard a dog barking in the background.

"I'm sorry to bother you. I'm investigating an incident in the neighborhood that took place maybe a month ago."

"Can I see some identification? Though you seem harmless enough, in these times you can't be too careful."

"I understand completely," I said, as I handed him my card. He looked at it for a moment.

"So, what's this about?"

"I'm investigating an attempted robbery, and I'm canvassing people in the neighborhood."

"How can I help you?"

"Would you mind if we step inside?"

"I'd rather not. Let's make this brief."

"I was wondering if a few weeks ago you might have seen or heard anything suspicious in the area after dark, maybe from the Franklins' house?"

"Well, every day around 9:30 p.m. I walk my dog. You say about a month ago. I'd have to think a little bit.

That's quite a while ago. I can hardly remember what happened yesterday," he said chuckling.

"Maybe someone milling around in the back of their house?" I said, trying to get him to focus.

"*Hmm.* Not that I can recall. Well, wait a minute. Now that you mention it, I do remember hearing some voices by the side of their house a couple of weeks ago. At the time, I thought it was a little odd that the Franklins would be back there."

"Why did you think that was unusual?"

"Well, it was kind of dark out, so what would they be doing there at that late hour?"

"Can you identify if the voices were male or female?"

"I can't be certain. I'm sorry. Did something happen? Did they get robbed?" he said, as his jaw dropped and his eyes opened wide.

"No, nothing like that. I'm sorry to have taken up any of your time Mr. ..."

"Mr. Burns."

"One last question. Do you happen to remember the time you heard these voices?"

"Like I said, I take Butch out for a walk between 9:30 and 9:45 p.m. every night. I'm just not sure whether it was when I first left or when I was on my way back from my walk."

"Well, thank you, and if you recall anything else, please contact me."

Why would the Franklins be by the back of their house at such a late hour? That's odd, unless it was someone else back there who didn't want to be seen on camera.

Unfortunately, since Mr. Burns couldn't remember the exact evening he heard people talking, I didn't know how it would help my investigation.

***

Later that day, I was sitting in my office having a cup of coffee, thinking about the case, when I heard the door open. I slowly reached into my desk drawer and pulled out my gun. Like the man said, you can never be too careful.

In front of me stood two police officers. I slid my gun back into the drawer.

"Are you Maddie Landon?"

"Yes. How can I help you?"

"I'm Detective Jamison and this is Detective Ballard. We received a call from someone who saw you entering private property and looking suspicious."

I was surprised two detectives were sent to my office for such a minor matter, at least in my mind.

Detective Jameson was medium height and built like a bull. Detective Ballard was barely 5'7" and slender. She reminded me of when I was a newbie on the force.

"Why do you think it was me?"

"Are you denying it?"

"I'm just asking the question."

"Answer my question," Detective Jamison said, with a hard-nosed look on his face.

"I don't deny it. Now, can you please tell me how you knew it was me?"

"A neighbor saw someone jump the gate and watched as they got into their car and drove away. They had written down the license plate number. What were you doing on the Franklins' property?"

"As you already know, I'm a private investigator and I'm working on a case involving the Franklins' daughter. If you had looked me up, you would also know I'm a former police detective with the NYPD."

"That doesn't give you the right to be on their property."

"Probably not, but I didn't disturb anything."

"How do we know you didn't try to break into their home?"

"Whoever it was that saw me would know that I wasn't in the back long enough to break in. Would you guys like a cup of coffee?" I said, hoping to defuse the situation.

"It does smell good, but no thank you. By the way, do you have a permit for that gun you have in your desk drawer?" he said, hiding a smile.

"As a matter of fact, I do. Would you like to see it?"

"I don't think that will be necessary. Try not to go where you don't belong. We'll report back to the person who called it in, but I can't promise you if the Franklins find out, they won't file a complaint. I'll try to smooth it over, but only because you were a fellow officer."

"I appreciate it. Thank you. Can I ask why you dropped by instead of calling?"

"We were in the neighborhood."

It probably had more to do with the fact that Mia's family was rich. I doubted Mr. Burns called the police. It was probably someone who lived across the street and saw me jump the gate, or maybe someone's door I knocked on that had no intention of answering.

CHAPTER 14

Two hours later, I was finishing up a background check for a good client of mine. He asked me to look into a gentleman he planned on doing business with and wanted to make sure he wasn't getting involved with someone who would rip him off. Just as I was sending him my report, my phone rang. It was a number I didn't recognize.

"Ms. Landon, it's Detective Jamison. I wanted to give you a heads-up. I spoke to Mr. Franklin and you will most likely be hearing from him. Sorry I couldn't change his mind."

"Thanks for the warning. I appreciate it."

When we hung up, I wasn't that surprised. He probably wanted to know what the heck I was doing there. Hopefully, I could talk him out of filing a complaint.

***

The following morning, as I was walking to my office, I received a phone call from Mia's father, Stephen Franklin. His tone, to say the least, did not warm my heart. He practically demanded I meet with him. Actually, it might be an opportunity to ask him some questions. Whether he would answer them remained to be seen. I told him I would be at his office by 11:00 a.m.

His building was in midtown. When I arrived, I went through the rotating doors and was greeted by a man standing behind a huge desk looking very bored.

"Where are you going?" he asked me in a friendly manner.

"Washington Securities."

"Sign in and take the elevators on the right side. It's the 12th floor."

"If I decide to take the stairs, where can I find the door to the staircase?"

He looked at me as if I had a screw loose. I thought it best not to ask him when the elevators were last serviced, though I was dying to. He gave me directions to the stairs.

It's a good thing I'm in shape, though halfway up I did stop for a breather.

Washington Securities had the whole floor. I gave my name to the cute blonde receptionist who was dressed in business attire: a cream-colored suit with a black and beige striped silk blouse. I did not dress for the occasion, wearing my usual standard work clothes.

I sat where I was directed and waited approximately ten minutes before I was escorted into Mr. Franklin's office.

"Please sit," he said without shaking my hand. Mr. Franklin had rugged good looks. He was tall and solidly built. His blue suit looked like it probably cost more than my whole wardrobe.

"Ms. Landon, if it wasn't for the fact that Detective Jamison put in a good word for you, you wouldn't be sitting here. I would have gone ahead and filed a complaint. You have about two minutes to talk me out of it."

"I appreciate the courtesy, but I can assure you I had no intention of breaking into your home. My client is the boy your daughter has accused of raping her. Though the camera shows my client leaving your home a little after nine, I was curious if the side or back of your house had any cameras." I knew there weren't any, but he didn't have to know that. "I wanted to see if it would be easy for someone to enter your house from the side door."

"And is it?"

"Just from looking at it, yes. It appeared to be a simple lock. Maybe you should change it." I wasn't sure if he appreciated my advice.

"My daughter has no reason to accuse someone of such a serious crime if it weren't true."

I didn't want to argue the point with the man.

"Do you know why Mia didn't tell you or your wife about the rape immediately? It wasn't until the headmaster reported it to your wife that Mia admitted she was raped. By that time, all the DNA was washed away," I said.

"What are you getting at?"

"I can't imagine how traumatic this must be for your daughter, but I have a young man who's already been kicked out of school. His future is in jeopardy, and I intend to find out the truth no matter where it leads me."

"That's very admirable of you, but what you're telling me in a roundabout way is that my daughter is a liar."

"That's not what I'm saying. She's a kid and she's scared. Maybe there's more to it that we don't know about yet."

"Thank you for coming in to see me," he said in a harsh tone. "And don't come anywhere near my family or there will be consequences next time."

I left his office and found my way back to the stairs. As I walked down, I was fairly certain Mr. Franklin wasn't going to file the complaint. I know parents always want to believe their children. To think your child would lie, especially about something so serious, would be hard for any parent to swallow. I wanted to put some doubt in Mr. Franklin's mind. I'm not sure if I accomplished that.

Though the temperatures were in the seventies with a cool breeze, I wasn't in the mood to walk back to my office. Instead, I hailed down a cab and was dropped right in front of my building.

Sitting at my desk eating a strawberry yogurt, I was contemplating my next move when I recalled what the neighbor Mr. Burns had told me. At the time I had dismissed it, but what if it was the night of the rape that he heard the voices. I doubt it was the parents. They wouldn't have been home that early, and why would they go in through the side door. It didn't make sense. What if the voices were Mia and someone else who had been in the house with her after Jason left? Maybe someone she didn't want seen on tape. If that's true, why would she be protecting her rapist?

CHAPTER 15

I needed to speak with Mia Franklin, which, according to her father, was not going to happen. Instead, I thought I would take a crack at Tiffany Blake. I wasn't sure if Tiffany would talk to me, but I had to give it a shot. I needed to catch her off guard and away from her friends. My phone was buzzing.

"Ms. Landon, it's Nina Demsky." She sounded frantic. "It's Jason. He's in the hospital. He was beat up last night."

"Is he alright?"

"The doctors have been running tests. They say he has a concussion, so they're keeping him in the hospital to watch him. His arm is fractured, and his face is all bruised."

"Is he able to speak?"

"Yes, he's awake. The doctors gave him something for the pain."

"Did the police question him?"

"They were here earlier but Jason says he doesn't remember anything."

"I'd like to come by if Jason's up to it."

"Yes. I'd like you to see him."

I packed up and left the office. Since I didn't have my car, I took an Uber to the hospital. When I got to Jason's room, Nina was by Jason's side, holding his hand.

"Hi, Jason." He looked awful. Whoever beat him up did a good job on him. His right eye was completely shut.

"Can you tell me what happened?"

"I was leaving the grocery store where I work and was attacked."

"What time did you leave work?"

"About 9:00 p.m."

"How many people attacked you?"

"I think two, maybe three. I'm not sure."

"Were they kids from your school?"

"It was dark and I couldn't see their faces."

"Did they say anything at all?"

"If they did, I don't remember."

"Did they take anything, maybe your wallet?"

"No."

"Is there anything you can tell me about them? Maybe you saw what they were wearing."

"Like I said, it was dark."

"Were they taller or shorter than you?"

"I don't know. Why are you asking me all these questions?"

"Jason, are you afraid to tell me who they are?"

"I already told you; I don't know."

"I can't help you if you're not being honest with me."

"Please, I never saw their faces. Could you just leave me alone," he said, turning his head away.

I motioned to Ms. Demsky that I wanted to speak with her in private. We stepped out into the hall.

"I have a feeling Jason isn't telling me the truth. I think he knows who beat him up."

"But if he knows who these hoodlums are, why wouldn't he tell us?"

"Teenagers don't like to snitch. It was probably kids from his school who thought they were getting even for what happened."

"But he didn't rape that girl."

"It doesn't matter. They think he did."

"They're just going to get away with it?"

"For the time being, at least. Unless Jason tells us who they were, there isn't anything the police can do."

As I was about to leave, I saw Samantha and Marshal Berger walking toward us.

"Maddie, how's Jason?" Sam said, trembling slightly.

"He's pretty banged up, but he'll be alright."

"Hello, Marshal. I'm sure Jason will be happy to see you guys."

"You're not staying?" Sam said.

"No. I'll talk to you soon."

"He could've been killed. I'm not going to stand by anymore and do nothing. I don't care what you say."

"Sam…" But she had already turned her back and was walking into Jason's room.

I said goodbye to Nina and left. I had my doubts that Jason was going to tell Sam or Marshal who beat him up.

CHAPTER 16

The following morning, I was having breakfast and feeling guilty that I hadn't called my father back yet. I was his flesh and blood and he never knew I existed until recently. We were both in the dark, but for different reasons. I knew I couldn't wait too much longer. I was staring at the bottle of Cabernet Sauvignon that was sitting on the kitchen counter. I got up and quickly stashed the bottle in one of the kitchen cabinets.

***

Around 2:00 p.m., I took an Uber over to the school, hoping to get a shot at speaking with Tiffany Blake.

I didn't spot Tiffany right away. I noticed Sandra Carlson first. They both had their school uniforms on. Their blue pleated skirts came at least three inches above their knees. They left the school walking closely together and chatting away down Fifth Avenue. I followed at a distance, hoping at some point Sandra and Tiffany would go their separate ways.

When they got to Saks Fifth Avenue, a high-end department store, they went inside. I did not follow them in. I waited where I could see the exits. Forty-five minutes later, they came out with no packages in hand. Maybe they were just browsing.

Two blocks later, they stopped at a coffee place. When they sat down, I noticed Tiffany took what looked like a T-shirt out of her bag. She showed it to Sandra and they both started giggling. I wondered if she stole it. She was rich and could easily afford a T-shirt, but I guess she did it for the thrill of it.

When my parents died, I was angry at the world and didn't know what to do with the rage I felt inside of me. I started stealing, first taking a bag of candy from the supermarket. Then it was a sweater and a pair of jeans from a department store. It was during that time I started getting panic attacks and my aunt took me to seek professional help. Though I still get panic attacks, they're usually not as severe as they once were. Eventually the stealing stopped.

When Tiffany and Sandra finally left, they walked together for a few blocks and then parted ways. I decided not to approach Tiffany right away but to wait and see where she went. She walked up to 57th Street and got on the crosstown bus. After a few other passengers hopped on the bus, I got on. Thankfully, I had the right amount of change. She got off at Broadway and 57th and from there walked up Columbus Avenue. At a certain point, Columbus Avenue changes, the streets get wider, and the neighborhood becomes more affluent. I thought she probably lived in one of the townhouses we were approaching.

"Excuse me," I said as I caught up to her. "My name's Maddie Landon. I'm investigating the alleged rape of Mia Franklin."

"I know who you are. Sandra warned me about you. You think Mia's lying about Jason."

"I'm not saying that at all. I'm looking into what happened."

"I don't want to talk to you. Actually, what I will tell you is that Jason raped Mia. Now leave me alone."

"Were you the one who told the school that Mia was raped?" Tiffany had a weird look on her face, as if she didn't know what I was talking about. She quickly walked away without answering my question. I noticed she entered one of the townhouses down the street. The good news was I wasn't too far from where I lived. The bad news was I didn't know much more than when my day first started.

Walking home, it dawned on me that both Sandra and Tiffany believed that Jason raped Mia; that or they were both very good liars. *If I'm assuming Jason is innocent, why is Mia lying to her best friends?*

I stopped on the way home to pick up some Chinese takeout. My little TV was on in the kitchen as I was eating. Though the TV was talking to me, I was thinking about Mia and why she would lie. I didn't think whoever raped her was a perfect stranger. There was no forced entry, and I doubted if a sixteen-year-old girl would open a door to someone she didn't know, especially at a late hour and at the side door.

If that's the case, and she did know this person, was she being threatened? If she was, I could see how she would be scared and even traumatized. If the threat was to her family, she might have been desperate enough to come up with the first person that came to mind.

I brought a glass of wine into the living room and sat in my father's chair. I pulled out the telephone records I had from Mia's cell phone. The one other number she called a few times was to a Benjamin Bradley.

I googled Benjamin Bradley. Though I couldn't find an address for him, his name was associated with a Jonathan Bradley. I went into my databases and found a Jonathan Bradley. His age was fifty-two, Maryann Bradley, presumably his wife, was listed as forty-four and son Benjamin, twenty. They lived in a six-million-dollar house in Scarsdale off of Weaver Street. Jonathan Bradley worked at Washington Securities. *That's interesting.* Mia's father also worked there. Is it possible that's how Mia knew Benjamin, through her father, and they've been in contact? Though they both had attended the same school, Benjamin was four years older than Mia, so it's likely the connection was through her father.

Why would Mia be in contact with this guy Benjamin? Maybe she looked up to him as a big brother. Could she have confided in him? *I think I need to talk to this guy Bradley.*

CHAPTER 17

I had no idea where to find Benjamin Bradley. If he was attending college, he could be anywhere in the country, or the world for that matter. Though I had his cell phone number, I would prefer not to call and give him a heads-up. The element of surprise is always better. I knew his parents lived in Scarsdale. I guess that would be a place to start.

***

The next day, around 4:30 p.m., I drove up to Scarsdale, taking the Hutchinson River Parkway, and followed my GPS instructions to their address.

The Bradleys' house was quite elaborate. It was a huge brick center hall colonial, though it was hard to see with the high hedges partially obstructing the view. I was unable to drive up to the house since there was a closed wrought-iron gate at the entrance. I knew I couldn't stay on the street without someone calling the cops. I punched in the Bradleys' cell phone number. A woman's voice answered, "Can I help you?"

"I'm looking for Benjamin Bradley."

"He's my son. What do you want with him?" As would be expected, Mrs. Bradley sounded like a protective mother.

"My name's Maddie Landon and I'm investigating the alleged rape of a young girl who's a friend of your son."

"Ben isn't here. He lives in the city where he attends college. Why do you need to speak with him?"

"Your son appears to know the victim, and I'm talking to everyone who may have a connection to her."

"I feel very uncomfortable giving out his personal information."

"I'm pretty sure he wouldn't mind. I know he would want to help with the investigation."

"Even so, I'd rather not."

"Would you tell him that I stopped by, and can you please give Ben my telephone number in case he wants to contact me?"

I gave Mrs. Bradley my number and left. Well, at least I knew he was still living in the city and not some far-off place. Though I had Ben's number, his mother didn't have to know that. I was pretty sure Mrs. Bradley was texting or calling her son at this very moment to tell him about my unexpected call. I'm banking on the fact that he would contact me. If not, I would have to call him. So much for the element of surprise. Without having an address on him or where he goes to school, it would be like looking for a needle in a haystack.

As soon as I arrived home, I poured myself a glass of wine and called Jesse.

"Hey, babe," Jesse said when he picked up. "I was just going to call you."

"If I only had a nickel for every time I've heard that line," I said.

"Either you were very popular or you were getting the brush off quite a bit."

"I'd like to think I was popular but we both know that's not true."

"I like a woman who knows herself."

"How's life in Chester?"

"Not as much fun without you. Since we have no trials coming up, I have some breathing room."

"Does that mean I have your undivided attention for the whole weekend?"

"It does. How can I serve you?"

"Let's talk in the morning. I'm going to take a shower and pamper myself so I'll look fabulous when you see me tomorrow."

"Can't wait. Love you."

"Me too."

As soon as I hung up, my phone was ringing. It was a number I didn't recognize.

"Is this Maddie Landon?"

"Yes."

"This is Ben Bradley."

"Thanks for calling me. I was wondering if we could meet. I'm investigating the alleged rape of Mia Franklin and I had a few questions."

"How did my name come up in your investigation?"

"I noticed Mia texted your number a few times."

"I see. Sure. Anything to help."

I didn't want to wait till Monday when Jesse left. "How about sometime tomorrow, wherever you say?"

"I'm meeting some friends around 1 p.m. at a restaurant on Columbus Avenue between 71st and 72nd Street. How about 12:30 p.m.? I'll text you the exact address."

"Great. See you then."

I was looking forward to speaking with Ben, and I was hoping he may have information that could be helpful to the case. So far, I was getting nowhere. I had zero leads and I was running out of people to talk with.

Before falling asleep, I let myself imagine what it would be like if Jesse and I lived together. The fantasy was lovely. It was the reality that I was grappling with.

CHAPTER 18

Saturday morning, I was up bright and early and went out to get fresh bagels, knowing how much Jesse loved our New York bagels.

"Wow, is that the wonderful smell of bagels?" Those were the first words out of Jesse's mouth when he came in.

"I think I was just insulted," I said, grinning.

Jesse pulled me close to him and kissed me deeply on the lips.

"Yum," I said after we broke apart. "Do you think you can wait a little while before having breakfast? I know it's a hard choice for you."

Jesse was moving his head back and forth as if he was mulling it over.

"Very funny," I said, as I pulled him into the bedroom and pushed him down on the bed.

Forty-five minutes later, we were sitting and munching on toasted buttered bagels and scrambled eggs. As I was sipping my coffee, I relayed to Jesse everything I found out so far on the case.

"If you think this girl was threatened, why did she confess to her mother she was raped? She could have just said nothing."

"She didn't confess. The nanny told me someone from the school called Mrs. Franklin and told her that her daughter had been raped."

"So, you think she said the first name that popped into her head?"

"She had already told her friend the night it happened that it was Jason. If she wanted to pin it on someone, he would be the most likely candidate since he was there that night and he would be caught on camera."

"Your theory only makes sense if Jason didn't rape her."

"I know. My gut says he didn't do it."

"You still need to be open to the possibility that this boy Jason is guilty."

"By the way, there's someone I need to interview and he was able to do it today. I'm supposed to meet with him at 12:30 p.m."

"How is this person connected to the case?"

I explained to Jesse how his number popped up on Mia's cell phone records and how both his father and Mia's father worked at the same place.

"He's a twenty-year-old college student, and she's only a sophomore in high school. What could they possibly have in common?"

"Well, if they've known each other for years because of their fathers' work connection, they might just be friends. Maybe she has a crush on him."

"You might be right. Let me do most of the questioning. I don't want him to feel he's being ganged up on."

"Aye aye, Captain! I'll only ask him a question if I think it's really important."

***

We arrived at Ella Social a few minutes before noon. From the description Ben had given me of himself, I spotted him seated at the bar right away. He got up as he saw me approaching.

"Ben, I'm Maddie and this is Jesse. He's also a private investigator." They shook hands.

"I've never been here before. It's a really cool place. Would you mind if we sat at one of the tables?" I said. The place was fairly dark. A lot of wood. The bar had a brick wall behind it and a great structure with lights hanging down from the ceiling.

We headed over to one of the wooden tables and sat down. Ben was a good-looking kid with large blue eyes, a great head of dirty blonde wavy hair, high cheekbones, and a fair complexion. He had that preppy look, wearing beige khakis and a blue button-down cotton shirt. He was built like he might have played football or still did.

The waitress came over and we ordered beers all around. She asked for some form of ID from Ben. When she left, I decided not to ask him if it was fake. I was pretty sure Ben was only twenty and not twenty-one.

"What can I answer for you?" Ben said. I could tell from the way he spoke and handled himself that he was very self-assured, maybe bordering on cocky. Being brought up privileged might have had something to do with his attitude.

The waitress set down our beers.

"As I had mentioned to you, I noticed you're in touch with Mia."

"Well, she sometimes texts or calls me."

"How do you know each other?"

"We've known each other for ages. Our fathers work at the same place, and through the years we've seen each other at office parties, like at Christmas."

"Is your father a partner at the firm?"

"He's a senior partner."

"And Mia's father, what's his position?"

"I believe he might be a junior partner, but I'm not positive."

"With the age difference, what do you have in common with Mia?"

"I think Mia sees me as an older brother."

"Did she tell you she was raped?"

"No, I found out through my father. Mr. Franklin told him that Mia had been raped."

I thought I heard some hesitancy in his voice before he answered my question. I was curious why Mia didn't tell Ben she was raped. You would think that might be something she would have told him if she thought of him as an older brother or had a crush on him.

"Have you had any contact with Mia since the rape?"

I looked over at Jesse. He seemed content just to listen. I knew if there was something he wanted to ask, he would speak up.

"I haven't. I thought if she wanted to talk, she would call me."

"I see. Did she ever mention the name Jason Demsky to you?"

"No. Is that the boy who raped her?"

"That's the boy who was accused of raping her."

"Why don't you ask Mia what happened?"

"At some point I may have to, but at the moment I'm talking to people she knows." I didn't want to mention the fact that her father warned me against speaking to his daughter.

"Well, if you really want to talk with her, maybe I have some influence."

"I'll think about it and if I decide, I'll give you a call. By the way, your mother mentioned you go to college in the city. What college do you attend?"

"Drake. It's uptown."

A guy about Ben's age walked over to our table. "Ben, when you're finished, I'll be at the bar."

"Excuse me," Jesse said, before Ben's friend walked away. "My name's Jesse Monroe. Glad to meet you. What's your name?"

"Mark Jordan."

"Nice meeting you, Mark."

At that point, Ben said he was joining his friend at the bar if we didn't have any more questions.

We paid the check and left. "What was that all about?" I said to Jesse.

"You never know if you might need to question one of Ben's friends down the road. He might have some information on your victim."

"Good thinking."

We walked up Columbus Avenue and stopped at a little café that had outdoor seating. We each ordered a cappuccino and a French pastry.

"What was your take on Ben Bradley?" I said.

"He's a pretty smooth character, but other than that, I had no gut reaction," Jesse said.

"I got the feeling he thinks a lot of himself."

"Not a bad trait."

"There was something I couldn't quite put my finger on. I'm not sure I believed Bradley, but what reason would he have to lie?"

"Maybe he's more than friends with Mia," Jesse said.

"That's interesting. It didn't cross my mind. She could be a very mature sixteen-year-old."

"It's probably not as uncommon as you think," Jesse said.

"He seemed pretty sure he could set up something so I could speak to her."

"Might not be a bad idea."

"I'll think on it. So, did you ever date a teenager when you were twenty?"

"A person who's twenty is barely out of their teens. But to answer your question, I never did. As I told you, I was a late bloomer. I concentrated on my studies and didn't really start dating until I was in my mid-twenties."

"Wow, you were practically an old man when you lost your virginity," I said, trying to keep a straight face.

"I said I was a late bloomer when it came to dating. It would be a mistake to confuse dating and sex," Jesse said playfully.

"I see. My mistake," I said, suppressing a smile.

Our cappuccinos and pastries came. I dug into my napoleon and eyed Jesse's blueberry/raspberry tart.

"Don't get any ideas, young lady," Jesse said.

"Listen, I've been thinking. You know I'm not too keen about meeting my stepbrothers, but my father has asked me to come out to California and I haven't given him an answer yet."

"I think you should go. You might even decide that you do want to have a relationship with them. You have to keep an open mind."

I knew Jesse was talking more about us and not about my stepbrothers when he said I have to keep an open mind.

"I was thinking I would go out to Los Angeles next weekend if my father's not busy. I hate to admit this, but I've never flown by myself. To tell you the truth, I'll probably need to take something so I don't freak out and jump off the plane as we're flying thirty thousand feet up in the air." Jesse laughed.

"You laugh, but when I was six years old, my parents and I flew out to Chicago where my aunt, my mother's sister, lived. Going home, we flew right into a storm. I was so scared when the plane started shaking. My parents tried to reassure me, telling me it was just turbulence and nothing to worry about, but I could see the concerned look on their faces. I remember thinking I was never going to step foot on an airplane again."

"Do you plan on parachuting out if there's any turbulence? Otherwise, I think I'd take my chances on the plane. If you take anything beforehand, just don't overdo it."

I wondered if Jesse was hurt that I didn't ask him to come out to California with me.

CHAPTER 19

I woke up to ferocious rain smacking the outside of my air conditioner. Jesse was still sleeping. I eased out of bed and made a pot of coffee. When I went back into the bedroom, Jesse was stirring.

"Are you coming back to bed?" he said.

I slipped in next to him and gently stroked his hair.

"Are you upset I haven't asked you to come with me to California?"

"No. It's the first time you're meeting with your stepbrothers and you don't need me there as a distraction. You'll have enough to deal with."

"Thank you for being so understanding. That answer is going to get you really lucky."

***

After Jesse left on Monday morning, I went for a quick run, showered, and had breakfast before going into the office. I called my father at 11:00 a.m. California time. I could hear it in his voice he was happy I was coming out to see him and to meet his sons. I wasn't sure how any of this was going to turn out, but I knew it was something my adoptive parents would have wanted me to do.

Lately I've been thinking about what it would be like if Jesse and I moved in together. I've lived by myself for so long, it's hard to imagine what my life would look like sharing it with someone else. I'm not good at compromising or having someone else's stuff around, though for a guy, Jesse is very neat. I think I'm more afraid Jesse will realize all the baggage I come with and will bolt. The phone interrupted my thoughts.

"Did you find out anything yet?" Samantha barked into the phone.

"No and hello? Sam, investigations take time. You remember how long it took to eventually find out what happened to your mother?"

"Can't you force Mia into telling the truth?"

"At this point, I can't talk to her."

"Why not?" Sam demanded.

"Her parents won't allow it. I'm not the police, so I can't just waltz in and question her."

"But I can. Maybe she'll tell me."

"I think Mia is going through a rough time. I don't want you to make things worse. Please let me handle it."

"I don't care if she's having a hard time. Look what they did to Jason. They could have killed him."

Samantha did have a valid point. Though I didn't think Mia would talk to Sam or confess to her that she lied, if that's what she actually did.

"Sam, I don't think it's a good idea."

Next thing I knew, the phone went dead. Sam had enough of my sermon.

For the next hour or so, I wrote down everyone I had talked to regarding Jason's case and what I had learned so far. At this point, the police only had Mia's word that Jason raped her and a camera showing Jason entering and leaving Mia's house the night of the alleged rape. Though there was no forensic evidence, there was a ton of circumstantial evidence. If Mia was telling the truth, then why did she ask her nanny to wash her bedsheets. There might have been DNA evidence on the sheets that could have proved that Jason raped her. The only conclusion I could come to is that Mia lied about who her rapist was. Maybe I should take Ben Bradley up on his offer and meet with Mia if she agreed to it.

***

"Hey, I was thinking about you," Annie said when she answered the phone. "What's going on?"

"I thought I'd tell you the big news. I'm going to California on Friday to see my father and his family."

"Wow! That is big. Are you going by yourself?"

"I am. I was thinking of asking Jesse to come, but then I decided I would be anxious enough without having to worry how Jesse was getting along with everyone."

"Are you going to be alright flying?"

"As long as the plane stays in the air." Annie laughed. "Right now, I'm more concerned with finding out who raped Mia."

"And you're sure it wasn't your client who did it?"

"As sure as I can be. This kid is definitely hiding something, but I don't think it has anything to do with Mia's rape."

CHAPTER 20

That night, as I was brushing my teeth, I remembered how Ben Bradley learned of Mia's rape. It was from his father who found out about it from Mia's father, Stephen Franklin. It makes sense since they both work at Washington Securities. I wonder what else Mia's father shared with Jonathan Bradley.

Since I didn't want my face shown anywhere near Stephen Franklin's office, I had to think of another way to get to Jonathan Bradley. I thought the best approach would be to wait until he came home from work. There was only one problem. Where Mr. Bradley lived in Scarsdale, it was going to be impossible to wait near his house without any neighbor contacting the police. I'd have to show up later in the evening and hope he would be home.

***

The next day I was up in Scarsdale and in front of the Bradley's six-million-dollar home at 7:30 p.m. It was probably rude to come unannounced to someone's house at that hour without calling ahead of time, but I didn't want to give Mr. Bradley a heads-up since he might mention my call to Mia's father.

I left my car in front and walked through the wrought-iron gate, praying it wasn't going to electrocute me. The brick center hall colonial was massive. There was a pond on the front grounds with giant-size goldfish swimming around. I had to walk maybe seventy-five feet before I reached their front door. I rang the bell.

Though I was pretty sure the person who was standing in front of me was Jonathan Bradley, he looked nothing like I expected. He was about my height, maybe an inch taller, lanky, and wearing wire-rimmed glasses. His hooked nose was too big for his face, and he had the unfortunate luck of having pockmarks, most likely from childhood acne. But there was something about him that commanded a presence.

"Can I help you," he said.

"My name's Maddie Landon. I'm a private investigator," I replied, giving him my card. "I'm sorry to disturb you at your home and during the dinner hour, but I would like to speak with you about Mia Franklin. Can I please come in for a few moments?"

"I can give you five minutes of my time."

The foyer was larger than my bedroom. The sheen bounced off the polished wood spiral staircase leading up to the second floor. A beautiful Persian rug took up part of the foyer. Mr. Bradley showed me to his study. The walls were lined with built-in bookcases. Underneath my feet was an oriental rug in shades of red and blue. Jonathan Bradley asked me to sit while he sat opposite me behind a mahogany leather desk.

"I spoke to your son, and he mentioned that Mr. Franklin told you that Mia was raped."

"Why were you speaking to my son?" he said in an accusatory tone.

"In the course of my investigation, I learned that your son and Mia Franklin had been in contact. I've been speaking with everyone who is acquainted with Mia Franklin."

"What did my son tell you?"

"He had no information for me, except that he thought Mia might think of him as a big brother."

"I see. So how can I help you?"

"I was wondering what Mr. Franklin might have told you about that night?"

"As my son already mentioned, just that Mia had been raped."

"And you didn't ask him any questions?"

"I may have. He told me it was some kid from her school that was there on a scholarship."

I could hear the disdain in his voice. "Nothing else?" I said.

"You're working for the family, I presume?"

"Yes, but my main priority is finding out the truth wherever that leads. Did you know your son was in contact with Mia?"

"I don't see how that's relevant."

"Oh, I didn't know you had company." I turned around and saw a beautiful woman standing by the door. Though I only got a quick glimpse, I presumed it was Mrs. Bradley. I could see where her son got his good looks. She was taller than her husband, maybe by a few inches, with a model's figure. Her blonde hair was short but stylish.

"We're just about through," he said to her in a dismissive tone, and she left.

"Your wife is beautiful," I said.

"If you'll excuse me, I have dinner waiting. I'll show you out."

I was sitting in my car rehashing the brief conversation I just had with Mr. Bradley. This is a man who is fairly wealthy and believes he's in control. He strikes me as someone who was probably bullied as a kid and took his revenge by becoming very successful. There was a definite air of superiority about him. Now I knew where his son got his cocky attitude from. I wondered what his wife saw in him. I'd been told that women like to be with powerful men.

Though Mrs. Bradley was a very handsome woman, there was no spark in her eyes. Maybe Jonathan Bradley's charm had finally worn off after years of marriage.

As I was driving, I heard my phone buzzing. It was from an unknown caller. "Hello. Hello," I said, and then hung up. It was probably a wrong number.

***

The following day, as I was typing out my report on what I'd found out so far, I saw that Jesse was calling.

"Hey, babe," I said.

"Are you all packed for your trip?"

"If you mean are my toothbrush and underwear in my backpack yet, then the answer is no."

"I like a girl who travels light. Is Annie taking you to the airport?"

"I have an early flight so I'll take an Uber. Listen, in case I never make it back, I'll have my typed interviews and notes on the case in my desk drawer. Will has my key. I want you to take over the investigation. If you don't, Sam will probably kill you. I'd watch your back if I were you."

"Can I take time off to grieve for you?"

"Can't you wait till after you find out who the rapist is?"

"I'll try." I could hear it in Jesse's voice that he thought all of this was very amusing.

"I'll call you from the airport on Friday. I love you."

"Madds, you'll be fine. Besides, I think you owe me a chess rematch, so don't plan on skipping out on me. Sleep tight."

CHAPTER 21

I was up by 4:30 a.m. on Friday. My Uber was coming at 7:00 a.m. It didn't take me long to pack, throwing whatever I needed in my shoulder bag. By 6:00 a.m. I had nothing to do but wait for my Uber. I had already drunk three cups of coffee by the time my driver was downstairs. Probably not a good idea since I woke up feeling anxious.

Though LaGuardia Airport was closer, it had no direct flights to Los Angeles. Instead, I was flying out of JFK Airport. I had no intention of taking off and landing more than once on my trip out to California or worrying about making a connecting flight.

I waited in line with all the other travelers to get through security. All the coffee I drank was kicking in and I was getting antsy. I took off my shoes and my belt and put them in one of those ugly gray containers, along with my shoulder bag. My stuff went through first and then I walked through the metal detector. I was praying I wasn't going to catch any diseases from walking barefoot. As soon as I got on the other side, I collected my bag and my laptop and slipped on my shoes. I followed the signs to the Delta area and parked myself at my gate.

Before boarding, I called Jesse and Annie and told them I didn't chicken out, at least not yet. I heard someone saying the flight to Los Angeles was now ready for boarding. I waited till they called my section and walked onto the plane along with the other passengers like good little children. As I was passing the cockpit, I did a quick check to make sure the pilot looked alert and wasn't under the influence.

I found my row and seat and threw my shoulder bag in the overhead luggage compartment. I specifically took an aisle seat in case I had to make a run to the bathroom or wanted to jump out of the plane.

The woman who was sitting next to me was very chatty. I tried to ignore her and kept my head in my book, but she was having no part of that. She just kept on talking. When the pilot announced we were next to take off, I squeezed the armrests so tight I thought I would lose the feeling in my fingers.

When the plane lifted up off the ground, I breathed a sigh of relief. Now all it had to do was stay up in the air. I tried to read, but between chatty Kathy and my anxiety about meeting my father's family, I wasn't having much luck.

Since I wasn't sitting in first class, the only goodies the flight attendant offered me were water, juice, tiny, tiny pretzels, and two cookies. Instead, I ate one of my power bars.

My thoughts wandered to my Aunt Lucy, my birth mother's sister. For the past few months, we'd been talking on the phone every so often. Before I left, I told her I was going out to California to meet my father's family. She was really happy for me, but I also had the feeling the whole situation might be sad for her knowing her sister, my mother, would never know me.

During the course of my search for my biological mother, I found out she had gotten pregnant when she was sixteen. Her god-fearing parents sent her to live with an aunt until I was born and then she was forced into putting me up for adoption. Unfortunately, I never had the opportunity to meet her since she died a few years ago of sepsis. Though knowing the reason I was given up for adoption was like a weight lifted off my shoulders, those scars remain with me.

By the time the plane landed, I knew that chatty Kathy was divorced twice, had horrible husbands who treated her badly, had two grown kids who rarely talked to her, and worked for a transport company as an administrative assistant in a suburb of Los Angeles.

My phone was ringing as I was attempting to find my way out of the airport.

"Hello."

"Maddie, it's Dad. I'm waiting at Arrivals, standing outside my car."

It was weird hearing Harris Tyler calling himself dad to me. It made me feel kind of uneasy. I had a father who I was close to and loved for the first twelve years of my life. I hope Harris had no illusions that I would be calling him Dad.

"I should be there in a few minutes." The one and only time we met was about two months ago when he came to New York with his wife, and we got to know each other a little bit. Ever since then, we'd been emailing and talking on the phone. Unfortunately, he never knew I existed. I can't blame him for that. If he did know, my life might have been very different. In a strange way, I'm glad it worked out as it did. I wouldn't have traded my parents for anyone else, but when they died, something broke inside of me.

As soon as I got out of the airport, I spotted him. He waved.

"I'm so glad you're here," he said, as he took my shoulder bag from my arm and placed it into the trunk of his car.

"How was your flight?" he said, giving me a quick hug.

"Thankfully uneventful. I'm not a fan of planes."

"That's probably because you rarely take them. It gets easier the more you fly, but I can understand how it could be scary. I thought we would grab some lunch, just the two of us before heading back to the house."

My birth father was a tall and very handsome man. We both had high cheekbones, large almond-shaped eyes, and a square chin. His eyes were dark brown. I took after my birth mother with green eyes.

"How is Jesse? I thought he might come out with you."

I didn't want to tell him it's hard enough just by myself. "I thought maybe next time or if you come to New York again."

"Maddie, I realize this isn't easy for you, and I don't want you to feel I'm trying to take your father's place because I know how much you loved him. I just want us to be in each other's lives, if that's what you want as well."

"When my parents were killed, my Aunt Jenny, my mother's sister, came to live with me. She died when I was nineteen and I've been on my own ever since. There have been only a few close people I've shared my life with. I've gotten used to it and I like my life the way it is." I could hear Dr. Goldberg whispering in my ear, saying: "You have to keep an open mind."

"I understand, I really do. Let's give each other a chance. That's all I ask."

We had lunch outside at a really nice café. In New York, it's hard to find places to eat outside with all the noise and the fumes from the traffic in the city. While we were eating, my father told me about his childhood. I was interested in knowing more about my grandparents.

"What were your parents like?" I said.

"I was fortunate. My parents were very supportive. They always encouraged me to dream big. I remember one time my father was teaching me how to play basketball. I was maybe seven and I was getting really frustrated because I couldn't get the basketball in the hoop. I was so mad I threw the ball and it hit this kid in the leg. My father calmly told me to walk over to the boy and apologize. When I retrieved the basketball, my father said we were leaving. I could tell by the look on his face he was disappointed in me. When we got home, he sat me down and explained to me that not everything came easy. If I wanted to become good at basketball, it would take practice like everything else. Getting frustrated didn't help. I always remembered what he told me."

Harris talked about my birth mother again and how they had to keep their relationship a secret because her parents were so religious. Though he was easy to be with, talking about my mother was too painful knowing what she went through and then dying so unexpectedly without ever meeting her.

CHAPTER 22

Before going back to his house, we drove around the streets of Los Angeles. He took me to Rodeo Drive and the Beverly Hills Hotel. How did I not know that the outside of the hotel was painted pink and green? I hadn't traveled very much, and I was enjoying seeing places that were so different from New York.

My father lived in a suburb about twenty minutes outside of Los Angeles. The street we turned into had beautiful palm trees on both sides of the road. We drove onto a paved driveway and stopped in front of dark brown garage doors. I had never seen a house like this before except in photos and in the movies. My father said it was a Spanish/Mediterranean-style home with terracotta roof shingles and painted white over flat stucco walls. The walkway leading to the front door had several large rectangular slabs of stone, with pebbles in between each slab and colorful shrubs on each side of the walkway.

When my father opened the door, I walked slowly inside. There were no walls between the rooms. I think they call it an open concept. My father saw me staring at the floor and told me it was Brazilian Cherry solid hardwood flooring. It was throughout the main floor. There was a staircase with a wrought-iron railing leading up to the second floor. The windows were from floor to ceiling.

Walking around, I was surprised that the furnishings were very modern, but comfortable looking. The walls were all white but the artwork throughout gave the large room warmth.

"Hi, Maddie. I'm so happy you're here," my father's wife, Jennifer, said to me. "We want you to feel comfortable while you're staying with us." Jennifer Tyler was very attractive. She looked a lot younger than her fifty-five years.

"Why don't we go out back where we can relax on the patio, unless you want to unpack first?" Jennifer said.

"As you can see, I travel light," I said, looking down at my shoulder bag sitting on the floor.

"I'm going out to get us something for dinner," my father said. "Do you eat meat?"

"I eat everything."

"Great," he said. "I'll be back soon."

We walked out onto the back patio. I was staring at a rectangular built-in swimming pool. When I was a kid, my mother signed me up for swimming lessons. She instilled in me how important it was to know how to swim. Though she never told me why, I knew she was afraid of the water. I took to it right away. As an adult, I hadn't been swimming in years until Jesse and I started dating. When we'd go out fishing, we usually tied up the boat by an inlet and swam.

"Wow, it's really beautiful out here."

"How about if we have something to drink. Any preference?" Jennifer said.

"Do you have any white wine?"

"My thoughts exactly."

My phone buzzed. "Hello." Whoever was at the other end said nothing, and then they hung up. This couldn't be a coincidence.

"Is everything alright," Jennifer said.

"Of course."

"You look upset."

"No, it's nothing."

Jennifer brought out two glasses of white wine, which she set down on a colorful ceramic table. When she came back out again, she was carrying pretzels, chips, and almonds. I wondered if this was a life I could get accustomed to.

Outside, I could see the blonde highlights in Jennifer's hair. She wore it short, but it suited her.

"Can you talk about your case?" Jennifer asked as she sat down.

"Sure. It's a rape case. A seventeen-year-old boy was accused of raping a sixteen-year-old girl. They both attended the same private school except he was there on a scholarship, otherwise he wouldn't have been able to go there. Whether my client is guilty or not doesn't play a part in my investigation. In this case it's my job to find out who actually raped the victim or to find enough evidence to put doubt in a jury's mind in order for my client to be found innocent."

"That's so interesting. Are you making any headway?"

"Unfortunately, not yet. I've been told I can be a little obsessed when I'm working a case. It can stress me out at times."

"Well, maybe being here will help you relax."

We can only hope, I thought to myself. My mind was not far from New York and Jason Demsky.

"I'd love to meet Jesse. From what you've told us about him, he seems like a wonderful man. Do you have any marriage plans?"

The question took me by surprise. "I haven't really thought about it." I was feeling uncomfortable being asked about my plans with Jesse.

"So what's the holdup?" she said in a way that didn't come off as being nosy.

"I've been on my own for most of my life. I'm not sure I'd be good at sharing it."

"I remember when I first met Harris. He was gung-ho on getting married, but I was more interested in a career. I had just finished college and wanted to work in journalism."

"So what happened?"

"We broke up." I was surprised at her answer. "I eventually got a job at a local newspaper. It was a start, and I was happy. My love life was another story. I dated quite a bit but nobody I wanted to marry. It was by accident that your father and I met again. It was at a friend's party a few years later. The funny thing was I almost didn't go. I was supposed to be on a blind date that night, but my friend begged me to come. She said I could bring him along."

"Did you?"

"I did. But the moment I saw your father at the party, that was it for me. Fortunately, he wasn't dating anyone seriously at the time."

I wondered if there was something I was supposed to take from her story.

"Did you give up your career once you got married?"

"No. I made it clear to Harris that I was going to pursue my journalism career. I did take time off when each of the boys was born. I worked for the *Los Angeles Times* for many years, and now I work part-time for the *Los Angeles Daily News*."

"Do you think if you never ran into my father again you would have regretted that you didn't marry him when he asked you to?"

"It's hard to second guess the decisions you make. At the time, I knew I wasn't ready."

"I'm back," I heard my father say from behind me. I was relieved. I knew Jennifer was just trying to get to know me, but I'm always uncomfortable talking about myself to people I'm not close to.

CHAPTER 23

During dinner, we chatted about life in New York and California. Thankfully, we kept the conversation light. I kept looking at this man who was talking. I felt like an outsider, someone who didn't belong here. After waiting thirty-seven years to look for my biological father, I wasn't sure what I wanted from this person. Did I really want a relationship? But I knew I had to give him a chance.

***

I was sitting on the back patio the following afternoon, taking in my surroundings. My father was casually dressed in black shorts and a white polo shirt. Jennifer was wearing a sundress showing off her well-toned arms. I was wearing denim shorts and a white T-shirt. A man wheeling a baby carriage suddenly appeared. I knew it was Adam, the older of the two brothers. He looked like his father, square chin, and high cheekbones. His hair was straight, light brown, almost blonde, just like mine. I was amazed at how much we looked alike. He was coming straight toward me.

"Hi, Maddie, I'm Adam and this is my daughter Kate," he said, looking down at her. "This must be awkward for you because it certainly is for me." He must have been nervous since he kept on talking.

"I can definitely see the resemblance. When my dad first told me he had a daughter he never knew about, it kind of threw me for a loop. I'm sure it came as a surprise to you."

"I knew I had a father out there, but I wasn't actually sure I'd find him."

At this point, we both sat down. Where was Adam's wife?

"I can't imagine never knowing who my parents were. My father told me that your birth mother died. I'm sorry."

"I had wonderful parents." Adam started fidgeting with the baby. "What kind of work do you do?" I asked him, changing the subject.

Adam picked up Kate and was bouncing her on his knee. Kate was maybe a year old. She was smiling at me.

"I'm in real estate. My dad says you're a private investigator. That must be fascinating."

"I like it. I get to meet all sorts of people."

"Is it dangerous?"

"Do you know that's the number one question people ask me when I tell them what I do."

"Well, I wouldn't want to disappoint you." We both laughed. "And what's the number two question they ask you?"

"Do I carry a gun. The answer is yes, but only in New York. So you're safe." Adam smiled.

"Hey, guys," my father said, lifting Kate off of Adam's lap. "Do you know where Andrew is?"

"He'll be here. He's running late." I thought I saw something between them. Not sure what that was about.

"Is Dana coming?" Dana was Adam's wife.

"She wasn't feeling well. She might pop in later." My father didn't look too pleased. I was curious about what was going on. Did they have a problem with my presence?

"I'm going to take Kate for a while. I think your mom wants to spoil her more than she already does." My father left me and Adam alone.

"Does your brother have a problem with me?" I asked.

"My brother has a few issues. He's really a nice guy. When my father first told us about you, Andrew was skeptical. He thought you were taking advantage of our dad."

"So he doesn't believe I'm your father's daughter? Do you believe I am?"

"After my father told us about his relationship with your mother and what happened to her, and seeing your photo, I believed you."

"I asked your father if he wanted us to take a DNA test and he said no. Look, I'm not interested in your father's money, if that's what you or your brother are afraid of. I have a great life in New York and that's where I plan on staying. To tell you the truth, it was your father's idea for me to come out here and meet his sons." I was ticked off. I got up and started to walk away.

"Please don't go. I'm glad you came, and I know my parents are."

As I was about to turn toward Adam, I saw a young man who I presumed was Andrew in what appeared to be a heated discussion with my father.

"Why don't I get us something to drink," Adam said. "What would you like?"

I was still angry but I knew Adam meant well. "A beer if you have."

"Two beers coming up. I'll be right back."

I sat down again, looking out toward the tall trees that surrounded the backyard. I was getting the feeling that the only person besides my father and Jennifer who wanted me here was Adam. It never dawned on me that there could be any resentment from anyone in the family. Maybe I shouldn't have come. I heard footsteps behind me.

"Maddie, this is my son Andrew." I got up and shook Andrew's hand. It felt clammy. Just then, Adam came back with our beers. None too soon. I took a gulp as soon as the cold beer was in my hands. My father whispered something in Andrew's ear and walked away, leaving me alone with his two sons.

CHAPTER 24

Andrew was about four inches shorter than Adam, maybe 5′9″, straight nose, thin lips, a narrow chin, large dark brown eyes, a full head of curly dark brown hair, and an olive complexion. His dimpled cheeks gave him a boyish look. He didn't look me straight in the eyes.

"It looks like you guys are having a good time," Andrew said with a scowl.

"Grow up, Andrew," Adam said. "Dad asked Maddie to come."

"Look, Andrew, I have no idea how this is going to turn out. Maybe we'll never be friends or have a relationship, and that's okay. Right now, I'm trying my best to get through this day. It isn't easy for me either." I was trying to keep my emotions in check since I didn't want to make a scene. Andrew seemed to back off a little.

"Your father told me you're in law school. Have you decided what type of law you want to practice?" I said to Andrew.

"Trust and Estates. Next month I'm taking the Multistate Professional Responsibility Examination and then I have to pass the California Bar. My father said you used to be a police detective. How come you quit?" Andrew said.

"It's kind of complicated. I decided I wasn't willing to go along with the office politics. Being a private investigator suits my personality. I don't like to take orders." Though Andrew seemed less confrontational, I didn't get the impression we would be good buddies. That was okay with me.

Around six o'clock, we all sat down for dinner outside on the patio. My father had grilled chicken and vegetables and Jennifer had made a big salad. There was yummy-looking bread in the breadbasket. I could see that my father was happy that we all seemed to be getting along. I had two glasses of wine, which made everything better.

When my brothers left, my father sat down next to me. "I'm sorry if Andrew was rude to you earlier."

"It's fine."

"After Adam was born, we were told it might be difficult for us to conceive again. During the two years before we learned that Jennifer was pregnant again, we went through all sorts of tests. We were just about to start in vitro fertilization when we got the good news.

"Because we thought Andrew was our miracle child, we made the mistake of spoiling him. When he was fourteen, he started using drugs. We had no idea he was using until a police officer showed up at our house with Andrew completely out of it. He had been caught trespassing on private property. Fortunately, there were no charges pressed. We put Andrew in rehab kicking and screaming. It took several years before he finally kicked the habit. When I told him about you, I think he felt threatened, though he had no reason to. He'll come around."

"I'm glad you told me. I don't want to cause any trouble in the family. Maybe I shouldn't have come."

"Don't be ridiculous. We all want you here." I doubted that was true but I didn't want to debate the point.

"Before you leave tomorrow, why don't we spend the day together, just the two of us."

"Sure," I said, forcing a smile.

It was after twelve midnight in New York by the time I called Jesse. When he picked up, I knew he had been sound asleep.

"Hey," he said in a gravelly voice.

"I should never have come. Nobody wants me here except for my father and his wife."

"What happened?"

"I think they believe I'm after their father's money. They don't trust me. Well, that's not entirely true. The older one, Adam, was at least friendly, though his wife never showed. And I got the feeling Andrew doesn't want me in his father's life."

"Does your father know all this?"

"Yes. He apologized for the way Andrew acted." I went on to tell Jesse about Andrew and his earlier problems with drugs.

"Madds, what's important is that your father has made it perfectly clear that he wants a relationship with you. Don't worry about his children and what they think."

"It took me by surprise. I didn't think my father would invite me out here knowing how his children felt, or at least how Andrew felt."

"Maybe he didn't realize it himself. He probably thought by the time you got out there, everything would be smoothed over. Just keep your eye on what's important."

"I can't wait to see you."

"Me too. Don't worry. Sweet dreams."

***

On Sunday, my father and I spent the day together. I enjoyed his company while he was showing me the sights. We did some of the tourist attractions, including Universal Studios, and we stopped for dinner at a restaurant at the Santa Monica Pier.

After ordering, my father looked at me. "Is something on your mind, Maddie?"

"When I first decided to look for my mother, I didn't know what to expect. My whole life I had it in my head that my biological parents didn't want me. I thought my parents may have been junkies or my mother had been a prostitute. But when I found out what really happened to her, it was very painful for me. I know you didn't know any of this, but she told her parents she was raped." My father looked as if he was slapped in the face. I continued.

"She thought if she told her parents she was raped, they couldn't blame her. Lydia was banking on the fact that her parents wouldn't force her to report the rape to the police since they would feel so much shame. The only other person who knew her secret was her best friend, Janie Berg. Lydia's parents sent her to live with her aunt until I was born and adopted by my parents. All because they were strict Catholics, and their religion was more important to them than their own daughter."

"I don't know what to say. I wish Lydia would have told me."

"I think she was too ashamed and couldn't face you. I want you to know I don't think any of this was your fault. I know you had no idea what my mother went through."

"Still, knowing the pain you feel hurts me."

We ate in silence. I was glad I told him. I knew it was weighing on me and he needed to know.

Harris dropped me off at the airport at 7:00 for my 9:00 p.m. flight back to New York. We hugged and promised to keep in touch.

On the ride back, I tried to sleep but it was difficult. I dozed every so often. In between dozing, I thought about my time with my father and his family. Though not everyone accepted me, it didn't really matter. I knew if I wanted a relationship with my father, however that looked, that's what he wanted too.

CHAPTER 25

When the plane touched down, I was happy to be on dry land. I took a taxi home and dropped my overnight bag in the foyer, took off all my clothes, and was fast asleep as soon as my head hit the pillow.

Something woke me up. When I looked at the clock, it was almost twelve noon. I kept hearing this buzzing sound. I finally realized it was coming from my phone that was in my overnight bag. There were three anxious calls from Samantha wondering where I was and why I hadn't called her back, and one call from Annie. I called Annie first.

"How's my California girl?" Annie said when she answered.

"The good news is I made it there and back safely. The bad news is apparently I'm a gold digger."

"Would you elaborate, please?"

"One of the brothers, Andrew, has doubts whether I'm really Harris's daughter. The other brother I have my suspicions about. He came but his wife mysteriously took sick and was a no-show. I'll tell you about it when I see you. I did like what I saw of LA, though I am definitely a cardholder New Yorker."

"How about drinks tomorrow? I'll meet you at The Dead Poet at 6:00 p.m."

"Sounds good. How is everything here?"

"I gotta go. A client is anxiously waiting to see me. Love you."

"Right back at you."

I made a quick call to Jesse to tell him I was safely home and would call him as soon as I had a chance.

My first priority was to call Marshal Berger. Maybe I didn't push him hard enough the first time. If he was close to Jason, he may know more than he had originally told me.

Marshal answered on the first ring.

"Marshal, it's Maddie Landon. Do you think you might have some time to meet with me after school today. I'm worried about Jason."

"I'm worried as well. I'm finished with school at 2:30 p.m. There's a Starbucks on Lexington and 68th. I can be there by 2:50."

Another call was coming in as I hung up. It was from an unknown caller.

"Hello," I said cautiously. "Did you have a nice time in California?" they replied and then hung up. The voice was disguised so I couldn't identify who was calling. How would this person know where I was? Was I being followed and didn't even realize it?

I didn't want to admit it to myself, but I knew the calls were getting to me. For now, there wasn't anything I could do about it. I wasn't going to let a few phone calls stop me, if that was their intention.

***

I was waiting inside Starbucks for Marshal. I ordered a latte, gave the barista my name, and sat down. I spotted Marshal coming in, his backpack slung over his shoulder. I got up and walked over to him.

"Hi, Marshal. Thanks for meeting me. Can I order you something?"

"A cappuccino, thank you." The first time I met Marshal, I walked away thinking how mature he was for his eighteen years. Though I was practically on my own at his age, I wasn't nearly as mature or self-assured as this young man. Once we got our drinks, we sat down.

"The last time we spoke, you told me that Jason couldn't have raped Mia. You seemed very sure. Why is that?"

"When he found out Mia had accused him of raping her, he told me he had been studying with her earlier at a friend's house and walked her home. He was about to leave when Mia asked him to come in because she wanted to talk to him about something."

"Did he tell you what transpired?"

"Her mother was getting on her case because she wasn't doing well in school and thought Mia was paying too much attention to boys, and not enough on her studies. Mia asked Jason to tutor her. She said she knew he could use the money."

"What was Jason's response?"

"He said he would. They discussed when and where, and then Jason left. He was completely blindsided when she accused him of raping her."

"Do you think he could have been mad at her because she refused to go out with him, and maybe things got out of hand?"

"Like I originally told you, Jason wasn't interested in dating Mia. He only asked her out because those jerks dared him to."

"Did Jason tell you he wasn't interested in Mia?"

"Not exactly."

"Then how do you know?"

"You'll have to ask Jason."

"I told you Jason isn't talking. If I don't find out what he's hiding, your friend could be in serious trouble."

Marshal looked down.

"I understand if you don't want to betray what Jason may have told you, but I need something to help him." And then it dawned on me. I was pretty sure I knew what Jason was hiding.

"He's gay. Is that it?"

His silence told me I was right.

"Are you lovers?"

"Does that matter? Is this going to help Jason?"

"I'm not sure. The prosecution could say that Jason was angry at Mia for rejecting him in front of everyone, so being gay might not be relevant. He wanted to hurt her like she hurt him."

"Why the hell did Jason have to take that stupid dare. It's not as if he even wanted to. Are you going to tell Jason you know?"

"At this point, I have no reason to. My main priority is to find out who raped Mia. Is there anyone you can think of?"

"I wish there was."

"Okay, if you think of anything else, please call me."

Instead of going back to the office, I went home, changed into my running clothes, and jogged to the park. The temperature was still warm for the end of September, and I was already sweating by the time I got there. I passed the playground where the kids looked like they were having a great time without a care in the world. I noticed the nannies watching over them carefully. A few years ago, there was an incident in the park where a baby was taken. Thankfully, there were cameras all around and the guy was caught. The story goes that his girlfriend, who was mentally unstable, had a miscarriage and forced her teenage boyfriend to kidnap the baby from the park.

As I was on my second loop around, my thoughts switched to Jason. The one thing that could possibly help Jason, he was ashamed to tell me. Now I get why he went along with the dare. I guess it doesn't matter whether you're in private school or public school, bullying doesn't discriminate. At the moment, I had no other suspects and wasn't able to talk to the one person who knew exactly what happened that night. Now what?

I called Sam back as soon as I left Starbucks. She picked up right away.

"Where have you been? I've been calling. Any news?"

"Hello to you too. I've been out of town for the weekend. Did you know that Jason was gay?"

"He made me promise. How did you find out?"

"That doesn't matter. Who else knew he was gay?"

"I think just Marshal, but I'm not sure."

"Why do you think Jason didn't want anyone to know? It seems being gay nowadays is very different than it used to be. People are more accepting, especially among their peers."

"You would have to ask him." I intended to.

"Are there any other secrets you're keeping from me?"

"No, I swear. You see why Jason couldn't have raped Mia."

"Actually, if Jason was angry enough because he felt humiliated in front of his classmates when Mia refused to go out with him, he might have been provoked."

"But they made up."

"That's a good point, except Mia was using Jason because she was getting bad grades and her mother was on her case. If for some reason they got into it when he brought her home, and in the heat of the moment she told him the truth, it could have set him off."

"You think he did it?" Sam said accusingly.

"That's not what I'm saying, but I have to be open to all possibilities. I've been doing this long enough to know what people are capable of in certain situations. I promise you I'm keeping an open mind. If you hear anything, let me know. In the meantime, don't pick any fights." I then heard the familiar sound of the click without a goodbye.

CHAPTER 26

When I got back to my office, I took out my notes on everyone I'd contacted and spoken to regarding the case. Basically, no one was being very cooperative. Any one or all of them could be lying. Maybe someone knew more than they were willing to admit to. For now, I had to go in a different direction.

Without being able to talk with Mia or her mother, it was going to hamper my investigation. Since I had no physical access to Mia Franklin yet, I thought I would follow her for a few days. I didn't know what I was hoping to accomplish but my investigation was at a stalemate. I had nothing at this point.

***

The next day, I was at her school by 2:30 p.m. I just had to hope wherever Mia was going, it was on foot. I saw Sam talking to a few kids and I was glad she didn't look in my direction.

I spotted Mia with her two friends, Sandra and Tiffany. It was the first time I had seen Mia but I recognized her from the description Sam had given me. From a distance I could see she was about 5'7", with straight blonde hair that came a few inches below her shoulders, a milky complexion, and a wiry body. When I was sixteen, I looked like a wreck. I was still wearing braces; I was completely flat chested and hadn't had a growth spurt as yet. I was what they called a late bloomer. Until I was eighteen, I tried to stay away from mirrors.

Mia was talking to her friends for a while and then went off on her own. I waited a minute or so and then started following her, keeping a good distance between us. She walked down Madison Avenue for several blocks and then she entered a jewelry store. Since we had never met, I followed her inside. One of the salesmen asked if he could be of assistance but I told him I was just browsing. Mia was looking at the bracelets. I knew the jewelry in this store was very pricey.

I heard Mia ask the salesman to see the bracelets that were in a case behind the glass counter. He took out the case and placed it on top of the counter. Thankfully, the store was small enough that I could overhear what was being said, yet I was able to keep a safe distance.

I saw Mia try on several bracelets until she had decided on one. The salesman said it was $1,200 plus tax. Mia rummaged through her backpack and took out several bills, counting out the exact amount for the bracelet. She told the salesperson it didn't need to be wrapped since she was going to wear it. He gave her the receipt and she left. I followed a few moments later.

Where the hell did a kid her age get that kind of cash? I knew her parents had money, but somehow, I got the distinct impression this was not her parents' money. If it was and they knew about it, wouldn't she pay by credit card?

Mia walked two blocks to Lexington Avenue and waved down a taxi. Shit. I waved the next one and got in. Though I've heard these words on television, I never thought I would be saying them—"follow that taxi." I have no idea if he thought I was crazy but he did as I said.

Mia got out at 59th Street. I knew exactly where she was headed. I threw a twenty at the driver and told him to keep the change.

Mia entered Bloomingdale's and I followed. The last time I was in Bloomingdale's was maybe five years ago. It was for their delicious frozen yogurt they serve in their restaurant. Since I was last here, they remodeled the store. Mia was moving at a pretty fast pace, as if she knew her way around. We covered the Sportswear Department, the Shoe Department, and the Lingerie Department, where she was on a buying spree. She paid cash whenever she bought anything. Where did she get all this money from? Maybe she had a rich boyfriend, though I doubted it.

I called it quits when she got into another cab. It was almost five-thirty. Hopefully, she was heading home.

* * *

I was at The Dead Poet on the dot of 6:00 p.m. Annie was already inside, seated at a table. I leaned over and gave her a kiss as I sat down.

The waiter came right over.

"I'll have a Cabernet Sauvignon and a couple of sliders with an order of sweet potato fries." Annie ordered a glass of Merlot.

"Does sweet potato fries count as your vegetable for the day?" Annie said, laughing.

"As a matter of fact, it does."

"So tell me all about California."

"I was surprised how pretty it was. Did you know that the Beverly Hills Hotel is pink and green?" Annie just rolled her eyes. "You should have seen their house. It was beautiful. Spanish/Mediterranean-style with a pool in the backyard."

"I'm jealous."

"It was very nice but it's not New York. I wouldn't want to live there; it's too spread out and I would miss all the seasons. Besides, you're not there," I said.

"Thank heavens."

"You're not getting rid of me that easily."

"So tell me more about those big, bad brothers."

"I actually liked Adam. He's the older one. I'm not sure what the issue was with his wife. She never showed."

"Maybe she thinks her father-in-law is going to change his will to include you. Less of the pie for them."

"*Hmm*, I wonder if that's what had Andrew all bent out of shape?"

"How do you feel about your father?"

"I was really surprised how much I enjoyed being with him. He's very thoughtful and easy to be with. Even though it'll be a long-distance relationship, we'll talk on the phone."

"I'm so happy that after all these years, something good came out of it."

"By the way, interesting developments on my case." I went on to tell Annie how I found out Jason was gay and what I learned from following Mia.

"I'll have to tail her for a few more days. Maybe I'll figure out what's going on with her. I'm certainly not making any headway with anyone I've talked to so far."

"It's early. Baby steps."

"On that note, anything new?"

"Doug and I decided to go for counseling. We need to be able to talk about the baby issue without fighting. And I need to figure out what I really want."

"That's a load off. I was getting worried there."

"Before you get too excited, I know you, Maddie, and you'll want to grill me every five minutes on how Doug and I are doing."

"Well, I do think you're exaggerating just a tad bit, but I'll try to refrain from being a nuisance," I said, chuckling.

"I promise if there are any developments, you'll be the first to know."

"Let's toast to new beginnings."

CHAPTER 27

I was nearing my apartment building after leaving Annie when my phone rang.

"Hi, Lucy," I said when I saw who it was. I knew my aunt, my birth mother's sister, was calling to find out how everything went when I was in California. "I'm sorry I haven't had a chance to call you. It's been hectic here since I got back."

"I figured as much. How did everything go?"

I recounted what transpired with everyone and how much I enjoyed my father's company.

"Did he mention your mother?"

"Yes. He told me that they had to keep their relationship a secret because your parents were very religious."

"I never forgave my parents for what they did. I don't think I ever told you this, but Lydia and I never spoke to our parents again once we both left for college."

"I didn't know that. Sometimes I wish I had never looked for my birth parents. It's upsetting knowing what my mother went through."

"Lydia would never want you to feel that way. And she would be so happy that you now have a relationship with your birth father. I know I'm grateful that I got to know you."

I didn't know what to say.

"I should be in New York in the next couple of weeks. I'll call you then."

Every time I think about what my grandparents put my mother through, I wanted to scream. My mother must have felt so helpless and so alone when she was sent away to live with her aunt before I was born.

I poured myself a glass of wine and called Jesse as soon as I got in.

"Hi, babe," Jesse said when he answered.

"Hi to you too. How was your day?"

"All the bad guys are safely in jail," Jesse said.

"If only I had your optimism. I know it's my turn to come up to you, but I was wondering if you wouldn't mind coming here. I'll owe you."

"What's going on?"

I rehashed to Jesse what I found out when I was tailing Mia. "Don't you think that's really odd? Where would she get all that money? I can't imagine her parents gave it to her."

"That is weird. What does that have to do with the case?"

"I don't know if it does. I thought you can assist me with some surveillance. Are you game?"

"Sure, sounds like a perfect way to spend a Saturday evening."

"I'll take you out for ice cream afterward."

"You certainly know how to show a guy a good time on a Saturday night."

"I knew you'd like it."

"Sleep tight."

***

In the morning, I decided I would pay Jason a call. I was hoping his mother wasn't home so I could talk to him alone. I rang his buzzer at 10:15 a.m. At first there was no answer so I buzzed again.

"Who is it?" Jason said. I could hear the caution in his voice.

"Jason, it's Maddie Landon. Please let me in."

"My mother's not home."

"I want to speak with you." For a few moments there was silence and then I heard the buzzer. I opened the door and took the stairs to the fourth floor and rang the doorbell. When the door opened, Jason looked a lot better than the last time I saw him.

"How are you?" I said, as I stepped into the foyer.

"Okay."

"Can we sit for a moment?" Jason led me into his room where he sat at his computer and I sat on his bed. He didn't ask me how the case was going. Maybe he was resigned to the fact that he was going to be convicted.

I looked at his computer screen. It was dark.

"Your mom says you're on your computer a lot. Anything you particularly like to watch or do?"

He lit up the screen. "Right now I'm playing this game, trying to figure out how to get out of this maze. There are all sorts of obstacles that you have to get past in order to finally get out."

He was so animated. It was like watching a different person. "I'll show you," he said. I watched him as he tried to maneuver his way out of the maze.

"It must be hard for you not being able to go to school. Are you keeping busy?"

"I like to read. I've been downloading books." I was glad to see he wasn't doing anything destructive with his time, like learning how to build a bomb.

"Jason, why didn't you tell me you were gay? I wouldn't have said anything. I don't know if it'll help your case or not but it's something I should have known about."

"How did you find out?" he said, his eyes opening wide.

"That doesn't matter."

"Please, don't tell my mother," he said, almost in tears.

"Why?"

"Because she's religious and probably thinks it's a sin."

I was hoping that Jason was wrong. I didn't want Jason to go through what my grandmother did to my mother. I couldn't believe Nina Demsky wouldn't accept Jason being gay.

"From the time I've spent with your mother, I know she loves you very much, and I can't believe she would love you any less if you were gay."

"She talks about having grandchildren someday. I don't want to disappoint her."

"I'm not going to tell your mother if that's what you're worried about, but you should."

"I can't."

"This is going to eat you up if you keep hiding it. I'm sure the kids at school probably have some idea. Maybe if you didn't keep it a secret, they would feel differently toward you."

He didn't respond.

"Jason, would you happen to know why Mia would have a lot of cash on her?"

"No. How do you know that?"

"That's not important. Listen, I want you to think about our conversation. If you need my help, just call me."

"Thanks."

"Have you thought any more about seeing someone to talk with?"

"I'm thinking about it."

I felt bad for Jason. Though I didn't know anything about Nina Demsky's religious beliefs, I found it hard to believe she wouldn't accept him knowing he was gay. Everything she was doing was for Jason.

As I exited the building, I started walking. I didn't believe that Jason's sexual orientation would help him in court. There was too much circumstantial evidence against him and no one else to point the finger at. For Jason's sake, I had to find out why Mia lied.

CHAPTER 28

I was back at Mia's school waiting for her to come out when my phone rang.

"Maddie, it's Larry Banks." Larry is the criminal attorney who occupies one of the suites on my floor. A few months ago, he helped me on a case I was working on.

"What's up."

"If you're available, I need you to track someone down. The thing is, you won't find him in any of your databases. He's a witness in a case that goes to trial next week. He was supposed to be in my office yesterday so I could prep him, but he never showed. I need you to find him as soon as possible since the trial starts on Monday."

"Where's your investigator?"

"On his honeymoon. My witness is not such an upstanding citizen, so be careful. I can send you a photo and the name of the place where he might hang out. That's all I got. Can you do it?"

"I'll squeeze it in."

"Thanks."

A few minutes later, I was staring at the picture of this guy, Miguel Garcia. Larry texted me the name of the Bodega in the Bronx where Garcia hangs out.

I almost missed Mia as she was leaving the school. She was alone. I followed her to 77th Street and 2nd Avenue. A dark blue car pulled over and Mia got in. I snapped a photo of the license plate. It was hard to get a look at the driver. All I could make out was that he was white with dark hair and definitely a lot older than Mia. They were deep in conversation for a few minutes and then she got out of the car and he drove off. I thought I saw her put something in her backpack but wasn't sure. She walked back up to Madison Avenue and hooked up with a few friends. They stopped at one of those trendy coffee places and went inside. At that point, I decided to discontinue my surveillance. I wanted to get back to my office and run the guy's license plate. What was Mia doing with him and who was he?

On the way in, I picked up a tuna fish sandwich and a container of coffee and brought it back to the office. I got my computer up and running and conducted a NYS Department of Motor Vehicles License Plate search. His name was Dominick Santiago. It listed his address and date of birth. The car was a 2017 Chevy Impala. At one point, his license had been suspended for several speeding tickets and driving under the influence.

"Hey, Jerry. When you get a chance, can you give me a call, it's Maddie Landon." Jerry was someone I knew from my days on the police force. I was hoping he could run a criminal check on this guy; find out what he's been into.

I took my gun from my safe, cleaned it, and slipped it into my ankle holster. I locked up and grabbed a cab to my apartment to pick up my car. I drove to the address of the Bodega in the Bronx and found a parking spot one block away. Three guys were hanging around, none of them I would want to tangle with. My subject was not with them.

"Hi, guys." They surrounded me.

"I come in peace," I said, hoping my humor might charm them. "Would you happen to know a Miguel Garcia?"

"Why do you want to know?" The guy looked at me with his small, beady eyes.

"We were supposed to meet up last night but he never showed. I'm worried about him." I doubt if these guys believed me, but you never know.

"Yeah, how do you know him?" the skinny guy with a mustache and goatee said to me.

"I knew his sister." Thankfully, Larry Banks told me that he had a sister who passed away.

"What do you want with Garcia?"

"He was going to help me out with something, but I never heard back from him."

"I haven't seen him for a few days. Any of you guys seen him?" They all nodded no.

"Would you happen to know where I could find him?"

"What's in it for us?"

"How about I buy you guys a six-pack of beer and I'll even throw in a bag of pretzels."

"You're funny. Go ahead. We'll wait right here."

A few minutes later, I handed the skinny guy a six-pack and a bag of pretzels. I even threw in a bag of potato chips.

"He shacks up with some lady who lives on Grant Avenue and East 166th Street, second building. I only know her first name, Terry."

"Thanks, guys. Enjoy the goodies!"

As I was walking to the car, I noticed I had a call from an unknown number.

"Hello," I said anxiously.

"Maddie, it's Jerry. How are you?"

"Good. How's everything at One Police Plaza?"

"Same old, same old. How's the PI business?"

"That's why I'm calling you. It's a case I'm working on. I have a name and birth date of this guy who I think might be trouble. Can you run a criminal check on him?"

"Sure. Are you seeing anyone?"

"I am. He's also a private investigator. What about you?"

"I recently got married. We met on a blind date, of all ways."

"I'm really happy for you. I'll text you my email address. I owe you one."

"Take care, Maddie."

Jerry and I dated a few times back when I was a rookie. We liked each other but there were no sparks. We remained friends, but when I left the police department, we lost contact with each other.

I drove up to Grant and 166th Street and squeezed into a parking spot at the end of the block. The neighborhood was not what I expected. The buildings were well kept. No graffiti on the building walls. Since I only had a first name to go on, I wasn't sure how I was going to find her apartment. There was a directory as soon as you walked into the building. In order to get access to the apartments, you had to be buzzed in. There was a listing for a Terry Rhodes. I didn't see any other Terrys listed on the directory. I rang the buzzer, but there was no answer. Since

I wanted to leave my card by her door, I did something I hate doing, I kept ringing buzzers until someone let me in.

I walked up to the third floor and rang Terry's bell. Still no answer. As I kneeled down to slip my card with a note under the door, there was a very strong odor coming from inside the apartment. Unfortunately, I knew that smell from my days as a detective.

CHAPTER 29

I walked to the apartment across the way and rang the bell. An elderly lady opened the door with the chain on.

"Can I help you?"

"Do you know your neighbor, Terry Rhodes?"

"Only to say hello. She's not very friendly."

"Can I come in for a moment?"

"Who are you?"

"Sorry, ma'am. My name's Maddie Landon. There's a weird smell coming from her apartment. Would you happen to have the superintendent's number, or can you tell me where I can find him?"

"Oh my! His apartment is in the basement. He should be home now. I hope she's alright."

"Thank you. By the way, have you heard anything unusual coming from her apartment in the last few days?"

"You mean the terrible loud fighting? The way those two go at it. I reported it to the super, but it doesn't stop."

"If you happen to remember anything else, please call me," I said, passing my card through the small opening.

I walked down to the super's apartment and knocked. The door opened and the man standing in front of me was probably in his fifties, Hispanic with curly dark brown hair, and light brown skin. His uniform shirt had the name Roberto embroidered on it.

"Can I help you?"

"My name's Maddie Landon. I'm a private investigator," I said, handing him my card. "I was looking for Terry Rhodes who lives on the third floor. When I knocked, there was no answer, and I noticed a terrible smell coming from her apartment. I think there may be a serious problem. Can you open her door?"

"I can, but how do I know you don't want to rob the place?"

"You don't, but I believe there is someone in that apartment who is either dead or is in serious trouble. You can go in first if you like as long as you don't touch anything."

He took his set of keys, and we went up to Terry's apartment. Roberto knocked several times and called out her name, but no response. He unlocked the door. The smell hit us both right away. There were two bodies: one was my witness and the other one I was guessing was Terry.

"Call 911," I said. The poor guy was turning green. He went out into the hallway. Though I doubted they were alive, I checked for a pulse. Negative. It looked like Terry was shot twice in the chest and my subject was shot in the head. It was hard to tell how long they were dead since the windows were shut. The blood from the headshot had already coagulated. Though I had seen a few dead bodies when I was a police officer, you never got used to it, especially if they were innocent victims. I wrapped my hands around myself, trying to keep warm. I needed to remain calm until the police came. Since I didn't want to touch anything, I just took a quick glance around the room, spotting a black leather jacket with the symbol of a crow on it. What did the crow stand for?

I went out into the hall and asked Roberto if he knew the man lying on the floor.

"That's the boyfriend. He's no good. He sells drugs. I never knew what she saw in that creep."

I picked up my phone and called Larry Banks.

"Larry, your witness is dead and so is his girlfriend. Both most likely shot at point-blank range. I'm waiting for the police to arrive. What should I tell them?"

"Are you alright?"

"Yeah, just a little shaken. It's been a long time."

"Just tell them the truth and give them my name and number."

"Okay. I'll talk to you later. Not sure if I have to go down to the precinct or they just want my info."

As soon as I hung up, two male police officers arrived. One was tall and lanky and the other was short and slightly on the heavy side. The tall one seemed to be in charge.

"What do we have here?" the one in charge said.

I went on to explain who I was and why I was at the apartment. The other officer took notes. I told them I knew nothing about either of the victims except that Miguel Garcia was a witness to a crime.

"Did you touch the bodies?"

"Only to feel for a pulse but there was none."

I gave the officer Larry Banks' telephone number. Fortunately, I didn't have to go down to the station. They just took my information in case they had any further questions. I left, glad to get out of there. I sat in my car for a few minutes with the heater going. My right leg was shaking. If he was a drug dealer, why was he killed? Could it be that someone found out he was testifying? Well, it wasn't my problem anymore or so I thought.

CHAPTER 30

As soon as I walked into my apartment, I threw off all my clothes and took a hot shower, letting the water wash all over my body. I got out, wiped myself off, and wrapped myself up in a terrycloth robe. I poured myself a glass of wine and sat in my father's chair.

As I felt myself slowly relaxing, I called Larry.

"How'd it go?" he said. I explained how I found Terry Rhodes' apartment and what I told the police, which was basically nothing, except that Garcia was going to be a witness at a trial.

"Do you think he was killed because someone found out he was going to testify?" I said.

"It's possible. In the world he lives in, crap happens."

"Do you plan on looking into Garcia's death?" I said.

"I'll leave that to the police. It was a weak case to begin with. My defendant has been in and out of jail most of his life. Putting someone like Garcia on the stand was a gamble. He might not have held up once the prosecution cross-examined him."

"Expect a call or a visit from the police at some point."

"Thanks, Maddie. Good work. Send me your invoice."

After hanging up, I made myself a peanut butter sandwich and called Jesse.

"Hey, beautiful, how are you?" Jesse said when he answered.

"Besides finding two dead bodies earlier today, I'm fine."

"Whoa, back up and start from the beginning." Which I proceeded to do.

"You really stepped in a pile of shit."

"Yeah, except it's not my problem anymore."

"Are you okay?"

"I am now. I was pretty shaken up. I hadn't seen any dead bodies since I was with the police department. They were both shot. I took a quick peek around and noticed a leather jacket with the symbol of a crow on it. I'm wondering if he may have been part of a gang."

"You just said it's not your problem anymore. Leave it alone."

"Yeah, you're right."

"I'm still hung up on why Mia was with this guy Santiago in his car. I'm having a friend from my days on the police force run a criminal check on him. I'm curious if he has a record."

"Before you let that imagination of yours run wild, let's wait before you go off half-cocked. I'll see you Saturday. Please be careful," he said.

"Nice to know you care. You might get doubly lucky when I see you."

"I have to take a cold shower. Sleep tight. I love you."

I fell asleep watching television with Olivia Benson, the detective on Law & Order: Special Victims Unit, talking in my ear.

***

The sound of buzzing woke me up. I was groggy and reached for my phone.

"Hello." All I heard was deep breathing. "Whoever the hell you are, stop calling," I said, and I hung up. I looked at the clock. It was 2:00 a.m. My frustration level was rising. I had no clue who was making these calls. Though I kept going over in my mind who it could be, I was coming up empty. After about an hour, I gave up and fell back to sleep.

***

I smacked the radio, hoping it would stop beeping. It was 7:00 a.m. The rain was coming down pretty hard. I wanted to turn over and go back to sleep but I knew that wasn't going to happen.

I put on the coffeemaker and made myself some breakfast. I tried to put the hang-up calls out of my head. When I turned on my computer, I noticed an email from Jerry with an attachment. I opened it up and looked at Dominick Santiago's criminal record. He did two years for selling drugs to minors. He also did a year for criminal possession of a firearm without a license.

I called Jerry, hoping he might be able to get information on Santiago that wasn't in his criminal record. I left a message in his voicemail. Now that I knew Santiago was selling drugs, I was very curious what Mia's relationship to Santiago was. Did she have anything to do with selling drugs? Could that be where she got all that cash? Maybe now would be a good time to call Ben Bradley and set up an appointment to meet with Mia. I picked up my phone and called Bradley's number. He answered right away.

"Mr. Bradley, it's Maddie Landon. I want to take you up on your offer. Can you arrange a meeting with Mia?"

"I'll set it up and let you know where and when."

"Thanks, Ben." I was hoping this meeting wouldn't get back to Mia's parents.

My phone rang. I saw it was Jerry.

"Jerry, thanks for getting back to me and thanks for the info. I have a question."

"Shoot."

"I was wondering if you could find out if anyone at the precinct might know more about this guy Santiago that wasn't in his criminal record."

"I'll ask around."

"Thanks, I really appreciate it."

Though I wasn't sure what I was looking for, I was hoping Jerry could provide me with some answers.

CHAPTER 31

If Mia was either buying or selling drugs, the only way I would know was to keep tabs on her. While I was waiting for her to exit her school, I noticed Sam arguing with Mia's friend Tiffany. What was that all about? A minute later, Mia pulled Tiffany away from Sam and got into a very heated exchange with her. A few minutes later, Mia left by herself, looking upset. She walked a few blocks and met up with a girl that I had never seen before. I snapped a photo with my phone. I thought I saw some sort of exchange between the two of them, but I was too far away to see what it was.

At that point, Mia left and walked up Madison Avenue. She stopped in front of one of those fancy bakery places that sold tiny cupcakes that were the rage. A boy about Mia's age came up to her and they walked around the corner into a side alleyway. It was hard to get close enough to see what they were doing. A minute later, the boy left. I took a photo of him as he was leaving.

Mia came out a few seconds later. I followed her back to her house and stayed about forty-five minutes before I left. Was it possible Mia was involved in selling drugs to high school kids? But if she was, how was it connected to Mia's rape? At this point, I didn't see a connection.

On my way home, I called Sam. She picked up right away.

"Jason told me you spoke to him," she said without saying hello. "Why aren't you talking to Mia. I know she's hiding something," Sam said in a defiant tone.

"I can't talk to her right now. Trust me, Sam, when the time is right, I will. Now I have a question for you. What were you arguing with Tiffany about?"

"Were you spying on me?"

"Of course not." I didn't want to tell her I was following Mia.

"I was trying to find out the truth from her. She must know who raped Mia."

"Sam, listen to me. Tiffany is her best friend. Why would Tiffany betray what her friend told her in confidence? Would you?"

"I'm angry and it just came out."

"I know, Sam, but let me handle it. I told you when the time comes, I'll talk to Mia. Before you hang up, has anyone ever approached you to buy drugs?"

"You mean like cocaine or marijuana?"

"You tell me?"

"I think kids take prescription pills. Why are you asking?"

"I was just curious. Sam, are you using drugs?"

"Of course not. Do you want me to ask around if anyone is selling drugs in our school?"

"No, Sam. I'm guessing drugs are prevalent in all schools. I'll talk to you soon."

I really wasn't interested in going into my office. Instead, I walked around for a while before stopping for a cappuccino. I thought about Mia, and if what I recently found out had anything to do with Mia being raped.

As I approached my building, I saw Louis' smiling face.

"Hi, Miss Maddie. I haven't seen you for a while."

"I know. I've been working nonstop. How's everything? Anybody in the building giving you a hard time? Because you know I can fix that…" I said, smiling.

"Oh no! They know better than to complain to me."

"I'm sure they do. Have a nice weekend if I don't see you."

When I got upstairs, I changed and went for a quick run. As I was making my way around the third loop, I thought about Louis and how he always seemed upbeat. I knew he didn't have an easy life but he had a wonderful family. It got me thinking about Jesse and my future with him. I couldn't imagine if he wasn't in my life, yet I still got anxious thinking about making that final commitment. I kept running faster and faster.

CHAPTER 32

I heard the familiar knock on my door Saturday morning. Jesse stared at me with those beautiful eyes of his and I reached for him, closing the door behind him. I held him closely as he lifted me up and brought me into the bedroom.

As we were lying in bed after taking turns satisfying each other, my thoughts turned to Dr. Goldberg's words: "What is more important, my relationship or holding on to the fear?" I pushed that thought aside.

We left the house at 6:00 p.m. With surveillance, you never know what to expect. Mia may or may not be home when we arrive, and if she was home, would we be waiting for several hours before she came out? The joys of surveillance. We parked where we could see the entrance to Mia's brownstone and waited.

It was 10:00 p.m. and still no sign of Mia. I knew it was a Saturday night and teenagers go out pretty late, but I was having doubts whether she was even home, and we missed our chance. Just as I was about to tell Jesse that we should leave, I spotted Mia coming out of her house. She stood outside waiting for someone.

Mia was wearing a very short black leather skirt with high black boots, and a white sweater that revealed her flat midriff. I wondered if her parents were home and allowed their daughter to go out dressed that way.

A black SUV came and Mia got in. We followed, hoping we wouldn't lose her in the city streets. The car turned onto the FDR Drive and eventually we found ourselves exiting in Bronxville. The homes in this town are worth in the millions. The car made several turns until it finally stopped in front of a huge colonial-style home. We drove past the car and stopped at the end of the street. When the car left after dropping Mia off, we turned around and went back toward the house. Fortunately, the place across the street looked like it was in the middle of major renovations and nobody was living there. The houses were far enough apart that anyone who lived in the area most likely wouldn't notice we were watching the house across the street.

Jesse opened the trunk of his car and took out a camera with a telephoto lens.

"This is so cool," I said, looking through the lens. I could see into the window of the house. "I never used one of these when we were tailing anyone back on the force."

"If you do a lot of surveillance, you need a camera where you can observe your subject from a distance."

Luckily, the curtains weren't drawn. "It looks like there's a party with a lot of teenagers," I said, peeking through the lens. "I doubt if the parents are home."

"What would be the fun in that," Jesse said.

"I was a boring kid."

"Same here."

"So, you never did anything wild or got into any trouble?" I said.

"My mother would have killed me. I wasn't exactly a saint. I smoked marijuana for a period and did some drinking, typical teenage stuff, but that was about it. Since I knew my mother couldn't afford the tuition for my college education, and I didn't want to have loans when I got out, I stayed home most weekends studying in order to qualify for scholarships."

"I'm very impressed. You would not exactly say I was the studious type. I did enough to get by. I guess I was fortunate that the money I had from my parents paid for my college tuition."

Jesse gently touched my knee, knowing how much I wished they were here instead of the money they left me.

At one point, one of the girls came out and puked in the bushes. She was half naked.

"So, this is what rich kids do on a Saturday night," I said.

We watched and waited. I knew if I didn't tell Jesse now, I would chicken out. My palms started to sweat, and my mouth went dry. It was at that moment when I blurted out: "My name's not Maddie."

"Aha! I knew it. I'm sleeping with a spy. Wait till I tell the guys about this," Jesse said, grinning.

"My real name is Amanda."

"It's a beautiful name. How come you never told me?"

"The only people who called me Amanda were my parents. After they died, I never wanted anyone else calling me by that name. The only two people who know are Annie and Will."

"Why are you telling me now?"

"Because I want us to live together and I figured you should know my real name," I said quickly before I got cold feet and backed out.

Jesse was speechless.

"Why the sudden change?" he finally asked.

"It's not so sudden. I've been thinking about it for a while. I realized if I don't take a chance, I won't know what I'm missing. But I want you to know I'm not easy to live with. I'm set in my ways and I hate to compromise."

"Gee, this is all news to me," Jesse said, suppressing a smile.

"Are you sure you have no doubts about living with me? Because I can understand if you do."

"Absolutely not. I'm trying to figure out how we can arrange this," Jesse said.

"So now that we are going to be roomies, is there anything I should know about you that you haven't already disclosed?" I said.

"Is this when I admit to all my flaws?"

"Yes, so fess up."

"I like my drawers neat. I fold everything, including my underwear."

"Wow! That might be a deal breaker," I said with a straight face. "You better not be looking in my drawers. Is that it? Anything else I should know about?"

"I think it's better if we learn about each other as we go along, otherwise there won't be any surprises."

"I'm not a surprise kind of gal. And please, no surprise birthday parties."

"Duly noted."

Though I was relieved I finally told Jesse I wanted to live with him, I didn't tell him everything. I was afraid if he knew, he might change his mind.

CHAPTER 33

"Jesse, look!" I spotted Mia and a teenage boy, maybe around the same age or a little older, coming out of the house arguing. I took several photos. I gave the camera to Jesse, hoping he could make out what they were quarreling about. At one point, the boy grabbed Mia's arm and she pushed him away. She ran back into the house and he went after her.

"Could you tell what they were arguing about?" I asked.

"I couldn't make it out."

When I looked at the time, it was a little after 1:00 a.m. We were debating whether to leave when I noticed the boy who had words with Mia earlier, leaving the party in a hurry.

"I think we should follow him. If he has a beef against Mia, maybe he'd be willing to talk to me," I said.

"Let's go."

We followed him to an apartment building in the Bronx. I watched him walk into the building and noted the address. Though I didn't know his name, I had his photo. I figured someone in the building would know who this kid was. Maybe he would talk to me.

On the way home, we found an all-night diner. While we were waiting for our food, Jesse and I were floating around ideas how we could make our living arrangement work. I thought our home base should be in New York and we could stay at Jesse's place on the weekends. The hard part was deciding what Jesse would do about work— would he be able to continue working where he was now, or would he work for criminal attorneys in New York? Was it fair to Jesse that I wanted to stay in New York? He suggested that until he decided what he would do, we should keep the same arrangement.

"Changing the topic, if Jason is innocent, why did Mia accuse him?" I said.

"He could be the first person that came to her mind. If she had to pin it on someone, Jason would be an easy target, especially since he was at her house that night and Mia knew he would be caught on camera," Jesse said.

"Okay, but the real question is why did she lie? My theory is that the person who raped Mia also threatened her. Maybe this person had something on her that she was afraid if it came out would have serious consequences for her."

"My question would be, why didn't she just deny she was raped when her parents confronted her?" Jesse said.

"That's a good question. She's a kid; maybe she couldn't keep it in when her mother kept pressing her. The housekeeper/nanny said Mia had been acting strange. Also, she did tell her best friend that she was raped."

"Well, now all you have to do is find out who threatened her."

I gave Jesse my best: "You have to be kidding look."

***

Monday morning I set the alarm so I could give Jesse a proper send-off. After he left, I went for a quick run. As I was making my way back, I was kicking myself for not telling Jesse that I couldn't have children. He had a right to know before we moved in together. I had to tell him.

When I got back, I showered and tried to put my fears aside for the moment. My phone rang as I was drying myself off. It said unknown caller. I didn't answer it. If it was someone who needed to get in touch with me, they'd call back.

CHAPTER 34

I was thinking of taking a ride up to the Bronx to check out the young man who was arguing with Mia at the party Saturday night when I heard my phone beep.

"You want to meet for a drink later?" Annie said when I answered.

"How about the Vanguard Wine Bar, 6:30 p.m."

"See you then."

My phone rang again. It was a number I didn't recognize.

"Hello."

"Ms. Landon, this is Ben. I have it arranged for 3:00 p.m. There's a park not far from Mia's school. It's on 86th Street and East End Avenue. We'll meet you by the entrance," he said and hung up.

***

I was waiting by the entrance when I saw Ben Bradley and Mia Franklin walking toward me.

"Hi, Mia. Thank you for coming. Why don't we find a place to sit in the park." Mia was quiet and avoided eye contact. She had on her school uniform and her backpack was slung over her shoulder. Mia was slowly walking a few feet behind us as we approached a very pretty area with an open garden and a bench where we could sit. Mia and I sat while Ben stood. She was rocking back and forth.

"I'd like to ask you a few questions." Mia looked pale. "Are you okay?"

"Yes." I noticed Ben was watching on. Maybe he was being protective of Mia.

"Can you tell me what happened the night Jason came over?"

"Jason walked me home and then he came up. He was still angry that I wouldn't go out with him. He said mean things." Mia's right leg was bouncing up and down and her eyes were darting all around.

"Like what."

"That I thought I was better than him and I was stupid. Then he just freaked out. Before I knew it, he was all over me and he raped me."

"Why didn't you report it right away?"

"I was scared of him. He threatened to hurt me if I told anyone. Are you through? I don't want to answer any more of your questions."

"Why were the sheets washed if Jason's DNA was on them?"

"I told you I didn't want to report it. I was afraid."

"Mia, is there someone else you're afraid of? If there is, I can help you."

"It's Jason. There is no one else."

Mia got up quickly and walked away.

"Why can't you just accept the fact that Jason raped her?" Ben said.

He went after Mia and I stayed for a few minutes. I didn't believe her story, but she wasn't going to change it. Someone who is telling the truth is more detailed and they don't avoid eye contact. Why was she lying?

***

The inside of the Vanguard Bar was dimly lit. It had a great-looking bar with high-back chairs that were very comfortable. The menu included small plates with a French influence. I was seated at a table sipping a glass of red wine while I waited for Annie. I spotted her walking in and waved. The waiter came right over and Annie ordered a glass of wine. I chimed in, ordering a few appetizers.

"I told Jesse I wanted us to move in together," I said, the words spilling out, "but I didn't tell him that I couldn't have children. I know I should have told right away but I chickened out."

"I can't say for sure, but I don't think it will matter to him."

"Why do you say that?"

"He's forty-five. If he wanted a child, he probably would have one by now."

"Maybe, but I still need to tell him."

"I can't believe you finally agreed to live with him. What did he say?"

"For a brief moment he was speechless. The only rub is his work situation. For now, until he figures out what he wants to do, we'll keep the same weekend schedule."

"I guess that makes sense."

"I still have no idea how we're going to solve our living arrangement. It's not really fair for Jesse to have to give up his job to come to Manhattan, and I certainly don't want to live in Chester."

"Jesse wants to be with you. I think he'd be willing to live here as long as he still has his place. This is big news. I think the four of us should celebrate."

"It's not as if we're getting married."

"I know, but this is a big step. I'm so proud of you. By the way, you have to taste these Smoked Salmon Tartines. They're so good."

I brought Annie up to date on everything, including my meeting with Mia.

"Wow, you've been a busy little beaver."

"You should have seen the poor super when we discovered the two dead bodies. He was turning green. I got him out of there as fast as possible since I didn't want him throwing up inside the apartment and contaminating the crime scene. I wasn't exactly thrilled to be there myself. Well, it's not my problem now. What I need to find out is who raped Mia and why she is pinning it on my client."

"Let's say Mia is selling drugs. How does it impact the rape case?"

"Beats me. At this point, I'm not seeing a connection unless the person who raped her threatened to expose her if she said anything."

"Did you expect her to change her story when you questioned her? She had to keep up the pretense," Annie said.

"I had to try."

"You'll have to dig somewhere else."

"I love advice with no solutions."

"Sorry, sweetie. I wish I did have some answers."

"That's okay. I'll figure it out. Hopefully, before my client winds up in jail."

I walked with Annie part of the way home before we said goodbye. I was trying to think what my next step would be when my phone buzzed.

"Hi, Harris," I said, when I saw who it was. I couldn't bring myself to call him Dad.

"How are you?"

"I'm okay. I finally told Jesse I'm ready to move in together."

"I know how hard that decision must have been for you. I'm proud of you. I'm assuming Manhattan is going to be your home base."

"I guess, but until we figure it all out, we'll hold off on living together."

"That's probably the right resolution for now. I wanted to apologize again for the way things turned out when you were here."

"You don't have control over your son. Don't apologize for him. I got to spend time with you."

"I'm glad. I've been meaning to ask you if you've been in contact with your Aunt Lucy."

"We talk on the phone every so often, and when she comes to New York on business, we usually have dinner together."

"That's great. How is she?"

"She's good. Very successful. She was happy to hear that I was able to connect with you."

"How is your case going?"

"Slowly. Unfortunately, investigations take time." I didn't want to go into the details.

"We'll talk next week. Be careful," my father said before we hung up.

It was hard for me to take in his words. Maybe I still couldn't believe that I found the man who was my father and he cared about me, after believing all those years that I was nothing to him. Someone he never wanted.

***

When I got in, it was after 9:00 p.m. I changed into my boxer shorts and T-shirt and got into bed with the latest Harlen Coben mystery book. My mind was on overload and figured one more glass of wine might not be a bad idea either. Before I met Jesse, I hadn't thought much about the fact that I couldn't have children, maybe because I never thought I would meet someone I wanted to share my life with. I wasn't as sure as Annie that it wouldn't drive Jesse away. Now I couldn't stop thinking about it.

At some point, I must have dozed off. The dream I was in seemed all too real. I was following Mia when I saw her go into what looked like an abandoned brick building in the middle of downtown Brooklyn. I snuck into the building, hoping I wouldn't be seen. There were sounds coming from a distance, but I wasn't sure what direction they were coming from. I walked cautiously through a maze, the sound of voices becoming louder. I spotted Mia talking to a man who looked to be in his thirties, unshaven, bushy dark brown hair, wearing baggy army fatigues and laced-up black work boots.

Inching closer, I could hear them in a heated argument but couldn't make out what they were saying. Then I heard shots and footsteps running. I quickly ran over and saw Mia lying on the floor with blood seeping out of her stomach. I tried to put pressure on the wound to stop the bleeding but I knew she was dying. She opened her eyes and was trying to tell me something. I leaned in closer. The only words she uttered were, "I'm sorry," and then she was gone. As I looked down at Mia's dead body, I had the horrible realization that I would never know who raped her.

CHAPTER 35

I jolted awake. My phone was vibrating. I answered but kept quiet.

"I'm going to teach you a lesson, bitch," and then dead air. My heart was thumping and I started to sweat. Who would want to hurt me? Was it someone who thought I was getting too close to the truth? I was so tired I just wanted to sleep.

I dozed fitfully until my alarm went off at 6:30 a.m. I was thinking of going back to sleep but I had too much to do. So I put on the coffeemaker and watched as it dripped into the pot. I remembered my dream and wondered if it was an omen of what was to come.

Two cups of coffee later, I almost felt human. As I was putting a spoonful of cereal in my mouth, my phone rang.

"Hey," I said when I saw it was Jesse. "What do I owe the honor of this early morning call?"

"Just thought I would check in on my almost live-in lady."

"I'm elevated to lady status. I'm honored."

"What are you up to?"

"I thought I would take a ride later to the building in the Bronx. Maybe someone knows who this kid is that we saw fighting with Mia at the party. By the way, I met with Mia. Ben Bradley arranged it." I went on to tell Jesse what Mia said; basically that she stuck to her story.

"What did you expect? She can't change the story at this point. Be careful. Now that you've succumbed to my charms and have agreed to live with me, I would be devastated if anything happened to you."

"Nice to know you care about my well-being."

"Let me know if I can help."

"Will do."

***

As I approached the Bronx address, I noticed two policemen coming out of the building. I watched as they left. I spotted a man who was wearing a blue, short-sleeve shirt and gray pants walking into the building. I approached him.

"Excuse me," I said. "Would you happen to live in the building?"

"Yes. I'm the superintendent, Joe," he said in a hurried manner. Joe was short and wiry, probably in his fifties, with a slight accent I couldn't place.

"My name's Maddie Landon. I'm a private investigator," I said, handing him my card. "I'm trying to locate this person," I continued, showing him the photo I took the night of the party.

Joe had a weird look on his face. I felt something in the pit of my stomach.

"I saw two policemen leaving the building. Did something happen?" I said.

"This boy Dante," he said, pointing to the photo, "he was beat up." So that's why the police were here, I thought to myself. A chill ran right through me.

"That's terrible. Is he alright?"

"I don't know. Somebody who saw what happened called 911. They took him to the hospital, but he's home now."

"Do you know when this happened?"

"It was yesterday. Why are you asking all these questions?"

I had to think of something fast. "He's a witness to an accident I'm investigating. Can you tell me his last name?"

"It's Ramos. I feel so sorry for his mother, but the boy, I think he's into drugs," Joe said.

"How do you know?"

"The times I ran into him, he looked high. I'm sorry I don't know anything else. I have to get back to work," he said as he rushed off.

I found Dante's apartment number on the building directory and climbed the stairs to the sixth floor. The woman who answered the door looked like she had been crying. Her eyes were red.

"Mrs. Ramos, I'm so sorry to intrude right now. My name's Maddie Landon and I'm a private investigator." I handed Mrs. Ramos my card. "May I please come in and talk with you?"

"Does this have anything to do with why my boy was beat up by thugs?" she said in broken English. "Thank God they didn't kill him." And she made the sign of the cross with her hand.

"I'm not sure. That's what I'm trying to find out. If it's at all possible, I'd like to speak with your son." We were standing in her kitchen. I noticed the edges of the yellow-colored linoleum were curling up. "I believe he may have gotten himself in trouble and I would like to help."

"How can you help?" she said, throwing her hands up in the air.

"It's possible a case I'm working on may be related to what happened to your son. I'm not sure, but first I need to speak with him."

"He's resting now. Maybe come back later."

"I'll be quick." She hesitated and then pointed to Dante's room.

"Hi, Dante," I said as I walked into his room.

"Who are you?"

Dante's face was all bruised and his arm was in a soft cast.

"My name's Maddie. I saw you at the party Saturday night having words with a girl named Mia."

"Why were you watching us?" he said, avoiding eye contact.

"I'm a private investigator, and I was there on a case I'm working on. I want to help you if I can. Can you tell me what happened?"

"Nothing. I was mugged." Dante was scared. I could see it in his eyes.

"Do you know who mugged you?"

"No. They were strangers."

"Is that what you told the police?" He nodded. "Did these people threaten you if you told anyone?"

"I have no idea what you're talking about."

"Okay. Can you tell me what the fight with Mia was about?"

"It was nothing. Just some stupid argument."

"Was it about drugs?"

"No! Why would you say that?" he said a bit too quickly.

"I don't know; why don't you tell me?"

"Can you please leave me alone right now. I'm tired."

"Do you owe money to these people? If you can't pay them, do you think they're going to just leave you alone?"

"Please go."

"If you want to talk, your mother has my card. If you need my help, please call me."

When I came out of Dante's room, Mrs. Ramos looked upset.

"Did he say what happened? He won't talk to me. I begged him to tell me what was wrong," Mrs. Ramos said.

"Do you think he's using drugs?"

"I don't know. I tell him every day to stay away from that stuff. I know what goes on. I see it in the neighborhood. Those horrible people selling drugs and I'm always afraid for him."

"Is there a friend of his that he's close to that might know what he's involved in?"

"He has one friend, Leon Mitchell. They're close."

"Do you know how I can get in touch with Leon?"

"I don't know where he lives but he and Dante play basketball at the schoolyard a few blocks from here."

"If you think of anything, please call me."

"Will you find out who hurt Dante?" she said with a pleading look in her eyes.

"I will try."

As I was walking down the six flights, I wondered if there was any connection to the fight he had with Mia and why he was beat up.

CHAPTER 36

After I left Dante's building, I drove past the schoolyard and saw some kids shooting hoops.

"Hey, guys," I said as I walked over to them. "Any one of you seen Leon Mitchell?"

"Who's asking?" A tall, skinny kid, covered with adolescent acne, approached me with a menacing look on his face.

"His friend Dante was beat up. You know anything about what happened?" I thought that would catch their attention.

"Are you for real, man?"

I nodded.

"He ain't here," the skinny kid said, skipping the attitude.

"Do you know where he lives?"

"Over on Park Street. Is Dante alright?"

"He'll live. Would you happen to know if Dante was in any trouble?"

"We don't know nothing."

"Thanks." And I walked away. I didn't think they would tell me anything, even if they did know.

I drove over to Park. It's a narrow street with attached houses on both sides of the block, each house situated on a small plot of land. Fortunately, it was a short block. I had no idea which house Leon lived in. As I was about to knock on someone's door, I saw a boy about ten or eleven years old on a scooter coming in my direction.

"Are you selling something?" the kid said, looking me up and down.

"No, I'm looking for Leon Mitchell. Would you happen to know which house he lives in?"

"Why are you looking for him? Is he in trouble?"

"It's about his friend who was in an accident. Do you think you can tell me which house he lives in?" The boy pointed to number 78 and left.

House number 78 had a red door. I rang the bell and a male teenager appeared before me.

"Hi, would you by any chance be Leon?"

"Yeah, why?" Leon was probably around fifteen. He was a sweet-looking kid with dark curly hair and a dimple in his chin.

"Is your mother or father home?"

"Ma," he yelled.

"What is it?" his mother said to her son as she came to the door. Seeing me, she asked what I wanted.

"My name's Maddie Landon. I'm a private investigator. I just came from Dante Ramos's apartment. Dante was beaten up pretty badly."

"Please come in," Mrs. Mitchell said.

I was led into the living room. There was a plastic cover on the couch. Wasn't that something people did in the '50s and '60s? The brown shag rug looked outdated. They sat on the couch, and I sat down opposite them on a worn brown leather recliner.

"What happened?" Mrs. Mitchell said.

"Dante said he was mugged. What do you think, Leon? His mother told me you were good friends." Leon remained silent.

"I know this is very difficult for you, but I need to ask you some questions."

"You think my son had something to do with Dante being beat up?" she said, raising her voice.

"Absolutely not, but Mrs. Ramos told me that something has been bothering Dante and I thought he may have told your son," I said, looking directly at Leon.

"Why are you involved? You're not with the police," Mrs. Mitchell said.

"I'm not, but I'm working on a rape case that may be connected to these guys that beat up Dante. Do you think I can have a word with you privately," I said to Mrs. Mitchell. We both got up and walked into the hallway.

"Is it possible for me to talk with Leon alone. Sometimes teenagers are hesitant to talk in front of their parents. I promise you Leon is not in any trouble." Mrs. Mitchell was contemplating what to do.

"I'll give you a few minutes with my son."

"Thank you." I walked back into the living room and sat down next to Leon.

"Leon, none of what is said here gets back to your mother, but I need to know the truth. It could help Dante."

"I don't know. I don't want to rat out my best friend."

"I admire you for that, but he's in trouble and he's scared. I want to help him, and I thought if you knew anything, I might be able to find out what actually happened."

He shrugged his shoulders.

"Right now, whoever did this to him just beat him up, but maybe next time he won't be so lucky. I need your help. Was Dante using drugs?" Leon nodded yes slowly.

"Dante and a girl named Mia were arguing at a party last Saturday night. Do you know what that argument may have been about?"

"No, but I know he owed people money for drugs."

"Do you know who these people are?"

He shook his head. "I have no idea."

"Are you using drugs?"

"No, I swear."

"I believe you." Whether I did or not didn't matter. I wanted him to trust me.

"Did he tell you anything else?"

"I think these guys may have threatened him."

"Why do you say that?"

"Just a feeling. He never actually told me, but he changed. He got moody and kept more to himself."

"So, you have no idea why Dante and this girl Mia were arguing?"

"I don't even know who Mia is."

"Thank you for talking with me," I said, as his mother walked back into the room.

After speaking with Leon, I had my doubts that Dante was mugged. If he did owe money to drug dealers, maybe they wanted to teach him a lesson.

I wasn't happy where this investigation was headed. Though how Mia was involved in all of this, I still had no answer.

CHAPTER 37

On the way back, I called Jesse.

"The boy from the party was beat up." I said when he answered. I briefed Jesse on everything I learned about Dante Ramos.

"If what his friend said was true, these drug dealers probably wanted to make an example of him," Jesse said.

"What if Mia was somehow involved. If she was selling drugs to Dante and he couldn't pay her, Mia might have reported it to Santiago."

"We have no idea what the fight was about. We know more about Dante from his friend than we know about Mia. Maybe take a run at her friends again. I gotta go. My subject is on the move."

My phone was buzzing as I was putting my key in the door.

"Maddie, I know you said not to talk to Mia, but I had to. I wanted to know why she lied about Jason."

"And you expected her to tell you?" I said, trying to keep the anger out of my voice.

"She told me to leave her alone. She looked scared. Why would she be scared?"

Good question, I thought to myself.

"What exactly did she tell you?"

"Just to mind my own business and that my friend is a rapist."

"Sam, please don't have any further contact with Mia. Promise me."

"Sure," I heard and then a click.

It was a guess on my part that Mia found out that someone beat up Dante Ramos. That might scare her if she was somehow involved.

After dinner, I decided to pull out my corkboard. I thought I would write down what I'd learned so far on 3x5 index cards. Maybe a pattern would emerge.

I tacked up Mia Franklin's name in the middle. On the right side of Mia, I put her friends, Tiffany, Sandra, Logan Kelly, and Ben Bradley. I put Jason Demsky underneath Mia. On the other side, next to Mia, I tacked up Dominick Santiago. What did we know about him? We knew he sold drugs to kids. Mia was in the car with him. Let's assume that Mia was selling drugs for Santiago. Underneath Santiago, I placed Dante Ramos.

According to his friend Leon, Dante owed money to drug dealers, probably why he was beat up. Mia and Dante were arguing at the party. Was he buying drugs from Mia? Dante was scared. He wouldn't talk to me. I needed wine. I poured myself a glass of Merlot. Maybe things would look clearer with wine.

From a distance, something struck me. Though Mia accused Jason of raping her, he wasn't connected to anyone on the board except Mia. Most of what was up there was about Mia and drugs. I was still missing pieces. How did Jason fit into this puzzle? Was he in the wrong place at the wrong time?

***

In the morning, I decided to take another run at Sandra Carlson. She seemed a little more vulnerable than her friend Tiffany.

I caught up with her waiting in line in Starbucks after school. She looked at me for a quick second and then it registered on her face who I was.

"Are you following me?"

"We need to talk now."

"I don't have to talk with you."

"That's true, but if you don't, I'm going to tell Mia that you were the one who snitched to the headmaster that she was raped." It was a gamble—but I was hoping it would pay off. She got her fancy coffee and we sat down.

"I know you don't believe me, but I'm trying to help Mia. I think she's in some sort of trouble. Do you know if she's selling or using drugs?"

"Are you crazy? No way."

"Are you sure?"

"Yes. I would know." I didn't doubt that she really believed it. I'm just not sure she knew.

"Okay! Would you happen to know why Mia would have so much cash on her?"

"How would you know that?"

"That doesn't matter."

"I have no idea what you're talking about."

Either she was a good liar or she was clueless.

"Why did you tell the school Mia was raped?"

"Because she wasn't going to say anything, and I wanted the bastard to pay for what he did to her." I wasn't sure I believed her but what would be her motive to lie?

"Do you know why she wasn't going to tell her parents?"

"She said she would have to testify in court, and she didn't want to put herself through all of that."

"So why did Mia finally admit to it?"

"Her mother wouldn't let it go. She kept badgering her until Mia finally said she was raped." That made sense.

"What exactly did Mia tell you about that night?"

"Just that Jason tried to kiss her, and he got aggressive. He was angry that she wouldn't go out with him. You're not going to tell Mia that I snitched on her?"

"No. Thanks for talking with me."

If I believed Jason was innocent, then why did Mia lie to her two best friends about what happened that night?

CHAPTER 38

Though Mia's father made it perfectly clear he didn't want me anywhere near his family, I had no choice if I wanted to get to the truth.

While driving to the Franklins' brownstone, I thought my best shot at getting Mia's mother to talk would be to catch her off guard, away from her familiar surroundings.

I found a spot on her street where none of the neighbors would get suspicious, yet I could see the Franklins' front door from a distance. Though I didn't know what Mrs. Franklin looked like, how many women in their forties would be coming out of her house. By 6:15 p.m. I was bored out of my mind and decided to call it quits and return the following morning.

***

I was back at Mrs. Franklin's place at 8:30 a.m. the following day, well prepared with power bars, water, and the Beatles music. As I arrived, I spotted Mr. Franklin and Mia leaving at the same time. I had no idea what Melissa Franklin did every day. Was she a stay-at-home mom? Did she work? Was she one of those rich women who spent their morning at a health spa and then met friends at Le Bernardin, a high-end restaurant, for lunch?

At 10:20 a.m. a tall, very attractive woman with dark brown hair pulled up in a ponytail, who I assumed was Mrs. Franklin, walked out the front door. I quickly got out of my car and followed. Mrs. Franklin was wearing black leggings, a white zip-up sweatshirt, and was carrying a gym bag. After walking a few blocks, Mrs. Franklin went inside the Equinox Sports Club. I debated for a moment whether I wanted to follow her in or approach her after she left. I opted for the latter.

Seventy minutes later, Mrs. Franklin exited the gym, now wearing jeans, a button-down blue and white striped shirt, and a blue blazer. She walked a few blocks and went into a very fancy coffee place and sat down. I didn't know if she was meeting someone but now was my opportunity.

"Mrs. Franklin," I said. She stared at me with a puzzled look on her face. "My name's Maddie Landon. I'm a private investigator."

"You're the woman who tried to break into our home."

"Just for the record, I did not try to break in. I was just looking around."

"You're working for the boy who raped my daughter. Leave me alone and stop harassing me before I call the police. My husband has already warned you to stay away from our family."

"You need to hear me out. It's about Mia. She may be in trouble." That caught her attention. The waitress came over.

"Not now, please," Melissa Franklin said, waving her away. She nodded for me to sit down. "What do you think you know about my daughter?" she said in a condescending manner.

"Let's start from the beginning. Do you know why it wasn't until several days after Mia was raped that she reported it to the police?"

"How did you know that?"

"During the course of my investigation, I found out a few things. Can you tell me why she didn't report it right away?" I said, repeating myself.

"I don't see how that changes anything. My daughter told us who raped her. Why would she lie?"

That's what I would like to know. "I'm trying to find out the truth. Maybe she was threatened and scared of the person who raped her."

Mrs. Franklin didn't say anything.

"I think your daughter may be selling drugs. A guy by the name of Dominick Santiago is a drug dealer. Your daughter was seen getting in and out of his car."

"Are you crazy," she said, rising out of her chair.

I quickly spoke, not wanting Mrs. Franklin to leave. "Did you know that your daughter walked into a very expensive jewelry store and paid $1,200 cash for a bracelet? She then went into Bloomingdale's and bought several things, also paying cash. Where would she get all that cash?"

Mrs. Franklin sat slowly back down.

"Why were you following my daughter?"

"I'm trying to find out who raped her."

"I know who raped her: Jason Demsky. He was caught on camera. Cameras don't lie. I think we're finished here."

Mrs. Franklin threw a $20 dollar bill down on the table and left. What did I expect? She would believe her daughter was selling drugs and lied about who raped her? What mother would want to admit that about their child? It was a gamble. I didn't think Mrs. Franklin would believe what I had to say but I had to try. Maybe she suspected something was wrong, but she would never allow herself to acknowledge that fact to me.

CHAPTER 39

Though I was pretty sure Mrs. Franklin wasn't going to confront her daughter about our conversation, it might be hard for her to ignore what I just told her. Maybe on some level she knew Mia was hiding things from her.

It was after 2:00 p.m. by the time I got back to my office. Could I be wrong about Mia? I didn't think so.

The phone startled me. "Hello."

"Maddie, it's Jerry. I think I have some information for you." I let out a slow sigh of relief. Every time the phone rang, I held my breath.

"Anything at this point would be great."

"This guy Santiago is part of a drug gang. The guy who runs it is looking to acquire more territory. There was a double homicide in the Bronx recently. The police think it's Santiago's boss that was involved, trying to expand his drug operation in the Bronx." Something inside of me went cold.

"Can I ask one more favor? Can you find out the names of the two people who were shot?"

"Okay, but why?"

"It's a little complicated. This lawyer asked me to locate a witness that never showed. A long story short, I found two bodies up in the Bronx: my attorney's witness and his girlfriend. His name was Miguel Garcia. I noticed there was a leather jacket in the apartment with the symbol of a crow on it."

"So, you think this guy Garcia was part of a drug gang that Santiago's boss was trying to take over?"

"I'm not sure, but it's possible. Would you happen to know who Garcia's boss is?"

"Wait a second." A few minutes later, Jerry gave me the name of the guy who ran the drug operation Garcia was part of.

When we hung up, I had this horrible feeling that Jesse was right, that I did step into a pile of shit. But what did any of this have to do with Mia's rape?

I tried to locate information on Luis Martinez, Garcia's boss. I didn't expect there would be much in my databases about this guy. After spending some time looking, I was able to obtain his date of birth. From there, I ran a NYS Department of Motor Vehicles record search. The car registered to him was a 2019 black Mercedes. I jotted down the license plate number and the address listed for him. If this guy's operation was being targeted, maybe he would talk to me. I was taking a gamble but I was tired of being jerked around by everyone involved.

**

In the morning, I drove up to Yonkers, a city in lower Westchester County, to the address I found for Luis Martinez. Though I wasn't expecting any trouble, I had my gun with me, just in case. Martinez's house was a split-level ranch similar to the other houses on the block. I thought I would wait till he came out before I approached him.

At a little after 11:00 a.m., a man in his late forties, with a solid build and a cigarette dangling from his lips, exited the house. I walked up to him slowly so as not to startle him.

"Excuse me, Mr. Martinez?"

"How do you know my name and who are you?" he said with an edge in his voice.

"My name's Maddie Landon." I gave him my card. "I'm not here to cause you any trouble, but we need to talk."

"Why would I want to talk with you? Get lost."

"Because I was the one who found Miguel Garcia and his girlfriend dead in her apartment."

"Why would I care?"

"Cause I know Garcia worked for you. Can we talk somewhere?"

"My car." I wasn't thrilled about getting in Martinez's car, but I had no choice if I wanted to find out what he knew about Santiago.

His car was parked two doors down from his house. He got into the driver's seat and I got into the front passenger seat.

"This better be good because otherwise you're wasting my time."

"I'm working on a rape case on an unrelated matter. I was asked to locate Miguel Garcia since he was a witness to a crime. That led me to his girlfriend's apartment and discovering their bodies. Without going into all the details, I came to find out that Garcia was killed in a drug war between your guys and someone I've been watching because of his involvement in my case." I stopped, waiting to hear if Martinez had anything to say. He didn't, so I continued.

"What can you tell me about Dominick Santiago?" For one quick moment his face gave him away. He knew the name.

"I have no idea who you're talking about."

"Look, as I said, I'm not here to cause you any trouble." I wasn't sure how much I wanted to reveal. "My subject may have some involvement with him, and I need to know what he's into."

"You are way out of your league. Now get out of my car before I do something I might regret."

"Please, is there anything you know about this guy Santiago?"

He opened the door and pushed me out. Before I had a chance to say anything, he drove off. He knew who Santiago was but he wasn't going to give me the satisfaction of telling me.

Before driving back, I called Jesse.

"What's up?"

I went through what transpired between myself and Luis Martinez.

"You took a chance seeing this guy."

"I'm worried that Martinez is going to get even and that means killing Santiago. He's not going to let Miguel Garcia's death go unpunished. I'm afraid Mia may get caught in the middle of this mess."

"Maybe it's time to confront both her parents with what you know. If they don't believe you, it's on them. At least you would be doing the right thing."

"You're right. I don't think I should wait till after the weekend. I'll go there tonight. Instead of coming to your place later, why don't I come to you first thing in the morning."

"How about if we switch weekends. I'll drive down to you in the morning unless you want me to come with you tonight for moral support?"

"I think I should do this by myself."

"Okay! I'll see you in the morning."

After hanging up, I wasn't sure which I was dreading more, talking to Mia's parents or telling Jesse that I can't have children.

CHAPTER 40

I pulled up to the Franklins' home at 7:45 p.m. I knocked on the front door. When it opened, Mrs. Franklin was standing in front of me.

"What are you doing here?" she said. If looks could kill, I'd be dead.

"You and your husband need to listen to what I have to say."

"Stephen, please come here," Melissa Franklin said, shouting.

"What's going on," he said to his wife. When he saw me, he said, "I thought I told you to stay away from my family."

"I'm sorry to intrude but your daughter might be in danger."

"What the hell are you talking about?" Mr. Franklin said.

"Please can I come in?"

"I don't think so."

"Stephen, let's at least listen to what she has to say."

I could see from the look on Mr. Franklin's face he wasn't too happy that his wife wanted to hear me out, but he didn't object. We went into the living room. I did a quick glance around. The room a mix of modern furniture and antiques. Mr. Franklin pointed to a light blue sofa and told me to sit. They sat opposite me, each on a blue and gray striped upholstered chair with a chrome frame.

"So, what's so important that you had to barge into my house at this time of night?" Mr. Franklin barked.

"Is your daughter home?"

"No, she's out," Mrs. Franklin said.

I began by repeating what I had told Mrs. Franklin when I had spoken to her. Then I went on to divulge what I witnessed between Mia and Dominick Santiago and what I found out about his involvement with drugs. I ended with finding the bodies of Miguel Garcia and his girlfriend and my conversation with Garcia's boss. I debated whether to mention that Santiago might be the next target in the drug war but in the end decided that they had a right to know.

"If what you're saying is true, and I have my doubts that Mia is selling drugs, why would you tell us when you're working for the boy that raped our daughter?" Mr. Franklin said.

"Mia is only a kid. She has no idea what she may have gotten herself involved in and I don't want to see her get hurt. Secondly, I don't believe my client raped Mia. I think Mia was in a bind and that's why she said it was my client."

"What kind of bind are we talking about?" Mrs. Franklin said, her hands nervously twisting.

"She was never going to tell you she was raped, but when you found out from the school, you forced her to," I said, looking at Mrs. Franklin. "I believe the person who raped Mia also threatened to expose the fact that she was selling drugs."

"What can happen to Mia if she is selling drugs?" Mrs. Franklin said with a concerned look on her face.

"We'll talk to our daughter and find out what's going on," Mr. Franklin said in an authoritative tone. It was apparent he didn't want to continue our conversation or hear anything else I had to say.

As Mrs. Franklin was walking me out, I strongly urged her to talk with her daughter. I sat in my car, digesting what had just transpired. I knew Mr. Franklin didn't want to believe that his daughter was selling drugs, but I watched Mrs. Franklin and could see she was troubled by what I had said from the reaction on her face.

***

It was after 9:00 p.m. when I got back to my apartment. After undressing, I made myself a peanut butter sandwich and got into bed. I turned the TV on but I was distracted. I kept rehashing what I could have done differently to convince the Franklins that their daughter's life might be in danger. Before I went to bed, I was debating whether to turn off my phone. Though I knew threatening phone calls couldn't harm me, they were disturbing, to say the least. But were they a warning of what was to come?

***

When I woke up, the TV was blaring. The clock read 7:30 a.m. and I knew Jesse would be here by 9:00. I turned off the TV and quickly showered and straightened up. While I was putting the coffee in the coffeemaker, I was thinking about what I would say to him. My mind was a blank. Would it be a deal breaker? My stomach was in knots just thinking about it.

CHAPTER 41

I heard the familiar knock on the door. I stared at Jesse for one moment before he walked in.

"What's wrong?" he said.

"Nothing. Why?"

"You had a funny look on your face when you opened the door."

"Really?"

"I know you, Madds. Tell me what's going on. Did you change your mind about us living together?"

"No, not at all."

"Well then, what is it?"

"I need coffee. Do you want a cup?"

"Sure." He sat down and I followed after pouring the coffee into mugs.

"Okay. I should have told you this a while ago, probably when we started getting serious." Jesse didn't interrupt. I was dreading the next words out of my mouth.

"I can't have children. When I was twenty-two, I was diagnosed with endometriosis. I'm fine but, well, it left me unable to conceive."

Jesse was quiet. "Please say something," I said.

"Madds, I'm forty-five. If I wanted to have a child, I would have had a discussion with you a while ago."

"But if you're with me, you can never have children. You might change your mind and then what? I don't want you to resent me."

"If we decide to have a baby, there's always adoption or a surrogate."

"Are you sure?"

"Absolutely. Now let's make a make-believe baby."

While we were having breakfast, I told Jesse everything that happened with the Franklins.

"Do you think they'll confront Mia?" I said to Jesse.

"I think they will. But first we still don't know for sure that Mia is selling drugs and if she is, I think she'll deny it. She's not going to admit she lied about Jason. Your focus should be on finding out who raped Mia."

"If anyone knows, they're not talking. I'm beginning to suspect that she lied to her two best friends. If she was threatened, she may have decided not to share who her rapist was with anyone."

"There has to be another way to find out."

"I'm all ears," I said.

"Let me think on it."

***

We spent the rest of the day walking around Soho, an area in downtown Manhattan with a variety of beautiful shops, restaurants, and galleries. We wound up having dinner at a place called Mamo, an Italian restaurant that we happened upon, and afterward we stopped at a café for a cappuccino and dessert. Except for going out for breakfast on Sunday, we spent the rest of the day relaxing and playing chess.

***

When Jesse left Monday morning, I called Paul Greer, Jason's public defender. I wanted to know what, if anything, he found out that could help Jason. My call went to voicemail, where I left a message.

I dressed, had breakfast, and walked over to my office. As soon as I opened the door, I knew something was wrong. The light in the reception area was on. I always shut all the lights before leaving. Then it hit me, a horrible smell coming from somewhere. It smelled like rotting flesh. I walked cautiously into my office and couldn't believe what I was staring at. There was a dead cat lying on my desk, completely cut open, with its guts all over the floor. My desk drawers were pulled out. Whoever broke in was looking for something. On the wall above my desk in large red letters, it said: THIS IS A WARNING. NEXT TIME YOU WON'T BE SO LUCKY!

I started to gag and barely reached the toilet before throwing up. I ran across the hall to Cousin Will.

"What's the matter?" Mary said. "You're white as a ghost."

I couldn't get the words out. Mary yelled for Will.

"Maddie, what is it?" I just pointed to my office. Will went across the hall and when he came back, he said we should call the police.

"I'm not sure we should do that," I said.

"Why not? You could be in danger."

"I don't think I want the police involved. They might screw up my case."

"You're worried about your case and I'm worried about you."

"Seeing that poor dead animal shook me up. I'll be alright. Let's see if we can get a cleaning service that handles this type of situation," I said.

A few calls later, Cousin Will found a company that would clean, disinfect, and dispose of the cat. A painter was coming in the following day. "They'll be here in an hour. I still think you should call the cops."

"No cops. I need to get some fresh air and I'll come back."

"Why don't you go home. I'll take care of it when they come."

"Are you sure?"

"Go ahead. It'll be fine."

"I don't think I'll be able to work in my office ever again."

"Don't worry, it'll be cleaner than it was."

"It's the image I might not be able to get rid of."

"You will over time." I gave Will a hug and left.

After my parents died, I stayed with Will and his parents until Aunt Jenny came to live with me. Ever since that night, Will has always been like a big brother to me. He and his wife Sophie and son Noah are the only family I have, and Will's the person I trust most besides Annie.

CHAPTER 42

I walked for blocks; the picture of the dead cat still stuck in my head. This person was escalating. It had to be someone who knew I was investigating Mia's rape and wanted to scare me off. My phone startled me. It was an unknown number.

"Hello," I said cautiously, holding my breath.

"Ms. Landon, it's Paul Greer. What can I do for you?"

I breathed easier.

"I'd like to stop by your office to talk about Jason Demsky's case. Would you have some time this afternoon?"

"I can squeeze you in at 3:00 p.m. You have my address?"

"Yes. I'll see you then." I was curious if he had done anything on Jason's case.

When I called Jesse, his phone went directly to voicemail. I left a message. About an hour later, he called me back.

"Hey, babe, what's going on?"

"I walked into my office and there was a dead cat on my desk with its guts all over the floor and a lovely threatening message on my wall."

"When was this?"

"When I got in this morning. I could smell the stench right away. It kind of freaked me out for a moment. Will called a cleaning service that apparently deals with these situations. I think I need to get a new desk. I don't care what they do to clean it, the image of that cat split open makes me want to puke."

"Did you call the police?"

"No. I don't want them poking around and asking me all sorts of questions."

I was reluctant to tell him about the phone calls. I didn't want to hear any lectures about how I need to be careful.

"Listen, I have to go. I'm in the middle of something."

I thought Jesse seemed distracted as I hung up the phone. I wondered if he was feeling stressed at work.

I stopped at a Starbucks for an espresso and sat down. I couldn't get the image of the dead cat out of my head. Though I had put on a brave front for Will, the words on my wall frightened me. Whose feathers did I rattle? Was it Luis Martinez, the boss of Miguel Garcia who was killed? Or Dominick Santiago? He could have found out I was looking into him. The only problem with Garcia and Santiago is that I didn't have any contact with them when the calls had started. Maybe the incident with the cat had nothing to do with them.

I was curious if there were any street cameras near my office that could be accessed. Since I didn't want the police involved, I needed someone on the police force who would help me and who I could trust not to say anything. I was hesitant to ask Jerry for another favor.

My phone rang as I was leaving. "Hello."

"Maddie, it's Jerry. The names of the two dead people are Miguel Garcia and Terry Rhodes." Though I wasn't surprised I was hoping I was wrong.

"Are you still there?" Jerry said.

"Yeah, just thinking. Thanks, Jerry. If you need anything just ask. I owe you big."

If Luis Martinez was planning on getting even because of the death of Garcia, Mia could get caught in the crossfire. Though I could easily say it's not my problem, I'm not sure at this point I have a choice. As long as Mia had accused Jason of rape, she was my problem.

**

Paul Greer's office was a few blocks from the courthouse downtown. It was located in a small building that looked like it was ready to be condemned. His office was on the second floor of a three-story walk-up. Before I had called him, I spoke to Nina Demsky. I wanted to know if Paul Greer had been in touch with her in the last few weeks. She told me she had spoken to him only once since he took the case, and he hadn't been returning her calls as of late.

"Mr. Greer, Maddie Landon." We shook hands.

"Please sit." he said. Mr. Greer looked to be somewhere in his late thirties. He was on the thin side, about an inch shorter than me, with dark wavy hair and a nose that was too large for his face. Looking around his office, there were files strewn everywhere.

"How's Jason's case going?" I said.

"As you can see, I have quite a few cases. Things work slowly around here. Public defenders don't have the money to hire experts. I'll try to get the best deal I can for Mr. Demsky."

"Why are you thinking about a deal at this point? You're assuming he raped her. Have you even talked to him since he made bail?"

"I spoke to him a couple of times."

I knew that was a lie and was clenching my fists at my side so I wouldn't reach across the table and strangle him.

"I don't think Jason raped Mia Franklin," I said.

"Do you have another suspect?"

"At the moment, no. Look, we're both on the same side. I don't want to see Jason go to prison when there's a possibility he didn't do it."

"You said yourself there are no other suspects. He was seen going in and out of the Franklins' home at the time of the rape."

"I know the evidence against him looks bad, but I still have doubts that he raped her. From what I've learned so far, Mia might be involved with drugs, maybe even selling them. If that's the case, it might be enough to create doubt in one juror's mind that someone other than Jason could have raped her. Can you look into it?"

"I'll see what I can do."

"Is there a trial date set?"

"As of today, it looks like it should be on the docket for January. I'm meeting with the judge and the assistant DA next week. I'll know something then. The later the trial, the better for Jason."

"Let me know what you find out."

I was trying not to gag on my last words as I walked out of his office. I had no faith that Mr. Greer would get off his ass to help Jason. I was hoping I was wrong but wasn't counting on it.

***

Before I left the police force, there weren't too many guys in my precinct who I was chummy with. Most of them didn't want me there. One guy wasn't a dick like all the others. Thomas Brooks went out of his way to be friendly toward me. I was crossing my fingers he was still on the force. I found a number for personnel. When I got through, I was informed he was still at my old precinct. The person at the other end of the line gave me his direct number.

"Brooks here," he said when he answered.

"Tom, it's Maddie Landon. How are you?"

"Maddie, great to hear from you. How's everything?"

I didn't want to get into the particulars over the phone. "Do you think we can meet for a drink?"

"Sure. Are you okay?"

"Yeah, thanks for asking. What's good for you?"

"I'm off duty at 5:30."

"Do you know Dive 75 on West 75th?"

"I'll see you there," he said.

***

The first thing that catches your eye when you walk into Dive 75 is a giant fish tank with tropical fish swimming around. Also, you couldn't help but notice all the TVs situated in different areas for watching sports. I was already seated when Tom arrived. I waved.

"You look great, Maddie. Private investigations agree with you," Tom said as he sat down.

"You don't look so bad yourself." Tom was a good-looking guy with high cheekbones and smooth caramel-colored skin. He was around six feet with a solid build.

"What are you drinking?" I said to him when the waitress came over.

"I'll have whatever light beer you have on tap."

"And I'll have a Cabernet Sauvignon. Shall we order a pizza?" I asked Tom.

"Sure, sounds great."

"How are things at the precinct?"

"Same. Not many changes."

"Who are you partnered with?"

"Do you remember Frank Griffin?"

"Yeah. He was okay. At least he left me alone. How is your family?"

"Great. It's photo time." He brought out pictures of his two boys who were now almost teenagers and his beautiful wife, Amelia. "What about you, married?"

"Not yet, though I am seeing someone who's also a private investigator."

The waitress brought over our drinks and left.

"Well, to old friends. So, what do I owe the honor of this meeting?"

I caught Tom up to date on everything I knew.

"Do you think the person or persons who may be on the camera had anything to do with your subject's rape?"

"I have no idea, but at least I'll know who I'm dealing with. Look, I don't want you to do anything that could jeopardize your job."

"It's easy enough to check the cameras. Just give me the exact location, date, and a timeframe you need covered. If I find anything, I'll send it to you as an attachment."

"Thanks. I really appreciate it."

On the way home, my phone rang. I answered it without looking to see who was calling.

"Did you like my present?"

"You're sick. Who are you?"

"That was only a warning," the voice said, and then a click.

My hands were shaking as I put down the phone. Whoever it was, wasn't going to stop. I knew I should probably call the police, but what could they do? I was on my own.

CHAPTER 43

Two days later, I was still working from home. Maybe I should hire a driver like the character Mickey Haller does in the Michael Connelly books who works out of the backseat of his Lincoln Navigator. Cousin Will had called and told me that my office was as good as new. I'm sure that's true. Maybe in time I won't be seeing a dead cat lying on my desk. I was thankful that two days had gone by with no harassing phone calls, though I was under no illusions that this person had any plans of stopping. I was having trouble sleeping, afraid of what was going to happen next.

When I opened up my computer, there was an email from Tom Brooks with an attachment. I quickly downloaded it, grabbed a cup of coffee, and opened it up. I watched the entire video and then went back and played it again from the beginning. The video was date and time-stamped. It read 10:08 p.m. Someone who was dressed completely in dark clothes with a hooded sweatshirt, carrying what looked like a brown package, was outside my building. I zoomed in but couldn't make out the person's face. His head was down. I was only able to tell that he was white, medium height and build, and was wearing glasses. Other than that, there was nothing else that caught my eye. He opened the front door and then he was out of reach of the camera. Unfortunately, there are no cameras installed in our hallway, and I was pretty certain getting into my office was not that difficult. I played it again and again and still nothing popped out at me. Was it someone who'd been here before? Maybe someone I gave my card to? Someone I interviewed? Too many possibilities. Shit, I was hoping the video would tell me who broke into my office. What now? I was still clueless to who raped Mia. I felt like I was in a sinking boat without a paddle.

"Can you meet later," I asked Annie when she answered.

"How about 5:30 p.m. at The Dead Poet?"

"Great. See you soon."

***

I was already seated sipping on a Sauvignon Blanc when Annie arrived at The Dead Poet.

"I definitely need one of those," Annie said before she even sat down.

"Hard day at the office?"

"You can say that. First, someone who was scheduled for a consultation canceled at the last minute without giving a reason. Then this guy I'm representing decides he and his wife are getting back together."

"Isn't that a good thing?"

"Not when you're trying to pay the bills."

"Ah, the mighty dollar speaks."

The waiter came over and Annie ordered a drink.

"I'm a terrible person," Annie said.

"Don't be so hard on yourself. I know what it's like to start a practice. Drink up. You'll feel better," I said when Annie's drink arrived.

"You always have such wise advice," Annie said, grinning.

"I had a lovely day." I went on to tell Annie all about the office break-in and the surprises that were left for me. I decided not to mention the phone calls. I didn't want her to worry since there was nothing she could do about it.

"That certainly was a shittier day than mine. Do you think this person was looking for something specific?"

"Not sure. Maybe notes on the rape case if he was the rapist."

"That makes sense. So you got nothing off the video?"

"I've looked at it over and over."

"Try again. Maybe there's a small detail that you might spot on the second go around, or maybe a second pair of eyes."

"I'll keep looking. I'm going to tail Mia again. I wanna see what she's up to. I think this guy Martinez isn't going to let the death of one of his dealers go without retaliating. It's possible Mia's supplier might be out of business soon. I didn't get the feeling after meeting with Mia's parents that they understood the seriousness of what their daughter is involved in or maybe they didn't believe what I had to say."

"Do you think you should contact the police and let them know what's going on? You don't have to implicate Mia."

"If I do, they're going to start asking questions, questions I might not want to answer."

"Well, think about it."

***

The next day I decided to brave going into the office. I slowly opened the door and walked cautiously to my desk. I looked all around. There were no traces of writing on the wall except in my head. I blinked several times as I looked at my desk imagining the cat was still there. I walked around to my chair and gingerly sat down. Before I had a chance to open up my computer, I heard the door open. I slowly reached down for the gun that was in my ankle holster when I saw Nina standing in my office.

"I'm so sorry to intrude without calling."

"No, Nina, it's fine. Please sit. I don't have any coffee yet. Can I offer you a glass of water?"

"No, I don't want to trouble you. I took a chance that you were here. I have a cleaning job in the city in an hour."

"What's going on?"

"Have you found out anything yet? Anything to clear my son?"

"There are some developments, but I can't share them with you at this moment. Is Jason alright?"

"I know he's hiding things from me but he won't tell me anything. He just ignores me when I try to talk to him. He refuses to see the therapist you recommended, and I don't know what to do anymore."

I was at a loss as to what to say to Nina that wouldn't break my promise to Jason.

"I think you need to talk with Jason again. Maybe he feels you would be disappointed in him if he told you the truth."

"Why would I be disappointed in him? Did he say anything to you?"

"No." I hated lying to her and was feeling a little uncomfortable.

"I would never be disappointed in my son. I love Jason no matter what he's done," she said forcefully.

"Maybe he needs to know that." I couldn't think of anything else to say that wouldn't betray Jason.

As Nina was getting up to leave, I told her everything would be alright. Did I believe it? I wanted to.

CHAPTER 44

After Nina left, I brought up the footage of the person outside my building. Was there something I missed? I played it again several times. I zoomed in as much as I could. There was something very small on the right side of the hoodie that I hadn't noticed before, but I couldn't make it out.

I called Jesse and left a message asking him to call me back as soon as he could. I kept staring at the hoodie but the camera on my computer wasn't sharp enough to see what the image was.

Two hours later, I still hadn't heard back from Jesse. As I was leaving the office, I saw Jesse was calling.

"Hey, I never heard back from you. Is something the matter?" I said.

"Nothing is wrong. Work's been really busy. Just tell me what's going on."

I clued Jesse in on the video. "I saw something that was on the hooded sweatshirt the guy was wearing but I can't make it out. Is there any way you can do something with the footage?"

"Send it to me. I know someone who might be able to clean it up. I gotta go," he said and he hung up.

I didn't know what to think. Maybe he was really busy and I was concerned for no reason, but it just wasn't like Jesse to be so abrupt. I was determined to put it out of my mind.

Even if I could figure out what was on the hoodie, how would that get me closer to the guy who broke in?

***

The following morning, as I was getting ready to head to the park for my run, my phone rang.

"Hey, you got something?" I said to Jesse, when I picked up.

"Unfortunately, no. The person I sent it to hasn't gotten back to me yet. It might take a few days. This guy is doing me a favor."

I was disappointed that I had to wait for the video.

"I just got a call from my boss. There's a problem with the case we're working on. Some guy we were watching who was going to be testifying Monday morning gave us the slip. He's a reluctant witness, but we need him for our case. All hands are on deck to find him, but that means I'll be working all weekend. Sorry, babe."

"Why don't I come up anyway. You can at least have my company in bed."

"As tempting as that sounds, I might be pulling all nighters. I'll try to call you if I get a moment," Jesse said before hanging up.

If I didn't know Jesse any better, I would think he was avoiding me. It wasn't like him to just hang up so quickly. Maybe I'm overthinking this. He could be distracted since he's on a deadline to find this person.

I was a little bummed out that I wasn't going to see Jesse. I was tempted to surprise him and drive up to his place on Saturday, but there was a part of me that was afraid to find out if there was something going on that Jesse didn't want me to know about.

Since I had no plans at the moment and I was waiting on the footage from the night my office was broken into, I had the whole weekend free.

The only time I left the house was on Saturday to see a movie at the Anjelika Theater downtown. It was one of these whodunit thrillers that kept me on the edge of my seat. The rest of the weekend it rained so I stayed in and watched Netflix movies and had Chinese food. I never heard from Jesse.

CHAPTER 45

Monday morning, as I was headed to the office, I was both annoyed and anxious that Jesse hadn't called. What was going on? Maybe Jesse had second thoughts after I told him I was ready to move in together.

"Hey, any luck finding your witness?" I said to Jesse when he answered. I tried to play it cool. I didn't want him to think I didn't trust him.

"We may have a lead. I'm tracking it down now. Hopefully, we'll have him in our hands by tonight."

"But if he doesn't want to testify, isn't he going to make a lousy witness?"

"He'll be a hostile witness but there's not much we can do about it. I still haven't heard back from my guy yet about the video. Soon I hope. Gotta go. I'll talk to you later."

My phone rang as soon as Jesse hung up.

"Nina, how are you?"

"It's Jason. He's gone." The desperation in her voice was palpable.

"Try to calm down. What do you mean when you say he's gone."

"I came home from grocery shopping about a half-hour ago and he wasn't here. He never goes out, and if he does he would leave me a note."

"Maybe he went to a friend's house."

"I called Marshal and he's not with him."

"Did you call Samantha?"

"She's still in school and she can't answer her phone."

I didn't want to upset her more than she already was, but I needed to know if anything would indicate there was a struggle in the apartment.

"Nina, can you tell if anything in the apartment was disturbed?"

"I don't think so."

"Can you go into Jason's room and let me know if there's something out of place or it looks like there was a struggle."

"You're scaring me."

"Just do it please."

A few moments later, I heard Nina say: "I'm in his room and everything looks exactly the way it always does."

"Okay. Is his cell phone there?"

"No. I've been calling him but he doesn't pick up."

"At least we know he probably left on his own accord. That's good. I'm going to make a few calls and then I'm coming over. Please try not to worry. I know it's difficult but you have to remain calm. It won't do Jason any good if you panic."

My first call was to Marshal.

"Marshal, this is Maddie Landon. I know Jason's mother called you. He's not picking up his phone. Do you have any idea where he might have gone? Did he call you?"

"I spoke to him yesterday and I could tell he was depressed. I tried several times to get him to see a therapist, but he wouldn't listen."

"Do you think he would try and harm himself?"

"I don't know, but I'm really frightened for him. He's petrified he'll go to prison."

"I'm going over to his apartment now. I need you to think of any place he might go to be alone. Call me right away if anything comes to mind. Also keep trying him. Maybe he'll pick up."

On the way to Nina Demsky's apartment, I called Sam and left her a message. As I was parking the car, I saw that Sam was calling me back.

"Hi, Sam. I'm just about to go up to Jason's apartment. His mother called me and she's worried about him. When she came home, he was gone. Did he say anything to you?"

"The last two times I called him, he didn't pick up. I should have gone over to his house."

"Sam, he's probably alright."

"You're just saying that."

"I spoke to Marshal. If you think of any place he may have gone, please call me. I'm on my way to see his mother. I gotta go."

When Nina opened the door, her eyes were all red.

"Did you talk to his friends?" Nina asked as soon as I walked in.

"Yes, they haven't heard from him. I'd like to see his computer."

I went into his room and turned on his computer. It asked for his password.

"Would you happen to know his password?"

"Jason doesn't know that I have it. Please don't mention it to him."

"I won't. What is it?"

I put in the password and the screen lit up. I went to the last internet search page, and I was surprised to see what he had been looking at. It was over-the-counter pills to take if you want to overdose. I shut it down before Nina could see what was on the page. This was not good. I had no way of knowing if he went to the pharmacy and got anything to take. My fear was that he left the apartment because he didn't want to kill himself where his mother could find him.

"Can you keep trying him," I said to Nina.

"What is it? You look worried. Please tell me."

"It's nothing."

Nina opened up the page and her hands flew up to her mouth. "Oh my God! He wants to kill himself." She started to cry. "You have to find him and stop him. This is all my fault. If I would have dragged him to the therapist instead of doing nothing, he would be here with me now."

"Nina, this is not your fault. You can't force someone to do something they refuse to do. We'll find him," I said with as much conviction as I could muster up.

My phone was ringing. It was Marshal.

"I thought of a place he might go. I just don't know if I'm right."

"Where? At this point, we have nothing else to go on."

"Forest Park. It's in Queens. There's a very secluded area where we would go to be alone."

"I'm at Jason's apartment now. When I get to the park, can you give me directions where to go?"

"I'm taking an Uber. I'll meet you at the Visitor's Center which is located at the intersection of Woodhaven Boulevard and Forest Park Drive," Marshal said.

"I'm coming with you. My son needs to know how much I love him."

We rode most of the way in silence. I was praying we would find him there and that we weren't too late. Twenty-five minutes later, I was parked in front of the Visitor's Center. Marshal arrived five minutes later.

"Let's go," he said to us. "It'll take about ten minutes to walk there."

When we got to the area where Marshal and Jason sometimes went to be alone, we all started shouting his name and headed in different directions. We were off the hiking trails where the terrain was overgrown with large old oak and tulip trees and grass up to my ankles. As I was walking, terrible thoughts were running through my head: What if Jason wasn't here? What if we were too late? I kept walking and shouting Jason's name. He could be anywhere. I could only pray that Marshal was right. I walked quickly through the brush, yelling out his name. It was then that I noticed something sticking out behind a tree about ten yards in front of me. I ran over. It was Jason, lying unconscious.

"Over here," I heard myself shouting. Jason was barely breathing.

"Hang on, Jason," I said. I quickly dialed 911. "My name's Maddie Landon. I need an ambulance at Forest Park. I have a possible overdose and his breathing is very shallow." I turned to Marshal and asked, "Where exactly are we?" I passed the phone to him. The last thing I heard was Marshal saying, "Hurry please."

CHAPTER 46

"Oh my God, Jason, I love you," Nina whispered to her son, tears streaming down her cheeks. "The ambulance is almost here. Please stay with me."

After what seemed like forever, I could finally hear the sirens nearby. Hurry, hurry.

"Please step aside," the paramedic said as he got out of the ambulance. "Do you know what he took?" the other paramedic said. The bottle of pills was lying on the ground.

"Where are you taking him," I said.

"Long Island Jewish in Forest Hills."

"I'm riding with my son," Nina said to the medic.

They placed him on the gurney. I could hear one of the paramedics talking to Jason as they were putting him into the ambulance, trying to keep him awake. Marshal and I raced to the parking lot.

Driving to the hospital, I told Marshal to call Sam and tell her what was going on. When we arrived at the hospital, I saw Nina pacing anxiously.

"Where's Jason," I said.

"Nobody will tell me anything."

I went over to the nurse's station. "There was a young man named Jason Demsky who just came here in an ambulance. Can you tell me anything?"

"Are you family?"

"His mother is right here."

"Mrs. Demsky, I have some forms for you to fill out."

"I need to know how my son is doing."

"The doctor is with him now. As soon as he's finished, he'll come out and talk with you. In the meantime, please fill out the forms."

Nina's hands were trembling as she took the forms from the nurse.

"Why don't you sit down. It'll be easier to fill them out," I said. We both sat down. Marshal was pacing. A few minutes later, Sam arrived. She ran to Marshal and they hugged.

"How is he," she said looking at me. Her eyes were damp.

"The doctor is with him now." It was the first time I saw Sam where she was subdued. I knew she was scared.

An hour later, the doctor came out. "Mrs. Demsky, can I speak to you in private?"

Nina could barely stand she was so frightened. I couldn't hear what the doctor was saying. A few minutes later, Nina turned and walked toward us.

CHAPTER 47

"They pumped his stomach," Nina said. "He's going to be alright, but the hospital wants to keep him overnight for observation. I can't watch him all day. What am I going to do?"

"Do you think he would be better off in a hospital where they can look after him and give him psychiatric care?"

"I don't want him in a mental hospital."

"Is he conscious right now?"

"Yes. The doctor said I can see him. What should I say to him?" Nina asked me as we were all taking the elevator up to the second floor where Jason's room was.

"You'll find the words."

The three of us waited outside while Nina went into Jason's room.

"Do you think he's going to be alright?" Sam said, shifting her feet back and forth.

"He needs therapy, someone he can talk to without feeling judged. And he needs your support."

Nina came out, her shoulders slumped as if she was carrying the weight of the world.

"Why don't you go in now," she said, looking at Sam and Marshal.

"How's he doing?" I said to Nina.

"I told him we couldn't go on the way things were. He agreed to see the therapist and I'm thankful for that. I couldn't stand how he just stayed in his room all day, but

I didn't push him because I felt so bad for him. I'm his mother and I couldn't protect him from all the hurt he was going through."

"It'll take time. I know this is hard, but you'll need to trust Jason and the therapist."

"Whatever you think is best. I can't thank you enough for saving my boy's life. I could never repay you," Nina said as she hugged me.

"I'm going to leave now. Can you get home by yourself?" I said.

"I'll be fine. I'm just so thankful that Jason is alright."

"If you need me for anything, just call."

***

By the time I got home, it was almost 8:00 p.m. and I was exhausted. I quickly undressed and poured myself a glass of wine. I took it into the living room, plopping down into my father's chair. The next thing I knew, I heard a buzzing sound. I was groggy and disoriented and had no idea where the noise was coming from until I realized it was my phone.

"Hello."

"Why do you sound as if you were sleeping? Did I wake you?"

"I must have fallen asleep."

"It's only 9:00 p.m."

"I've had a long day. I think something's going on with Jesse. I can feel it," I said, yawning. I told Annie how weird he's been the last couple of days and why Jesse wasn't coming down for the weekend. "And what guy wouldn't want his girlfriend in his bed with him when she offers him the opportunity."

"If he knew he might be up all night following someone. He probably didn't want you to be disappointed if he couldn't be with you."

"I guess that's possible, but he never even called, not even for a quick hello. It's just not like Jesse."

"Could you be overthinking this?"

"What if he's seeing someone else?"

"That's your insecurities having a field day. He's not. You have to trust him."

I wasn't sure I could, but I didn't say that out loud to Annie.

"So how come you had a long day?"

"Jason tried to kill himself. If Marshal hadn't figured out where he had gone, Jason would be dead. Before I left the hospital, his mother told me Jason had agreed to see a therapist. I'm hoping eventually he'll feel strong enough to tell his mother he's gay. It's weighing him down. Right now, I have to get back to focusing on the case."

"From what you've told me, it seems as though Mia's mother knows Mia is lying, or at least thinks she might be. You know, I used to tell my nanny stuff I never told my mother or father," Annie said.

"Lucia was the best. I was so envious that you had someone who doted on you. You might not know this, but I asked Lucia to teach me Spanish. Though she tried really hard, I was a hopeless case."

"I loved Lucia and cried when she moved back to Mexico. I wanted her to stay forever, but when I turned sixteen she was ready to go back home."

"I did get the feeling Mia's nanny wanted to tell me more but was afraid to," I said.

"Maybe take a run at her again and don't worry about Jesse. He's crazy about you."

***

The next morning, I was sitting at my office desk frustrated that the case was moving so slowly. I still had no idea who trashed my office or who raped Mia. I did have my suspicions they were connected. My phone rang.

"I have some good news," Jesse said.

"Good, I could use some."

"My guy was able to clean up the video, and I think you can get a clearer image, though you still won't be able to make out the guy's face because of the angle. I'm sending it as we speak."

"Please thank your source for me. Let me know if there's a charge for his services."

"Don't worry about it. I got you covered. Sorry, Maddie, I got to go. My boss is calling me."

I don't care what Annie said, something is definitely going on with Jesse. I wanted to confront him, but I was afraid of what he might say.

I quickly downloaded the video, noticing a logo on the upper right-hand corner of the sweatshirt. It was a small white outline of a dog. I had never seen that logo before. The glasses the intruder wore had black frames. Jesse was right; it was still hard to make out the guy's face. I played it several more times to make sure I hadn't missed anything else. Wait a minute, didn't I just see that logo somewhere recently. Oh shit! Ben Bradley was wearing a hooded sweatshirt with that exact same logo when I saw him with Mia. Don't get ahead of yourself. There must be a million guys who have that same exact sweatshirt. Let's think about this. If it was Ben Bradley that raped Mia, and that's a big if, why would she agree to meet me with Ben? That didn't make sense.

Looking up the logo on the internet, the hooded sweatshirt was made by a company called Rhoback. It sold for about $110. That's a pretty expensive sweatshirt, one that Ben Bradley could certainly afford. What about the glasses. I don't remember Bradley wearing glasses. Maybe he didn't have to wear them all the time.

I needed more than a hooded sweatshirt to even consider that Ben had any involvement in raping Mia. First, I had to find out if he wore glasses. It's possible he wore contacts and that's why he didn't have his glasses on when I saw him. An idea was coming to me.

Picking up the phone I dialed Ben's number. It went straight to voicemail.

"Ben, I have a quick question. Please call me back."

CHAPTER 48

I locked up and went straight to Mia's house. When I originally spoke to Mrs. Gomez, Mia's nanny, I had the feeling she knew more than she let on. I wanted to take another crack at her. I waited where neighbors wouldn't notice me since I had no desire for cops to come knocking at my door again. All I could do was wait and see if she would come out at some point.

An hour later, the front door opened, and Mrs. Gomez came out with her shopping cart. I did not approach her immediately. I wanted to be sure she was far enough away where Mrs. Franklin wouldn't be able to see us together if she was home.

"Mrs. Gomez." She turned and I saw the recognition on her face.

"Please, leave me alone. I don't want to lose my job."

"I can't do that. I know you're worried about Mia. I'm worried about her too. Maybe you've seen and heard things that could help her. I'm not sure the Franklins are taking what I've told them about their daughter seriously. I know about the drugs and I think you do too. She could be in danger." I stopped talking.

"Mr. Franklin doesn't want to see what's going on with Mia, and Mrs. Franklin listens to her husband. She doesn't like to go against him."

"Has Mia said anything to you?"

"I know she's scared. She hasn't been herself since she was raped."

"Has she mentioned Ben Bradley's name to you recently?"

"No. Why are you asking about him?"

"I was wondering if they were close."

"I don't know about recently but I know he's always been nice to her. She thinks of him like a big brother. Please leave; you can't keep walking with me. Someone will see us together."

"I'm leaving, but I know that Jason Demsky didn't rape Mia. If you know anything or have any knowledge that what I'm saying is true, please contact me. No one will know it came from you." I handed my card to Mrs. Gomez and left. She knew more than she was saying. All I could do was hope that somehow I got through to her.

On my way back to the office, I called Nina Demsky to find out how Jason was doing.

"He's home and I made an appointment for him to see the therapist tomorrow."

"Are you going with him?"

"Yes. She wants to see both of us. What if he doesn't want to go back?"

"He has to know he doesn't have a choice. He's a minor and you could have him committed to a psych ward."

"I'm not sure I can do that to him."

"He doesn't have to know that. I'll be in touch."

***

I was back in my office sitting at my desk thinking about Jason Demsky. I couldn't imagine what he must be feeling. His whole life had been turned upside down all because of one person's lie. If I didn't find out who raped Mia or somehow got the truth out of her, Jason's life would be ruined. I couldn't have that happen.

All of a sudden, I felt like I couldn't breathe and the walls were closing in on me. I got up, quickly grabbed my jacket, and closed the office door behind me. Once the outside air hit me, I started to feel better. I kept walking. Shit, I hadn't had a panic attack in a while. It might be the pressure of the case or was it these feelings I couldn't suppress that something was going on with Jesse? I heard my phone ringing.

"Hello."

"Ms. Landon, it's Ben Bradley. What is it?"

"Like I said, I just had a quick question. When Mia left in a hurry, there was a pair of eyeglasses with a black frame in a case on the ground where she was sitting. I forgot all about them until I saw them in my backpack. Would you happen to know if they may have been hers?"

"I'm pretty sure she doesn't wear glasses."

"They wouldn't by any chance be yours?"

"I don't wear glasses either."

"Okay. I'm sorry I bothered you," I said and I hung up.

So did this mean I could rule Ben out? Was I back to square one, with no leads and no suspects? Maybe it didn't rule him out completely. It's possible he had on glasses for a disguise; but why would Ben rape Mia? Wouldn't Mia welcome the advances of someone she had a possible crush on?

I went back to my office, retrieved my laptop, and left. At home, I changed and went for a run. I could feel the stress leaving my body as I rounded the corner on my third loop. After I finished, I sat down at a bench trying to quiet my mind, but it wasn't working. Between my suspicions that Jesse was avoiding me and the threatening phone calls, I was a mess. I had to keep it together. Jason was counting on me.

It was already dark by the time I got back. As I was scrambling some eggs for dinner, I heard a knock at my door. There were only two people that the doorman would let up without calling me first.

CHAPTER 49

When I opened the door, Jesse was standing there. He looked awful. His eyes were bloodshot and his shoulders were slumped.

"What's the matter?" was all I could think of saying. A feeling of dread came over me.

"Can't I see my favorite girl," Jesse said, as he walked in and kissed me fiercely on the lips. "God, you smell good."

"Tell me what's going on. You never just show up."

"I need a glass of wine."

"Now you're officially scaring me," I said, pouring each of us a glass of wine, my hands shaking. We sat in the living room on the sofa. I had this growing ache in the pit of my stomach. "Just tell me."

"About six years ago, I dated a woman named Karen for maybe a month. It didn't work out for either of us and we stopped seeing each other. I never saw or heard from her again until about two weeks ago, when she called me on the phone and asked if she could see me. I told her I was in a relationship and she said it was about something else. When we met at the diner in town, she told me she had been living with her mother in Florida for the past six years. She said she was pregnant when she left." My heart started racing. I knew where this was going. I wasn't crazy.

Jesse continued. "She told me I had a son, Leo. He's five. At first, I didn't know what to say. Of course I asked her how she knew it was mine, and she said about two weeks after we broke up she tested positive. I told her I needed proof. I wasn't going to just take her word for it. She got angry that I would even doubt that he was mine, but she finally agreed to a DNA test.

"I'm so sorry, Maddie, I was such an ass to you on the phone. I've been feeling so guilty keeping this from you, but I had to be sure Leo was my son before I told you. I don't want to lose you over this. Please say something."

"How come she never told you about Leo sooner?"

"She said she was conflicted and needed time to think about what she wanted to do while she was staying at her mother's. She made the decision to start a new life in Florida since she knew we would never be together. Karen was highly trained in the tech world, and she was able to get a good-paying job after the baby was born."

"Why all of a sudden did she choose to come back?"

"She said Leo had started asking questions about his father and she didn't want to deny him the opportunity to have me in his life."

Though I wanted to be supportive, all I could think about was how our relationship was going to change.

"It's so soon I haven't even processed how I feel," Jesse said. "I'm not even sure how this is all going to work out, but I want you to know this does not change anything between us. I love you and I still want us to live together. I'm so sorry I didn't tell you sooner."

"It may be unrealistic to believe things won't change. If Leo is going to be in your life, then you'll be spending time with him."

"I know this is a lot to take in, and I feel so awful dumping all this on you."

"Have you met him yet?" I said, gulping down my wine.

"I met him a few times. At first it was awkward; I think more so for me. He's a pretty inquisitive boy, not shy at all. It made it easier for me."

"Does he look like you at all?"

"It's hard for me to tell. He has dark hair and eyes like mine. Maddie, I know this is a lot to take in. You're right, it will change our relationship in some ways but that doesn't mean we can't still be together. You're the most important person in my life." His eyes were welling up.

I didn't trust myself to say anything. I knew how things could change on a dime.

"I'm going to take it slow with Leo. Let him get to know me. For now, nothing is going to change for us. I want you to meet him. Again, I know this is overwhelming for you but it is for me too."

This is one of those times I wish I was alone, yet I didn't want Jesse to leave. I knew what Dr. Goldberg would say: "Tell him how you feel."

"This was so unexpected. I need time to think about everything."

"Madds, don't shut me out. Talk to me. This was a complete shock to me, so I understand what a shock it must be for you."

"Do you mind if we don't talk about it anymore tonight?"

"Of course," he said, but his eyes looked sad.

"I'm starving," I said, even though the thought of food made me nauseous. "Since I didn't know you were coming, you'll have to settle for scrambled eggs."

"How about if I make us an omelet. I'm sure you must have something in the refrigerator that I can add to the eggs," Jesse said, as he poked around in the fridge. "Here we go; voilà, an onion, swiss cheese, and tomatoes."

While Jesse was working on putting together an omelet, I added another bagel to the toaster oven. I wanted to ask Jesse if he knew how she could have gotten pregnant, but did it really matter at this point? I was looking over at Jesse as he was busy making the omelet. Maybe I was being selfish, just thinking about myself and not how this was affecting him. While we ate, we made small talk. He told me how he finally found the guy who was avoiding court and I filled him in on what happened with Jason.

Jesse spent the night. I could feel the urgency in his lovemaking and I responded. When he left in the morning, Jesse told me everything was going to work out. I wanted to believe him, I really did, but as always, the nagging thoughts of being left reared its ugly head. I picked up the phone and dialed Annie.

CHAPTER 50

Annie answered right away. "I need to see you," I said when she picked up.

"Are you alright?"

"No, I mean I'm not sick. Can you meet me now?"

"I wish I could but I'm in court this morning. There's a pizzeria place two blocks from the courthouse. I can be there at twelve noon if that's good for you. I'll text you the address."

Terrifying thoughts of the night my parents died came rushing back. What I really wanted to do was hide under the covers but I didn't have that luxury. The case wouldn't wait. I put on a pot of coffee and took out the board with the names I had tacked up relevant to the case. With what I now knew, I took the cards with Mia's friends Sandra, Tiffany, and Logan Kelly and moved them to the far end of the board. I then shifted Ben Bradley next to Mia and on the other side of Mia, I put Dominick Santiago, the middleman who I was pretty sure Mia was selling drugs for. Under Mia, I left Jason's name. I moved Dante Ramos to the other end of the board. Could Dominick Santiago have raped Mia? It's possible, since he could have threatened to expose her drug involvement if she revealed he was her rapist.

***

I didn't realize the time. I took an Uber downtown. Though the place wasn't much to look at, pizza was not on my mind. Annie was already seated. The place had square wooden tables, a giant wood-burning stove, and red brick walls.

We ordered a Margherita pizza and a glass of Chianti for me.

"What's going on?" Annie said right after the waitress left.

"Jesse showed up at my door last night. I can't remember any time when Jesse appeared unexpectedly. As soon as I saw him, I knew something was wrong. He told me he has a five-year-old son he never knew about."

"Holy shit. Who would have seen this coming. I can't even imagine what was going through Jesse's mind when this woman told him he had a son. So tell me all the details."

Annie was listening intently as I relayed what Jesse told me.

"Fast forward five years and now Leo is asking questions about his father."

"Wow! So that's why she moved back here and told Jesse about Leo. Obviously, this is a big shock, but what is really upsetting you?"

"That the relationship is going to change. He won't be spending as much time with me. And I know that sounds selfish of me but that's how I feel."

"Relationships change all the time. Couples have babies. Other things happen."

"But not me. I can't."

"Maybe this is an opportunity. This little boy will change your relationship, but it doesn't mean it can't be for the better. Jesse isn't going to love you less because he now has a son."

I couldn't stop the tears from falling.

"You know how much you love Cousin Noah. When you get to know this kid, it won't be any different."

"It's just that the timing sucks. After finally committing to moving in with Jesse, this is going to change everything."

"Maybe it's going to slow things down a little, but it's not as if you were dying to move in together. For so long, you were scared to commit to Jesse because you were afraid he would eventually leave. But you were willing to take a chance. This child shouldn't change that decision for you."

"I'm just not as optimistic as you."

"It's easy for me to be optimistic when it's not about me. Take one step at a time. She does know about you, right?"

"Yes, Jesse told her right away. But what if she wants to renew their relationship? I mean, that would make sense since they have a kid together."

"Say she does, but that doesn't mean Jesse would. I know it's hard for you to trust but you have to try or else you'll drive yourself crazy."

"What if I'm terrible with the kid?"

"He's five, not a monster. It'll just come natural or not," Annie said grinning. "Are you going up to Jesse's this weekend?"

"That's the plan unless something changes."

"Always the pessimist."

After we polished off the entire pie, Annie had to get back to court. Before going back uptown I walked aimlessly, not sure where I was headed.

CHAPTER 51

My phone buzzed. It was Sam. I was going to let it go to voicemail but changed my mind. Sam started talking the second I picked up.

"Maddie, Maddie, Mia's been shot," she said crying.

"I can hardly hear you. Mia's been shot? How do you know?"

"I saw it."

"What do you mean you saw it?"

"Don't be mad, but I was following her. I couldn't just do nothing. She was hanging out by this car and some other car drove by and shot them. What should I do? I'm scared."

"Where are you now?"

"I'm still here. The police and the ambulance came."

"Listen to me, everything is going to be alright. How far away are you from where it happened?"

"About a block, maybe less. But it happened so fast I didn't see the car that shot at them. The man was killed. I saw that they put him in one of those black bags that you see on TV."

"What about Mia?"

"They took her away in an ambulance."

"Are the police there?"

"Yeah. They're questioning some people."

"If you didn't see anything just leave. Actually, I'll come and get you." Sam started crying again. She told me where she was and I grabbed a taxi.

***

"I'm sorry," Sam said, burying her face in my chest when I got there.

"It's alright, Sam."

"How are we going to find out what happened to her?"

"I'll make a few phone calls. In the meantime, I'm going to take you home. As soon as I find out any information, I'll call you. When you get home, you need to tell your parents what happened. You can't keep this to yourself. What you witnessed is traumatic and your parents will know how to help you."

"Are you mad at me?"

"I promise I'm not."

We grabbed a cab. We first stopped in front of Sam's house on the Upper West Side and then I had the cab drop me off at my office. When I thought of what could have happened to Sam if she had been nearer to Mia when the shooting occurred, I started to tremble.

The closest hospital to where the shooting took place was Lenox Hill Hospital. I waited about forty-five minutes before calling. I figured if Mia was there, it would take time before she was processed. The person I spoke with said I would have to call back later. At least I knew Mia was there.

"Can you at least tell me what her condition is?"

"I'm sorry, I can't give out any information over the phone."

When I hung up, I thought about my conversation with Martinez. This had to be his doing in retaliation for the death of Miguel Garcia. About an hour later, I took an

Uber to the hospital. I could only hope Mia wasn't seriously hurt.

When I got there, I asked about Mia's condition again, and I was told they couldn't release that information since I wasn't an immediate family member. I pressed and asked if she was in surgery and I got the same answer. If Mia was in surgery, her parents would be waiting somewhere. Maybe in the cafeteria. I was told it was located on the second floor.

I took the elevator up and found my way to the cafeteria. As I walked in, I saw Mia's parents from a distance. I didn't know what to do. It was at that moment that Melissa Franklin looked up and saw me. She started walking toward me. My heart was thumping so loud I thought everyone in the hospital could hear my heart beating.

"I'm so sorry," was all I could think of saying when she was standing in front of me.

"I think you're glad Mia got shot." Tears were streaming down Melissa Franklin's face.

I wanted to say, "I warned you" but I held my tongue. Instead, I said: "I can't even imagine what you're going through."

"No, you can't," she said, and she turned and walked away.

I watched her as she walked toward her husband and they held each other.

What I wanted to know was Mia's condition, but I knew no one at the hospital was going to give me that information. At this point, I needed to go to the police and talk with the person in charge of the case. I had to tell them what I knew. I wanted to stick around the hospital, but I didn't think that was wise.

I went back downstairs to the main lobby and walked out of the hospital. There was a bench I sat on while I made some phone calls. I found out that a Detective McGuire out of the 17th Precinct was in charge of the case. When I called and asked to speak with him, I was put on hold for a minute or so until I heard a voice say, "Detective McGuire speaking."

"Detective McGuire, my name's Maddie Landon. I'm a former police officer," I said, hoping that would give me some clout. "I have some information that might be relevant to the Dominick Santiago and Mia Franklin shootings."

"How is that?"

"I'm a private investigator working on a rape case that involves Mia Franklin. Do you have some time today."

"I'm tied up for about an hour."

"I'll see you then."

I took an Uber to the 17th Precinct located on 51st Street. On the way over, it hit me that if Dominick Santiago raped Mia, I may never be able to prove Jason is innocent.

CHAPTER 52

"Excuse me," I said to the desk officer when I arrived at the precinct. "I have an appointment with Detective McGuire. My name's Maddie Landon."

"Take a seat. He should be with you in a few minutes."

Ten minutes later, a police officer led me to Detective McGuire's office. We shook hands and I sat down. Detective McGuire was a big Irish guy with a ruddy complexion. Though you wouldn't consider him handsome by any means, he had a very appealing manner about him.

"I see you were with the 20th Precinct. How come you left the force?" McGuire said.

"Let's just say it was the office politics and we'll leave it at that."

"Okay. So what do you have for me?"

"I was hired to investigate the rape of Mia Franklin, the young woman who was caught in the crosshairs of the shooting death of Dominick Santiago. I've been following Mia Franklin on and off for a couple of weeks when I realized she may be selling drugs for Dominick Santiago. I went to her parents to tell them what I found out since I was worried about her."

I went on to explain to Detective McGuire that I had been hired on another case to find a missing witness. "When I finally caught up with Miguel Garcia, both he and his girlfriend were lying on the floor, shot to death. A day or two later, I went to see Garcia's boss, Luis Martinez. Though he didn't admit to anything, I know for a fact that Garcia was part of Martinez's drug gang."

"You really have been busy."

"I'm not sure what you mean, but I have a young girl who has falsely accused my client of rape and now she's lying in a hospital bed, and I don't know whether she's going to make it."

"You mean you think your client is innocent." I ignored his remark.

"Can you tell me the condition of Mia Franklin?" I said.

Detective McGuire looked at me. "I can tell you that Ms. Franklin was seriously wounded. A bullet went into her abdomen. They had to operate to try to stop the bleeding. I was told she lost a lot of blood. Right now, she's unconscious. Is there anything else you know about the shooting?"

"You might want to look into Luis Martinez. It's possible he tried to get even for the death of one of his men."

"I appreciate the information. Thank you for coming in."

"If you find out any updates on Mia Franklin's condition, please call me," I said, handing him my card as I got up to leave. I was pretty sure Detective McGuire wouldn't be calling me with an update, but I could always hope.

What happens to Jason if Mia dies? Would he still go on trial if there was no victim? Those were the questions I needed answers to. I picked up my phone and dialed Paul Greer. It went straight to voicemail. "Mr. Greer, it's Maddie Landon. I don't know if you've heard, but Mia Franklin has been shot. They had to operate to stop the bleeding, but she's unconscious. Call me back ASAP."

I was walking to my office when my phone vibrated. It was Paul Greer.

"What happened?" he said.

"Mia was shot during a drug gang killing. Unfortunately, she was in the wrong place at the wrong time. What does it mean for Jason if she dies before the case goes to trial?"

"There's a good possibility the charges would be dropped since the victim, Mia, was the only witness to the rape. If there isn't enough additional evidence, it could get dismissed. For now, we have to assume that she'll recover."

"I'll be in touch."

I was going over in my mind my conversation with Paul Greer. It was probably in Jason's best interests if I could find out who raped Mia. If she died and it never went to trial, Jason would always be a rapist in people's eyes. I was not sure he would survive that. I needed to ramp up the investigation. I was pretty sure that the person who vandalized my office was Mia's rapist. It had to be someone she knew. She wouldn't have let a stranger into her house, not at that late hour. The problem was it could have been anyone she knew from school or someone she may have met online. If her rapist was Dominick Santiago, and Mia died, that secret would die with her. With no other viable suspects, my frustration was mounting.

***

The following day, I was up very early. I did my three-mile loop around the park, showered, and had breakfast before heading into the office. I was interested in how I would be able to obtain more information about Ben Bradley. Right now, he was my only suspect, though I knew he was a long shot.

When I got to my office, I thought I would check social media sites. See what I could find out about Ben. Then I thought this might be something I could finally get Sam involved in, but with what she just went through, I was skeptical. On the other hand, it might take her mind off of what she had witnessed. I picked up the phone and dialed Sam's number. She answered right away.

"What did you find out?" she said without skipping a beat.

"Mia was shot in the stomach and lost a lot of blood. They operated but she is still unconscious. Hopefully she'll be awake soon. Sam, there are things I learned about Mia during the course of my investigation that I can't get into now, but I would like you to do some research for me."

"Really?" Her enthusiasm was unmistakable. "What do you want me to do?"

"Remember, everything is confidential. You're not to tell anyone about this."

"I know. I know. You don't have to keep reminding me."

"I want you to look into social media sites where a college kid might be posting and see what, if anything, you can find out. Is that something you can do?"

"This is definitely my area of expertise." I'm not sure if it really was or if she was just being overzealous.

"I'm sending you as much detail as I know about him."

"Is he a possible suspect?"

"No." I had no idea if he was or not, but Sam didn't need to know that.

"Okay. I'll do my best."

"I know you will."

"Wait, what's going to happen to Jason if Mia dies?"

"Let's not think about that now," I said as I hung up.

I gathered as much information I had on Ben Bradley and sent it to Sam in an email.

CHAPTER 53

I hadn't heard from Jesse since he left my apartment. I could call him but something was holding me back. Between work and now having to devote time to his son, maybe he was too busy to call me. Since I was heading up to his place the next day, I didn't want to panic. I wanted to speak with Dr. Goldberg but she was away for one more week at a conference in Chicago.

***

The following day I was on the road by 5:00 p.m. Jesse was about a two-hour drive from Manhattan. As I was driving up the Taconic Parkway, I noticed the trees were turning from green to bright shades of yellow, orange, and red, a sign that fall was here and with that, the cooler temperatures. I was admiring the vivid colors when I heard my phone ring. It was a number I didn't recognize. I answered the phone cautiously.

"Ms. Landon, this is Mrs. Gomez, Mia's nanny."

"I'm so glad you called. How is Mia?"

"There's been no change, poor girl. It hurts to see her in that state. I pray for her every day."

"I'm so sorry. Did you call to tell me about Mia's condition?"

"No. You asked me to call you if I thought of anything. I'm not even sure if it's important. I'm just afraid that someone will find out that I spoke with you."

"I can promise that whatever you're going to tell me will remain confidential."

"Two days before Mia was shot, Ben and his parents came over for dinner. Mrs. Franklin asked me to stay to help with the cooking and the cleanup. Normally I leave around 4:00 p.m. I noticed that Mia was very quiet during dinner. She told her parents she wasn't feeling well and needed to lie down. She hadn't said anything earlier that something was bothering her. Right before I was ready to leave, I went into her room to see what was wrong and she was crying."

"Did Mia say why she was crying?"

"She wouldn't tell me."

"Does she normally tell you when she's having problems?"

"Ever since she was a little girl, she always came to me instead of her parents. But I was surprised how quiet she was at dinner since I know she likes Ben. I guess ever since it happened, she hasn't been the same."

"In what way?"

"She's more withdrawn than usual."

"Did you ever find drugs in her room when you were cleaning?"

"Mia doesn't like me cleaning her room so I usually stay out. Was I wrong to tell you?"

"No, of course not. It probably doesn't mean anything. Like you said, she's been this way ever since the rape. Do you know if Mia has had any counseling since it happened?"

"The Franklins have appearances to keep up. I think her father would be against Mia seeking help and it's not my place to say anything. I think he believes you should be able to solve your own problems."

"What about Mrs. Franklin? Does she have any say in the matter?"

"She might, but in the end, it's whatever Mr. Franklin says."

"I appreciate what you've told me. If you think of anything else, please let me know."

I didn't know what to make of Mia's behavior. Maybe it was nothing. It's not unusual for a rape victim to have psychological problems, especially if they hadn't had any sort of therapy. Just from my one interaction with Mr. Franklin, I got the impression he was in charge.

I was nearing Jesse's house when my phone buzzed.

"Hello."

"Time is running out for you, Maddie. There's no place to hide."

"Go to hell," I shouted before he hung up.

I started to shake and pulled over to the side of the road. I sat for a few minutes trying to calm myself down. Though till now my stalker hadn't tried to physically harm me, I was worried that he was escalating, and was afraid he might try something.

I parked in back of Jesse's car and grabbed my overnight bag from the back seat. I was a little uneasy as I opened the front door and hoped it didn't show on my face.

"Jesse," I shouted.

"In the kitchen."

"Something smells wonderful," I said, as Jesse held me close, wrapping his muscular arms around me and kissing me deeply on the lips. I could feel my body relaxing.

While we were eating Jesse's phone rang.

"Hello," he said.

"Okay. I'll be there at 5:00 p.m. I know, you already told me. I'll see you Monday."

"Who was that," I said when Jesse hung up, though I was pretty sure I knew who it was.

"It was Karen reminding me that I was taking Leo out to dinner on Monday instead of Tuesday."

"Does she call you often?"

"I know where you're going with this, and I have absolutely no interest in Karen. Apparently, when there's a kid involved, you also have to deal with the other parent. I don't like it either. Look, Madds, I'm not going anywhere. You're stuck with me."

"Are you sure? Maybe you need time and I'm a distraction."

"A distraction that I'm going to ravage in about two minutes."

"Okay. I get it. Right now that ravaging part sounds good."

Lying next to Jesse as he was stroking my hair, I couldn't help but think about Karen. I knew Jesse was a big boy and could handle himself, but I also knew firsthand ways you could be tempted. I wanted to believe Jesse, but the fear of loss seemed to have a chokehold on me. I wondered if taking a break might be easier for me.

"I can feel you thinking," Jesse said.

"You cannot," I said playfully.

"What's going on and I don't mean the case?"

"Don't you think it would be better for you if we spent some time apart for a little while so you can spend more time with Leo?" I said.

"Is that what you want?"

"I don't know."

"Madds, you have to trust me. I'm not naïve to think Leo isn't going to be a big adjustment in our lives. I'm not in this alone. It's you and me together. That's how I think of it."

"I'm just not sure I'm parenting material."

"You don't have to worry about that now. Let's take one step at a time."

We made love again and when we were both exhausted, we fell asleep.

CHAPTER 54

In the morning, I woke up to the wonderful smell of bacon.

"Are you trying to win me over with your cooking?" I said as I walked into the kitchen.

"Is it working?"

"It always works with bacon."

"So now I know what I need to do; stock up on bacon."

"Where are you going to take Leo for dinner tomorrow?"

"I thought I would take him to a fancy steakhouse. That will win him over."

"You've never taken me to a steakhouse."

"That's because the honeymoon is over," Jesse said, planting a kiss on my lips. "Actually, Leo likes chicken nuggets and hot dogs. We'll have to broaden his palate."

I still didn't know how all of this was going to work out, but I was weary of trying to figure it all out.

"What's going on with the case?" Jesse said.

"I completely forgot to tell you, the drug dealer Mia was working for was killed in a drive-by. And unfortunately, Mia was with him and was also shot. They operated to try to stop the bleeding. Right now, she's unconscious. In some way, I think the mother blames me."

"I doubt that. She's just upset."

"I spoke to Jason's public defender. He thinks if Mia dies there's a good chance the case would be dismissed since there were no witnesses to her rape and there's no forensic evidence pointing to Jason. Everything is circumstantial. I'm just worried if I can't find out who really raped Mia it will have an effect on Jason. I don't want that hanging over him. I need to find the truth. And I'm concerned about Mia's parents, even if it is dismissed. They might not leave it alone."

"What about the video? Did anything show up on the tape that would be useful?"

"Two things, the symbol of a head of a dog on the hooded sweatshirt and black-rimmed glasses. Oh, and I could tell the intruder was white. That could fit millions of people."

"That's true, but it's most likely someone she knew," Jesse said.

"That's what I was thinking, but maybe it's someone she recently met or someone she met online."

"For now, let's exclude those two categories and go with someone closer to her. Any takers?"

"One possibility is Ben Bradley, the guy we met together who knows Mia because their fathers work at the same hedge fund company. When I recently saw him, he was wearing the same hooded sweatshirt but no glasses. When I used a pretext, he told me he doesn't wear glasses. Unless he wore them as a prop. It's a long shot."

"Anyone else?"

"Nope. I'm at a dead end. I did speak to Mia's nanny last week and told her the danger Mia might be in and that I suspected Mia lied about who raped her. I asked her to call me if she thought of anything." I relayed to Jesse what I recently learned from Mrs. Gomez.

"It's hard to say what to make of it. Rape changes a person. She could have psychological problems."

"So what now? The one person who could tell me the truth is unconscious."

"You just have to keep plodding along. You'll figure it out."

"I'm having Sam check social media sites to see what kind of online presence Ben has since I have no clue what goes on with these kids."

"I'm sure she was overjoyed."

"She was. I had to get her to promise me that she would keep her findings confidential. Let's hope she heeds my advice."

CHAPTER 55

On my way back Monday morning, I decided to focus on the case and not torture myself with what was going to happen between Jesse and me. I was worried about Jason and how I was going to prove he was innocent. I didn't want him to have to go through the ordeal of a trial. He was barely holding on now. I hadn't heard any news about Mia in the last couple of days. If I didn't hear anything in the next day or two, I thought I'd give Detective McGuire a call.

When I got into my office, I called Nina Demsky. I was interested in how their session went with the therapist.

"Nina, it's Maddie. How is Jason doing?"

"We went to see Mrs. Burns. I have no experience with therapists, but she was very kind and easy to talk with. I spoke with her first and told her everything that had happened in the past two months. She listened and took notes. Before Jason went in alone to see her, she told me not to ask him any questions about his session unless he volunteered. When Jason finished, I spoke with Mrs. Burns again. She told me that Jason was understandably very depressed but decided to hold off on having him take any medication until she saw him for a few more sessions. He has agreed to see her again. I am so happy I could cry."

"That's great news. There's something I have to tell you. Mia has been in an accident." I didn't want to go into details right at this moment. "Mia was shot. The doctors had to operate to stop the bleeding. Right now, as far as I know, she's still unconscious."

"That's awful. I don't wish anything bad on her. I just want her to tell the truth. What happens if she doesn't make it?"

I explained to her what Paul Greer told me.

"That's good news, isn't it?"

"I guess it is, but for Jason's sake, I think it would be better if he was found not guilty or we found out who really raped Mia."

"I see," she said quietly. "Is there any news?"

"I'm working on a few things, but nothing concrete. I'll let you know."

While contemplating what to do next, I saw I had somehow missed a call from Sam. I dialed her number.

"I'm three blocks from your office. I'll be right there," Sam said.

I heard my door open a few minutes later. Sam practically flew into my office with excitement. She quickly opened up her laptop.

"Pull up a chair," I said. "So, what did you find out?"

"Well, he definitely has an online presence," she said, barely able to contain herself. "He's all over social media sites, including TikTok. Let me show you."

Sam went on to TikTok and replayed one of the videos posted by Ben. It was a video of Ben with his shirt off and moving around in very suggestive poses, talking into the camera, bragging to women what a hunk he was.

"This one is really juicy. Ben's friend is saying how this girl doesn't want to screw him and Ben is telling him that all those bitches say that, but they really want it. On another video, Ben is bragging how women find him irresistible. It's nauseating. The rest of what he posted on different sites was about himself and what he was up to. For instance, this one shows him with a couple of friends at a bar."

"Let me see that." I remembered his friend from the first time I met Ben Bradley. *What's his name again?* I thought to myself.

"Does this help at all?" Sam said.

"It does. You did a great job." Sam gave me a lopsided smile. That's as close to showing me how much my praise meant to her. The truth is, I'm not sure how much Sam found helps my case.

"I can't believe the stuff people post," I said.

"This is nothing. There's a lot worse out there."

"Are you on any social media sites?"

"I am but I don't post anything sexual. Just everyday stuff. Does this mean Ben Bradley may be the one that raped Mia?"

"I really don't know, Sam, but remember, what I do is confidential and that means whatever you do for me is also confidential."

"I know. You don't have to keep reminding me," she said, sighing. "Did they find out who shot Mia and the other guy?"

"As far as I know, they haven't. How are you handling this?"

"Okay, I guess. Aren't you ever afraid?"

"Of course I am, but I've also had a lot of training in dealing with certain circumstances. It doesn't mean I'm immune from feeling afraid or getting hurt. That's why I didn't want you anywhere near Mia. You're not equipped to handle situations that might put you in danger." Sam didn't say anything.

"Have you seen Jason?" I asked.

"Marshal and I have been going over to his house after school."

"Do you think you could get him to go back to work at the supermarket?"

"I'm not sure he wants to be out there after what happened to him. He's really a whiz with computers. Maybe he can get some sort of job working for someone who needs a computer expert. This way he could do it from home."

"That's a great idea, Sam. Why don't you run it by him? In the meantime, I'll see if I know anyone that might be interested in hiring Jason."

"I gotta go."

"Thanks, Sam. I really appreciate it."

After Sam left, I remembered the video she showed me with Ben's friend. *What the hell's his name? Think, Maddie. It's Mark something.* I only met him once briefly and didn't know if Ben and Mark were good friends, but at this point, he was the only person I knew who was acquainted with Ben. *What is his last name?* I remembered he had the last name of someone famous. Aha! Michael Jordan, the famous basketball player.

I did a search in my databases to locate a cell number for Mark Jordan. After several attempts, I found his cell phone number and called him.

"Hello."

"Mr. Jordan, this is Maddie Landon. We met several weeks ago at Ella Social when I was talking with Ben Bradley. I'm investigating the rape of Mia Franklin."

"Yes, I remember you and your friend. How can I help you?"

I didn't want him to know I was interested in Ben. "I was wondering if we could meet. I've been talking to everyone who may have known Mia." He interrupted me before I had a chance to continue.

"I met Mia once but didn't really talk to her so I wouldn't be of any help to your investigation. Sorry, I gotta go." He hung up before I had a chance to ask him any questions about Ben Bradley.

It was a long shot anyway. Even if he knew something, he probably wasn't going to rat out his friend. But what still bothered me was why Ben would rape Mia if, in fact, he did? If he knew she was selling drugs, would that be enough to keep her quiet? I didn't think so. Maybe there was something else. But what? I needed to learn more about Ben Bradley.

CHAPTER 56

The next day, I headed up to Ben's college. Before going, I looked up the name of the Dean of Students. His name was Jonathan Murphy. When I arrived, the person at the gate directed me to where I could park and where the administration building was located. After spending ten minutes driving around the parking lot, I got lucky, someone was just leaving. I found the building several minutes later. I went inside and walked down a long corridor, looking for Jonathan Murphy's office. The third door on the right was marked in bold letters, **Dean of Students.** I was greeted by a woman in her fifties with blonde frizzy hair that was in need of a good hairstylist.

"Can I help you?" Her name plate read Jane Lombardo.

"I hope so. My name's Maddie Landon. I'm a private investigator and would like to speak with Dean Murphy."

"Do you have an appointment?"

"No, but I only need to take a few moments of his time."

She looked at me, debating whether she should call Mr. Murphy and present my name to him or give me some cock-and-bull story about why I couldn't see him.

"Do you have some identification?" I gave her my card.

She picked up the phone, spoke to someone, and then told me to sit. Though there were two chairs, I stood.

A tall man with gray, thinning hair, wearing a dark blue suit and a white shirt with a blue and red striped tie came out of his office.

"Hello, I'm Dean Murphy," he said, extending his hand to me.

"Maddie Landon."

"Please come in."

I walked into a warm and comfortable-looking office. It was fully carpeted with floor-to-ceiling drapes. On a credenza behind his desk, there were loads of family photos.

"Please sit, Ms. Landon." I sat on a green and beige upholstered chair located on the opposite side of his desk. "How can I help you?"

"I'm investigating the rape of a sixteen-year-old girl."

"What's her name?"

"She doesn't attend school here." He looked perplexed. "I'm looking into a student of yours. His name is Benjamin Bradley."

"I see."

"Do you know if he's been in any trouble or if anyone has accused him of inappropriate behavior with any of the female students?"

"I'm sorry, I can't disclose any information about our students."

"Are you saying you can't or you won't?"

"Ms. Landon, I have nothing more to say. Now if you'll excuse me, I have a meeting I'm late for. I think we're through here."

As I was leaving, I noticed a strange look on Jane Lombardo's face. I quietly said, "You have my card if you'd like to talk."

Walking to my car, I wondered if Jane Lombardo knew something but was afraid to say.

It was close to noon when I finally weaved my way out of the school campus. I knew the school didn't have to report rape allegations to the police. They keep it in-house and are more interested in protecting the school than the victim.

On my way back to the office, I called Detective McGuire to see if Mia had regained consciousness. He told me as far as he knew she was still unconscious, but as soon as she was able to talk, he would be questioning her.

I grabbed a tuna fish sandwich to go at the deli near my office. I put on a pot of coffee when I got in and took out my notepad. My primary and only suspect was Ben Bradley. So what did I actually know about him? For one, he and Mia knew each other. She looked up to Ben, maybe even had a crush on him. He would be somebody she would most likely let into her house late at night. He kind of fit the description of the guy who broke into my office, and when I had met him with Mia, he had been wearing a hooded sweatshirt with the same logo as the intruder was wearing. Lastly, Mrs. Gomez, Mia's nanny, said Mia had been acting weird the night Ben and his parents were at the Franklins' house for dinner; though she did say Mia hadn't been herself since the rape, which was understandable. According to Ben, he didn't wear glasses. That did present an obstacle unless the glasses worn by the intruder were a disguise. Without any other prospects, this was the rabbit hole I was going down.

CHAPTER 57

"Can you meet for a drink in about forty-five minutes?" I said to Annie when she answered her phone.

"What time is it now?"

"It's 5:00 p.m."

"Let me check with Doug and I'll call you back."

Five minutes later, Annie called and said Doug was playing racquetball after work. We decided to meet at The Dead Poet around 6:15 p.m.

I sat at a table and ordered a drink while I was waiting for Annie. I wondered how Doug and Annie were getting along; hopefully therapy was helping.

"There you are," I said as Annie approached the table and gave me a hug.

The waitress came over and Annie ordered a glass of Merlot. I chimed in, adding a few hors d'oeuvres.

"I know you hate me asking any questions about the baby issue but I can't help myself."

"It's alright. I'm working through it, and Doug and I have been talking instead of quarreling. I just need a little more time. How is Jesse handling fatherhood? More to the point, how are you dealing with the situation?"

"I was willing to give Jesse space so he could have more time with Leo but he wasn't having any of it."

"Good for him. I knew I was crazy about Jesse for a reason. For one, he has more common sense than you."

"Thanks a lot. I haven't told you the latest. Mia is in critical condition from a bullet wound that she sustained when her drug dealer was killed in a drive-by. I believe it was in retaliation for the murders I told you about."

"Wow! Poor Mia. What are her chances?"

"They operated to stop the bleeding but she's still unconscious. Hopefully, she'll pull through." I went on to explain everything, including how Mrs. Franklin lashed out at me. I also clued Annie in on my visit to Detective McGuire.

"Don't let Mrs. Franklin upset you."

"I'm not."

"How come you decided to go to the police?"

"Now that it will most likely come out that Mia was selling drugs, I don't feel I should keep what I know from the police. Besides, I have enough going on trying to find Mia's rapist."

The waitress came with Annie's wine and the sliders and olives I ordered.

"I went to Ben Bradley's college today to speak with the Dean of Students. I was curious if there were any complaints filed by any of the female students. He had nothing to say on the matter."

"Colleges don't have to report any incidents of sexual abuse to the police or talk to any outsiders. They only care about keeping it quiet. They supposedly do their own investigation. I'd be surprised if any of these young women would get justice unless they went to the police," Annie said.

"I was hoping to at least find out if there were any accusations against Bradley."

"Do you think he was the one that raped Mia?"

"I really don't know, but at the moment, he's all I got. I'm just not sure how to go forward with the investigation. On the bright—"

"Thankfully, there's a bright side," Annie said before I had a chance to finish my sentence.

"As I started to say, Jason is going to therapy. I think he realized he didn't have a choice, or at least one that he liked."

"His mother must be relieved."

"I'm just not sure how his life is going to turn out, even if I find out who raped Mia. I was thinking if someone would hire him to do computer work, he might feel useful, and it would lift his spirits. Apparently, he's a computer whiz."

"I'll give it some thought. For now, keep your focus on finding the rapist."

"I finally gave Sam something to work on. I asked her to see what kind of presence Ben has on social media sites. It turns out he's on TikTok and likes to flaunt his body."

"Really. I'll have to take a look," Annie said amusingly.

On my way home from The Dead Poet, I heard my phone ringing. It was a number I didn't recognize. I was debating whether to pick up, but in case it was about Mia, I answered.

"Hello."

"Is this Maddie Landon?"

"Yes, who is this?"

"My name is Jane Lombardo. We met earlier today at the dean's office. Is it too late?"

"No, what can I do for you?"

"I overheard you speaking with Dean Murphy, and I know you mentioned a student by the name of Benjamin Bradley. Can you meet with me? I may have some information that could be of interest to you." That was certainly unexpected.

"When are you available?"

"I work half days on Wednesdays. There's a coffee place in Yonkers called Mandy's. I'll text you the address."

"What time?"

"Is 2:00 p.m. alright?"

"I'll see you then."

After I hung up, I was chomping at the bit. What could she know? Being in close proximity to Murphy's office, she probably saw and heard things. But why would she risk telling me?

***

I found Mandy's with no trouble. It was in a strip mall on Central Avenue. Central Avenue extends through several towns in Westchester County. When I went inside, there were people sitting with their computers open, lost in whatever they were looking at. I couldn't help but notice the state-of-the-art coffee machines and scrumptious-looking pastries. Mrs. Lombardo was easy to spot with her blonde frizzy hair sitting at a table in the back of the room.

"Hello, Ms. Landon," she said. "Thank you for meeting me. They have wonderful coffee. As you can see, this place is a hotspot." Mrs. Lombardo appeared nervous, rambling a little bit.

"Why don't I get us coffee. Anything else?" I said.

"They have delicious almond croissants."

I came back with two coffees and two almond croissants.

"I don't know whether I should be telling you what I'm about to say, but if it wasn't for the fact that I need this job, I would have quit long ago. I'm hoping you will keep my name out of it."

"No one will know that I spoke to you."

"Benjamin Bradley's name has come to Dean Murphy's attention twice. Both serious charges. One was the alleged rape of a freshman student and the other was an attempted rape. According to the second allegation, the girl was able to get away before something happened. Unfortunately, the charges don't hold much weight because it's usually the boy's word against their word."

"Is there any sort of investigation done?"

"There is, but nothing usually comes from it."

"How come these girls don't go to the police?"

"I think they're made to feel intimidated, that maybe it's their fault or they won't be taken seriously by the police. And the administration does not have to report these incidents to anyone, including the police."

"That's unbelievable. Does this happen often?"

"Enough. Why are you looking into Mr. Bradley?"

"There's a possibility he may have raped a sophomore high school girl. She named my client as the person who raped her, but after investigating, I believe she wasn't telling the truth. Now I have to prove it. Unfortunately, I need something to go on."

"I'm not sure what else I can tell you."

"Mrs. Lombardo, I know this is a lot to ask, but can you give me the names of the two young women who filed complaints against Bradley? If I talk to these women, they might be willing to go to the police."

"Oh my! How will you keep my name out of this?"

"Mrs. Lombardo, no one has to know it came from you. If anyone asks, I could say I was talking to several of the students on campus and their names came up."

"I need to think about it."

"I don't want to put pressure on you, but a boy's life is at stake."

"I'm sorry, but I still need to think about it."

"I understand, and I know this has been very difficult for you. I appreciate your candor." What I wanted to do was scream and shake her until she gave me their names.

CHAPTER 58

On the way back, my heart was racing. There was a real possibility that Ben Bradley might have raped Mia. But the question was still why would Mia blame Jason? Why not just say who it was? He had to have threatened her, but with what? If it was only about the drugs, would she still keep up the charade? When you've told a horrible lie and you're in so deep, how can you then tell the truth? I wondered if there was something else that he threatened her with since I found it hard to believe no one else knew she was selling drugs. What else could it be?

My phone rang. When I saw the number, I couldn't help but feel let down. What did I expect, Mrs. Lombardo to have changed her mind in the last fifteen minutes?

"Ms. Landon, it's Detective McGuire. I wanted to give you a courtesy call and let you know that Mia Franklin has regained consciousness. I'm going to be talking to her tomorrow."

"That's great news. Thank you for telling me." Because McGuire wasn't the detective in the rape case, I knew he was just going to question Mia regarding the shooting. I wondered how Mia was going to get out of her drug involvement. I was sure the detective would be asking her questions about her association with Dominick Santiago. At that point, if her parents were smart, they wouldn't allow her to be questioned without a lawyer present.

I parked my car in the garage, and as soon as I got upstairs, I called Jesse.

"Hey, babe, what's going on?"

"I spoke to someone who works in the dean's office where Ben Bradley attends college. She told me that there were two women who came forward to file a complaint against Bradley."

"I'm surprised she told you."

"It was more out of anger at the way the school handled complaints. They basically did nothing, and they made these women feel that they were to blame."

"Ben Bradley! Wow! Do you think she'll give you their names?"

"I don't know. It would certainly help my investigation if I could hear their stories. If they don't want to cooperate, I'll have to figure out how to go after Bradley without them. By the way, Sam had mentioned that Jason is a whiz on the computer. A real tech person. He needs to have a job where he can work from home and use his skills. If he feels productive, it might be a big boost for his morale. If you happen to know anyone who might need someone part-time, let me know."

"Will do. Now that you know about the allegations against Bradley, why don't you lean on him. It can't hurt."

"Might be a good idea. How did it go with Leo on Monday?"

"Well, we settled on a diner where he had a grilled cheese sandwich and french fries. I tried to sway him into eating something healthier, but he wasn't buying it. I thought this was not worth arguing over. It felt kind of weird trying to make conversation with a five-year-old.

There are just so many questions I can think of asking him."

"Did he ask you anything?"

"He wanted to know why I didn't come to visit him in Florida."

"Oh boy! What did you say?"

"I have to admit, I'd rather be interrogated by the police. Leo caught me off guard. I wasn't sure if I should tell him the truth, but in the end, that's what I did. I explained to him that when his mother moved to Florida, she didn't tell me she was going to have a baby, and that it wasn't until he and his mother came back that I knew I had a son. He then asked me why his mother didn't tell him about me. I said that she must have had her reasons. I could see he was trying to understand, but I didn't want to overwhelm him with too much detail."

"I'm glad you were straightforward with him. It'll be easier for him to trust you knowing you won't lie to him."

"Is that insight coming from personal experience?"

"From early on, my parents were honest with me and told me I was adopted. I was young and didn't really understand the meaning of being adopted until I was a little older, but I was grateful that they never hid the truth from me."

"Yet you hid the truth from yourself for all these years."

"I wanted to keep the past buried. I guess I thought it would be too painful to dredge it up."

"Are you happy you did?"

"In some ways yes and some ways no. It was hard for me to learn about the psychological pain my mother lived with, and then dying without her ever meeting me."

"I don't think you can ever run away from your past. It seeps out at different moments and when you least expect it."

"I didn't know you were a philosopher."

"There are lots of things you don't know about me. You'll just have to stick around to find out more."

I could have mentioned Leo but decided against it. Instead, I said, "Nothing like stringing a gal along."

"I'll see you Saturday morning. I love you," Jesse said.

CHAPTER 59

Two days later, sitting in my office, I was debating whether I wanted to confront Ben Bradley when my phone rang.

"Ms. Landon, this is Jane Lombardo. I thought about what you said, and I need your word that my name will never come up when you speak to these women. I'm very concerned that I could lose my job if the school ever found out it was me that divulged that information."

"You have my word."

"The woman who was raped was Heather Paxton. She left the school after she was told that there was no case against Bradley and he would not be expelled. I have no idea where she is now."

"There must be a file on her with her parents' address."

"I'm sorry I don't have access to her personal file, but I believe she's from a town in Connecticut."

"What about the other woman?"

"Her name is Christine Dunn. She's still at school. I believe she lives in the East dorms."

"Mrs. Lombardo, thank you so much, and I promise your name will never be disclosed."

"I hope this information will help your case."

As soon as I hung up, I opened up my computer and did a Google search for a Heather Paxton in Connecticut. My first search showed no results. I then did an in-depth database search under her name, also in Connecticut. Still no results. What now? I did a search for anyone with the last name of Paxton in Connecticut. There were several. I went into each report until I found a Thomas and Emily Paxton with a daughter named Heather. Her age fit. I printed out the report and contacted my source to obtain Heather's cell phone number. A few hours later, I had an email with her cell number. I called Heather, hoping she would pick up.

"Hello," she said with hesitation in her voice.

"Heather, my name's Maddie Landon. I'm a private investigator looking into a young man named Ben Bradley who possibly raped a sophomore high school student."

"How did you get my number?" she said, sounding worried.

"I'm not trying to upset you, but I thought if we could just talk."

"I already reported him to the school and they didn't believe me. Why would anyone else?"

"How about if we meet and you hear what I have to say. You won't have to talk if you don't want to." There was silence for a few seconds.

"There's a Starbucks in New Canaan. I can be there by 5:00 p.m."

"Thank you." Heather texted me the address.

***

New Canaan is about an hour and a half from the Upper West Side. I left in plenty of time. It took a while to find parking and then I walked around the town. New Canaan was very pretty with high-end shops and expensive restaurants. I found the Starbucks on Park Street. I was waiting inside when I saw a thin young woman with straight blonde hair down to her shoulders, wearing jeans and a pullover white cotton sweater with black loafers come in.

"Heather?" I said. She nodded. "Hi! Thank you for seeing me. Can I get you anything?"

"A mocha latte, please."

I carried the drinks to the table and sat down.

"Do you work in the area?" I was trying to get her to relax since she seemed tense. Her eyes were darting in different directions and her left leg was bobbing up and down.

"I work in a bookstore in town until I figure out what I want to do."

"Would you like to go back to college?"

"I don't know. I haven't made any decisions." She took a sip of her latte.

"My client is a high school senior who was accused of raping a sixteen-year-old sophomore girl. They both attended the same private school, except he was there on a scholarship since his mother couldn't afford the tuition. He was arrested and is out on bail until his trial. The school asked him to leave and right now he's completely lost." I didn't tell Heather that he attempted suicide. "I believe the young girl who was raped lied because she was threatened. After weeks of investigation, I started looking into Ben Bradley. Without getting into what I found out, I went to the college and spoke with Dean Murphy. Though he would not give me any information, I subsequently learned that Bradley had two complaints filed against him. One was yours."

Heather looked straight at me. "How did you find out it was me?"

"Talking to people on campus. I'd rather not go into any details. I was a former police detective with the New York City Police Department, so I know how colleges handle these types of situations, and I know what it could do to someone who was raped. I'm sorry for the way the school treated you and that you didn't feel the police would believe your story." By the look in her eyes, I knew she was listening intently and taking in every word I was saying.

"I could try to get Ben to admit to what he's done, but without any concrete proof, I think Mr. Bradley will get away with another rape. Your story might help my client."

Heather looked down; her hands wrapped around her coffee cup. I waited to see if she would say anything. When she looked up, there were tears in her eyes.

"I wasn't lying. He raped me."

"I believe you. Could you tell me what happened? I promise you it goes no further if that's what you decide."

"We were at a frat party. I knew I had more to drink than I probably should have but I wasn't drunk." Heather was holding her cup so tight I thought at any moment the paper cup was going to explode.

"Did you come to the party with Ben?"

"No. We met there. I had seen him around but I had never talked to him. He asked me to dance, and I admit I was attracted to him. He was very charming and fun to be with. He asked me if I wanted to go upstairs to one of the rooms where it would be quieter so we could talk. I said okay. I know I sound pretty naïve."

"You had no way of knowing."

"As soon as we got into the room, he became very aggressive and I got scared." Heather was trying to hold back her tears. "I said I wanted to leave but he pushed me down on the bed. When I started to scream he put his hand over my mouth and pulled up my skirt. I struggled and tried to push him off of me but he was too strong." Heather stopped talking, trying to gain her composure. "When it was over, he got up, fixed himself, and left. I was so petrified I would run into him I was afraid to go back downstairs. I finally got up the courage and rushed down the stairs and out of the house. I practically ran to my dorm."

"Did he say anything to you before he left the room?"

"He said don't bother to report it since it's my word against his."

"Did you tell a friend or your parents what happened?"

"I told my friend Darcey when she got back to the dorm. She said I should report it. I didn't know what to do. I didn't think anyone would believe me since I had been drinking."

"When did you finally go to the dean's office?"

"A few days later. They said they would have it investigated but I have no idea what they did."

"Why didn't you go to the police?"

"Dean Murphy and another woman whose name I didn't know kept asking me questions, like how much I had to drink and did I go willingly with him to the room upstairs. By the time I left there, I felt like it was my own fault so I never went to the police."

"And you never told your parents?"

"When I left school and went back home, I told them that I wasn't happy and I needed time to think about what I wanted to do."

"So, they never knew you were raped?"

"No. I should have told them but I didn't know how they would react."

"It's your choice, but I know what this is doing to you and unless you take charge of your life, you won't be able to go forward. How long ago did this happen?"

"Four months. Is it too late to go to the police if that's what I decide?"

"Absolutely not, but I think you need to tell your parents exactly what you told me. You'll need their support. You didn't, by any chance, keep the underwear you were wearing from that night?"

"I just threw everything in the washing machine. What a mess I've made."

"This is not your fault and don't blame yourself. The only person to blame is Ben Bradley. If you decide to file a complaint, you would have to go to the police precinct in Manhattan where the school is located in. Are you still friends with Darcey?"

"Yes."

"If for some reason you don't want to tell your parents right now, maybe Darcey would go with you."

"Would you go with me if she doesn't want to?"

"Yes, but I really feel you should tell your parents. They're going to find out eventually. I'll check in with you in a couple of days, and if you need to talk, you can always call me."

"Thank you. I will."

I wanted to speak with Christine Dunn, the other woman who filed a complaint, but that would have to wait till Monday.

Driving home, I kept thinking about Heather and the trauma she'd gone through. I banged on the steering wheel a few times, trying to let out the anger I was feeling toward Dean Murphy. I knew proving rape would be difficult. Most of the time it's a he said, she said situation. It wouldn't be an easy road for her. Though I didn't want to seem too pushy, if Heather went to the police, it would give me more ammunition against Bradley. But since Mia incriminated my client, I would have to get her to change her story, which I doubt she would, or find a way to get Bradley to admit to raping Mia. I thought it was time to pay him a visit.

CHAPTER 60

I had no intention of giving Bradley a heads-up, but I had no idea where he lived. I remembered Mrs. Bradley saying her son lived near his school. Unfortunately, that didn't help me since he wouldn't be in any of my databases. Surveillance would be easier at his parents' house, but did he come home on the weekends?

"Hey, how's my favorite girl?" Jesse said when he answered.

"I spoke with the young woman who claimed she was raped by Ben Bradley."

"How did you manage that?"

I went on to explain how I tracked her down and what she told me.

"So what's the plan?"

"I thought if you were up for some surveillance, we could tail him on Saturday from his parents' house in Scarsdale. It's a crap shoot since he may not even come home on the weekends."

"I'm game. I'll see you tomorrow morning. Love you."

"Right back at you."

***

I was up at the crack of dawn. I made egg sandwiches and poured hot coffee into travel mugs. I heard the familiar knock. When I opened the door, Jesse pulled me close to him and I was like putty in his hands. If only we could stay like that, I thought to myself before we pulled apart.

"I made sandwiches and coffee for our trip."

"I guess we're off. You sure I can't talk you into a little foreplay before we leave?" he said with a broad grin.

"I'll make it up to you later, but for now, we have to hit the road."

"Yes, ma'am."

We drove up to Scarsdale in Jesse's car since he had tinted windows that were better for surveillance.

"We have to be careful since it's a very upscale residential neighborhood and neighbors don't appreciate unfamiliar cars sitting for a while," I said.

"When we get there, we'll figure out the best place to wait," Jesse said.

"I did a DMV search last night to see what cars were registered to Ben's father. He has two cars registered to him: a Blue BMW and a Black Mercedes Coupe, both the latest models. There were no cars registered in Ben's name."

When we arrived, we circled around until we found a spot where neighbors might not see us unless they were coming out of their long driveways. We had a visual on Ben's place. While we were waiting, we ate our egg sandwiches.

"This might be a complete waste of time since I have no idea if he's even home," I said.

"There's nothing we can do about it now. Hopefully he's here and at some point, he'll come out. There are days I just sit and wait with nothing to show for it."

"That sucks. That's why I try to avoid surveillance if I can," I said.

"Since I'm always tracking people down for one reason or another, I don't have that luxury."

"How do you want to play this if we get the opportunity to confront Ben?" I said.

"I think you should take the lead. I'll chime in if I feel it's appropriate."

"Look, someone's pulling out into the street in the Mercedes Coupe." We couldn't see who it was but decided to follow just in case it was Ben. We tailed at a distance, still not sure who was in the car. Since I didn't know the area well, I had no idea where we were headed. After driving for about twenty-five minutes, the car pulled into a driving range and we followed a few seconds later. I was relieved to see it was Ben that came out of the car. He opened the trunk and pulled out a golf bag.

"What do you think?" I said to Jesse.

"Let's wait till he's finished and then approach him when he gets back to his car."

"Did you ever play golf?" I said.

"A few times. I was pretty bad since I never took a lesson and nobody ever taught me how to play. I went with a couple of guys who dragged me along back in college. It's not my thing."

"What is your thing?"

"If we weren't waiting for your guy, I would show you."

"How about a sample?"

"Don't tempt me."

"You got any ideas how I can get under this guy's skin?" I said.

"I doubt he's going to incriminate himself, but you want to shake him up a bit, though don't count on him showing it. The best way to get under his skin is to keep pressuring him. If he's rattled, it might lead him to making a mistake."

An hour later, I saw Ben Bradley heading to his car.

"Hi, Ben," I said, as he was putting his golf clubs into the trunk of his car. He looked up and I swear the look on his face was complete disdain.

CHAPTER 61

"You remember Jesse from our first meeting?" I said to Ben.

"I see you brought the big guns."

"Why don't you shove the attitude."

"I told you before, I don't know what happened to Mia."

"Well, since we last spoke, a few things have come up. You might want to listen to what I have to say." Ben just stood there. "I spoke with a woman named Heather Paxton. She seemed to have quite a lot to say about you." Ben couldn't hide the shocked look on his face.

"Those accusations were dismissed. She was lying," he said, trying to recover.

"I found her believable and so will the police." That smug look he had on his face disappeared.

"Those charges were investigated and nothing came of it."

"We both know how those school investigations go. I think the police won't be so dismissive of what she has to say."

"I wouldn't count on it," he said, quickly getting into his car and driving off.

"You definitely rattled him. He couldn't wait to get out of here."

"I'm still back to square one. Even if Heather goes to the police, that doesn't help Jason. As long as Mia sticks to her story, Jason will be convicted."

"Then you'll have to get her to change her story."

"And how will I do that?"

"With your powers of persuasion."

"Very funny."

"Why don't we get some lunch."

"Typical man."

"I need to keep up my stamina." Jesse chuckled.

It was a beautiful fall day so we decided to take a ride up to a historic village off of the Taconic Parkway called Cold Spring, located on the banks of the Hudson River. Both sides of the street were lined with cute boutiques, antique shops, and places to eat. We went to a place called Brassiere Le Bouchon, a typical French bistro, and sat outside on a lovely covered patio with green shrubbery planted all around.

"You think we sufficiently rattled Ben?" I said, as we were sipping our wine.

"I wonder if he would be stupid enough to contact Mia to make sure she keeps her mouth shut."

"I'm curious whether Ben's parents know what their son has been up to," I said.

"I doubt it, since the school can't tell them without his consent," Jesse said.

The waiter brought over our mussels.

"If Ben's threat was about Mia selling drugs and now the cops are going to be looking into her involvement, wouldn't that remove the threat? What reason would she have to stay silent?" I said.

"For one, Mia isn't going to admit to selling drugs now that the dealer is dead. How are the police going to prove it?"

"That's a good point. I don't think the kids she sold to would admit to buying drugs. I still feel the threat goes beyond the drugs. If Ben is violent, which he may be if he was the one who decimated my office, then he would be capable of threatening harm to her parents. Also, he did mention that his father is the senior partner in a hedge fund firm. What if the threat was to Mia's father? Wouldn't that scare Mia into keeping her mouth shut?"

"Never thought of that," Jesse said.

"But I'm still back to square one. If I can't get to Mia, then how can I change her mind?"

"You're going to have to appeal to her mother. I think if you tell her everything you found out about Ben, she might listen and get her daughter to talk with you."

"Though she hasn't listened so far, it's worth a shot."

Before leaving, we stopped for ice cream cones at the creamery shop and then picked up two bottles of wine at the Flowercup Wine store.

***

Lying in bed that night, I could tell something was on Jesse's mind.

"Anything you'd like to tell me?"

"Would you like to meet Leo next weekend when you come up?"

"I thought you wanted to wait a little before you introduced him to me."

"I think it's time. And I promise he doesn't bite."

"How do you know I won't?" I said, as I playfully bit Jesse's ear.

***

On Sunday we woke up to pouring rain and decided to stay in. Jesse cooked pasta for dinner and we polished off one of the bottles of wine we had bought.

CHAPTER 62

In the morning after Jesse left, I went straight to my office. A woman who had come to me a while back had just emailed me information on her husband who was claiming poverty in a divorce action. The wife believed her husband was hiding money to get out of paying her alimony. If only I had a dime for everyone who tried to get away without paying their fair share. As I was sending the email with the information on her husband to my source in order to conduct an asset search, I heard the door open. Before I had a chance to step into the reception area, Jonathan Bradley was standing in my office.

"How can I help you?" I said, trying to keep my composure. "Would you like to sit?"

"I don't think that will be necessary since I won't be taking up too much of your time. I just came here to say it would be wise of you to stay away from my son."

"Is that a threat?"

"Take it any way you want as long as the harassment stops."

"Is that what he told you? Did he happen to mention the sexual complaints filed by two young women at his school?"

"That's none of your business."

"It is my business if your son was the one who raped Mia Franklin."

"If you continue on this road, I can guarantee this will not be the last you've heard from me. You never know what could happen to people who meddle."

"Get the hell out of my office." My jaw was clenched so tight I thought it would break.

What I couldn't figure out was why Ben would tell his father about the complaints unless his father already knew. But how would he have found out if the school didn't tell him?

A thought occurred to me. I looked up contributors to the college. There was his name: Jonathan Bradley. I was curious if Dean Murphy told Ben's father even though it was illegal. If that was true, then Jonathan Bradley knew his son was most likely a rapist. Did Ben tell his father these girls were lying and he was the victim? How far would Ben's father go to protect his son? The sound of the phone startled me. It was my father.

"Hi, honey," he said when I answered. "How are you?"

I could feel myself welling up.

"What's the matter?" he said when I didn't answer right away. "Maddie, if something's wrong you can tell me."

I broke down and told him about the case and then finding out about Leo. I didn't mention the threats.

"You're stronger than you think. How many people would choose a career as a police officer? At any time, you could've been in danger. I admire you and I know you'll do your best to make sure your client is proven innocent."

"What if my best isn't good enough?"

"It will be."

"Can I get that in writing?"

"Sure," he said, laughing. "Now tell me what's really bothering you?"

"I'm scared I'm going to screw things up with Jesse."

"Why?"

"I love Jesse and I can't see myself being with anyone else, but I've been so afraid of committing to him that when I finally did, I wasn't sure I did it for the right reasons."

"What do you mean?"

"I did it because I thought I would lose him and I was tired of being scared."

"Those seem like good reasons to me. The choices we make are not always for the right reason but that doesn't mean it's the wrong thing to do. Do you understand what I'm saying?"

"Yes. But then things got complicated when he told me about Leo. After all I went through to finally agree to live with Jesse, I now find myself having to include this child in my life. I didn't sign up for that, and I don't know if I want to."

"Well, again you have to decide what's more important to you. You might surprise yourself. Kids have a way of worming their way into your heart. Maybe that frightens you."

"Do you think that's what would've happened to you if you had known about me?"

"I would hope so. You know I've never told anyone this before, not even Jennifer, but when Jennifer was pregnant the second time, I was hoping for a girl."

"Really? Thank you for listening. It helped."

"I'm glad. I'm always here for you."

I hung up before I got too teary-eyed.

I needed a break. I locked up and walked a few blocks. The air was chilly and I hugged my sweater closer to me. I appreciated my father's words.

I ordered a cappuccino at Starbucks and sat for a few minutes. My phone rang. It was a number I didn't recognize. My heart was beating as I picked up the phone.

"Hello."

"Maddie Landon?"

"Yes."

"My name is Emily Paxton. I wanted to let you know that my daughter won't be going to the police."

"Isn't that her decision?"

"She doesn't need to be dragged through the legal system when she has no proof that she was raped."

"That doesn't matter. The police will investigate even if there's no physical evidence."

"I'm sorry, I don't want my daughter traumatized again. She's been through enough."

"You're making a mistake. If she doesn't file a complaint, she'll never get over it. She needs to take control of her life."

"I'm her mother and I know what's best for Heather. Please don't contact her again."

"At least get her help." I wasn't sure she heard me before she disconnected.

In some ways I didn't blame her mother. She thought she was protecting her daughter, but unfortunately, it was not in Heather's best interests to sweep it under the rug as if it never happened.

At this point there wasn't much I could do. I knew if Jason's case came to trial, we could subpoena Heather to testify if the judge allowed it. I was hoping Heather would go to the police, even if her mother was against it.

CHAPTER 63

My foot was going a mile a minute. I had to get Mia's mother to listen to me. Would my persuasive charm work on Mrs. Franklin? I wasn't so sure. I picked up my phone and dialed Mrs. Franklin's number.

"Hello."

"Mrs. Franklin, this is Maddie Landon. Before you hang up on me, I need five minutes of your time. You might want to hear what I have to say."

"I'm sorry, I'm on my way to the hospital."

"Can we please meet? It's really important."

She was silent. I almost thought she hung up when I heard her say, "I'll be at the main entrance of the hospital at 1:00 p.m."

"I'll be there." I would only get one bite at the apple. I had to make it good.

I parked and was at the hospital entrance by 12:45 p.m. By 1:15 p.m. I thought I was stood up when I saw Melissa Franklin walking toward me.

"There's a bench around the side," Mrs. Franklin said.

We sat down and she waited for me to speak.

"First, I want to say I'm very happy Mia is doing much better. When I spoke with you and your husband, I tried to warn you." Mrs. Franklin didn't say anything. I continued. "I have reason to believe Ben Bradley raped your daughter."

"I've heard enough," she said, as she started to get up.

"Please, Mrs. Franklin, hear me out. I don't think Mia meant to name Jason as her rapist. I believe she did it because she was threatened. I found out some things about Ben that you might be interested in. Two young women filed complaints about him to the Dean of Students at his school. One woman claimed Ben raped her and the other young woman said Ben attempted to rape her, but she was able to get away. I spoke to the woman who was allegedly raped. She said the school did their own inquiry and found there was nothing there. The young woman never went to the police because she was intimidated by the people who interviewed her and thought the police wouldn't believe her. Unfortunately, the school is not obligated to contact the police."

"Why would Ben rape my daughter? They were friends. She looked up to him."

"Because he's a rapist and he believes he can get away with it."

"Why wouldn't Mia say it was Ben? What reason would she have to lie?"

"For one, I believe Ben knew your daughter was selling drugs. But I'm betting the threat was more than drugs. I'm only guessing, but he may have threatened your family in some way. I'm not sure yet."

"This is your version of what happened. You don't know if any of what you just told me is true."

"You're correct, but this morning I got a visit from Ben's father, basically threatening me if I didn't drop my investigation into Ben." I let that sink in for a moment and continued. "If Mia did accuse Jason because she was scared, it would be difficult for her to back down now. It's hard to take back a lie once it's out in the open. Mia is definitely afraid and it's not Jason she's scared of."

"Are you through?"

"When Mia is home from the hospital, would you let me talk to her?"

"I don't think that would be a good idea."

"Will you at least talk to her?" I was frustrated but knew I wasn't going to get her to change her mind.

"I'll think about it."

We both got up, and I thanked her for listening to me, even though what I really wanted to do was wipe that smug air of superiority off her face. I had no clue whether she would talk to Mia. Even if she did, I didn't think Mia would change her story.

On the way back to the office, I thought about Jonathan Bradley's threat and wondered if I believed he would make good on it. I was curious about him. Did he have his own skeletons? I had the feeling he was a man who was used to getting his own way.

As soon as I got in, I began searching through my computer, looking for information on Jonathan Bradley. Bradley had impressive credentials. He got his undergraduate degree from Harvard University and his MBA from the Wharton School of Business. He was listed as a senior partner at Washington Securities, the same place Mia's father worked. I wanted to dig deeper into Mr. Bradley. First, I read as much as I could find online about him. Though there were several articles, there was nothing that could help with my investigation. I pulled up the originally report I had done a while back on Jonathan

Bradley and opened it up. At first glance, there wasn't anything out of the ordinary, but then when it came to people associated with him, there was a woman listed by the name of Patricia Bradley. Delving further, I found an address for this woman in Yonkers but was having a hard time locating a telephone number for her. I had no idea how she was related to Jonathan Bradley, but I thought it was worth the trip to find out.

When I arrived at Patricia Bradley's address in Yonkers, the area her apartment building was located was kind of seedy looking. I found Patricia Bradley's name on the building directory. She was listed in Apartment 4G. I had no intention of going into the elevator and instead found the door to the stairs leading up to the fourth floor. I rang her buzzer. I didn't hear anything for a few moments and then there were footsteps. I heard a voice say, "Who is it?"

"My name is Maddie Landon. I'm a private investigator and found your name associated with a Jonathan Bradley."

"Do you have any proof of who you are?"

"I'm slipping my card under the door." A minute later I heard the door unlock. The woman who was standing in front of me looked around sixty, but I had a feeling she was quite a bit younger. She was wearing a bathrobe and slippers, and her hair looked uncombed.

"What do you want?"

"Do you know a Jonathan Bradley?"

"Why are you asking about him?" she said in an angry tone.

"Do you think I could come in so we don't have to talk in the hallway?" I was surprised but she let me in. We were standing in the kitchen that probably hadn't been remodeled in many years, if ever. I sat on a yellow vinyl cushion chair around a yellow Formica table. She lit up a cigarette.

"Now, what were you saying?" she asked.

"Are you related to a Jonathan Bradley?"

"You could say so. I was married to the bastard for six years until he couldn't wait to dump me and leave me penniless." That took me completely by surprise.

"How long ago was that?"

"Maybe fifteen years ago." Something didn't add up.

"So Ben is your son?"

"He was until Jonathan got custody of him. He took me to court and said I was an unfit mother. It wasn't true. I loved Benny."

"How did he get custody?"

"He was working all the time and I was home with the baby. I started drinking and there were some incidents. I got into AA and had been sober for a few months, but that son of a bitch lied on the stand. He said I was still drinking and endangering our son. He had the best lawyers. I think he even paid my lawyer off to lose the case. I haven't seen Benny since then. He never gave me alimony and that's when I started drinking again. I'm not proud of myself. I know I'm weak."

"Have you ever tried to get in contact with your son?"

"Once, but his father made sure that wasn't going to happen. Why did you say you were here?" She crushed out her cigarette and lit another one.

How was I going to explain that I thought her son was a rapist.

"My client was accused of raping a young girl, but I've come to learn that your son might be involved." I thought she would be upset and accuse me of lying.

"Poor Benny, but it doesn't surprise me. The apple doesn't fall far from the tree."

"What do you mean?"

"Jonathan fooled around on me over the years. I think there may have been rumors that he raped someone, but when you have money, it's easy to get away with stuff."

"Was he physically abusive to you?"

"He was verbally abusive. There were times when he would threaten to hit me. I hope you're wrong about Benny. If anyone's to blame, it's his father. He's the criminal."

As I was leaving Patricia Bradley's apartment, she wanted me to tell Benny that she loved him. I didn't say anything. After speaking with Patricia, I knew Jonathan Bradley was ruthless and would do whatever it took to make sure Ben wasn't going to be implicated in Mia's rape.

By the time I got home, it was barely light out. I changed and went running in the park. All sorts of thoughts were swirling around inside my head. What I learned from Patricia Bradley didn't shock me. There aren't too many things that do. I've seen too much from my days in law enforcement and also from the years I've been a private investigator. I knew if I couldn't get Mia to admit that

Jason wasn't the one who raped her, how was I going to prove it was Ben Bradley?

* * *

In the morning, I headed up to the college to talk with Christine Dunn. When I arrived, I asked the person at the gate entrance where I could find the East dorms. Though he gave me directions, I still had to ask a student where the dorm was once I parked my car.

As I was approaching the front door to the dorm, there was a young woman who was just leaving.

"Excuse me, I'm looking for Christine Dunn."

"Fourth door on the right," she said, without even looking up.

The door was slightly ajar, but I knocked anyway.

"Come in. It's open."

"Are you Christine Dunn?"

"Who are you?"

"My name's Maddie Landon. I'm a private investigator," I said, handing her my card. Christine was petite, with short brown straight hair and milky white skin. She was lovely.

"I'm investigating the rape of a high school sophomore student. It's about Ben Bradley." Her eyes opened wide.

"What has this got to do with me."

"Is this a good place to talk?"

"Close the door."

"I've been making some inquiries into Mr. Bradley. I believe he's a suspect in a case I'm working on."

"How did my name come up?"

"I've spoken to a number of people on campus and your name was mentioned."

"I don't know how that's possible since I never told anyone."

"Well, I guess someone knew. These things have a way of leaking out." I hated lying but it's part of the job. "This conversation goes no further, but could you tell me what happened?"

"Please leave. I have nothing to say to you."

"I just want to—"

"If you don't leave right now, I'm calling security."

"You have my card if you change your mind."

"I won't."

I knew Christine didn't want to be reminded of what happened. For her, it was over. The school wasn't going to take action and since there was no actual rape, she wanted to forget the whole incident. It's not uncommon for victims to want to put the incident behind them. Unfortunately, it's not as easy as they think.

CHAPTER 64

After seeing Christine Dunn, I went back to my office. The phone rang as I was pouring myself a cup of coffee.

"Hello." I only heard breathing on the other end. I was about to hang up when I heard a voice say, "It's Heather Paxton."

"Heather, how are you?"

"Did my mother call you?"

"Yes."

"She thinks she knows what's best for me, but when you told me going to the police was the only way I was going to take control of my life, I knew you were right. Please help me."

"What do you want me to do?"

"Go to the police with me."

"What about Darcey?"

"I would feel better if it was you. I just need you there for moral support. Even though I know it's the right thing to do, I'm so nervous. What if they don't believe me?"

"Let's take one step at a time. I'll pick you up at the train station and we'll drive to the precinct together."

I was totally surprised to hear from Heather. I wasn't sure it would actually help my case, but it would certainly get both Ben Bradley and his father's attention.

When we walked into the station, we went up to the front desk and Heather told the officer she wanted to report a rape. She was told to wait until a detective could see her. We sat down and Heather took hold of my hand.

"Try not to worry. Just tell them what you told me. I'll be waiting here until you come out."

"You can't go inside with me?" she said with an uneasy look on her face.

"I know you'll do fine."

A woman was walking toward us. "Are you Heather?"

"Yes."

"I'm Detective Slattery," she said with a warm smile on her face. "Is this your sister?"

"Maddie is a friend."

"Can you please come with me? Your friend can wait here for you."

As Heather was walking with the detective, she looked back at me. I was glad that it was a woman detective that was handling the interview. Hopefully, she would put Heather at ease. Approximately fifty minutes later, Heather was walking toward me.

"How did it go," I said as we were leaving the precinct.

"She listened and asked me a lot of questions. I told her what the school said and that I didn't think the police would take me seriously so I never reported it. Detective Slattery asked me why I changed my mind, and I told her what you said. What do you think is going to happen next?"

"Ben will probably be brought in for questioning, most likely with a lawyer which his father will insist on."

Though I didn't want to scare Heather, I was thinking of Ben's father and would he try to intimidate her. I had a feeling I might be the brunt of his rage.

"You need to tell your parents that you went to the police. They have to know." I was hoping now that she reported the incident, her parents would support her no matter what.

I dropped Heather off at Grand Central Station and told her to call me any time, day or night. It was a little after 5:30 p.m. when I got home.

"You got time to brainstorm with me?" I said when Annie picked up the phone.

"I was going to call you. There is someone who might be interested in hiring Jason part-time. The guy who set up all our computer software said he can use someone like Jason and Jason should give him a call. I'm texting you his contact information."

"You're a lifesaver. This will give Jason something to focus on instead of just sitting in his room playing video games."

"How's Jason's therapy going?"

"He's going, so that in itself is a miracle."

"I have some news," Annie said. "I really want to have a baby."

"Mazel Tov! What tipped the scales?"

"You know I always wanted to. I just got derailed when I lost the baby. I didn't want to face that pain again, but I realized that was the grief talking and not me."

"Doug must be ecstatic."

"He is. He's already picking out names. I'm still a little scared."

"I know you are, but I'm always here for you. I'm so happy. I can't wait to spoil that kid."

"Let's not get ahead of ourselves. You're forgetting I still have to get pregnant."

"A minor matter. By the way, Jesse wants me to meet Leo this weekend."

"That was quick. How are you feeling about that?"

"Scared. Not sure I'm up for it. Hopefully, I won't turn out to be the big, bad stepmom."

"This kid will have you eating out of his hands."

"Now the serious stuff." I caught Annie up to date on the case. "Any ideas how I'm going to nail this creep?"

"The only way I see is to get Mia to talk."

"And how do you suppose I'm going to do that? Her mother and father made it perfectly clear they don't want me speaking with their daughter."

"When does that ever stop you? Mia isn't going to be in her house forever. She's vulnerable now. Her mother must have mentioned the conversation you had with her. Mia has to break sooner or later."

"You think so?"

"It's probably eating her up and she just needs a push," Annie said.

"I don't know. She's a pretty strong kid. Don't forget she was selling drugs."

"Do you think she got into selling drugs by accident? Maybe it was Ben Bradley who got her into it."

After hanging up, I opened my refrigerator and saw there was nothing to eat. I thought I would do a quick run to the Thai Restaurant near me. The fresh air would probably do me some good.

It was dark out by the time I left the restaurant. The streets were deserted, yet I thought I heard footsteps in the distance. I looked over my shoulder but no one was there. I quickened my pace. When I looked back again, there was a shadow of a man in a hooded sweatshirt maybe a half a block away or was I imagining it. As I walked faster, the footsteps came quicker. My heart was racing. I had no idea if I was overreacting but I didn't want to take that chance. I saw an alley and ducked into it. It was quiet. I didn't hear anything and then all of a sudden he was there. Instinctively, I started kicking and punching him. I didn't see the knife at first until it plunged into me, and then I felt this horrible, searing pain coursing through my body. I fell to the ground and heard footsteps running away. I crawled the few feet back to the street. I opened my mouth to yell for help but no sound came out. And then everything went blank.

"Can you open your eyes?" Someone was talking to me. I tried to say something but I couldn't speak. There were people all around me. Then darkness.

When I opened my eyes again, I was lying on a bed being wheeled by two men wearing green costumes. Who were they? The next thing I remember is a mask being placed over my face and then nothing.

CHAPTER 65

My eyes opened and there was a man standing over me.

"Glad to see you're awake. Do you know where you are?"

"No," I said, barely audible.

"You're in the hospital. My name is Dr. Greenberg. You were stabbed and we had to operate to stop the bleeding. You're going to be fine, but very weak and sore for a while. Is there anyone we should contact for you?"

"Annie," I said in a whisper. I croaked out her number.

"We'll call her. Try to get some sleep."

I woke up disoriented. It was dark in the room. I tried to move but it hurt too much. I must have fallen back to sleep since next time I woke up, there was light peeking through the curtains.

"Good morning, young lady." A woman who was probably in her mid-fifties, on the plump side, with rosy cheeks and a warm smile, asked me how I was feeling. Her name tag said Margie. "How are we doing?"

"My stomach is hurting. Can I have something for the pain?" I felt like shit.

"Let me see what I can do. In the meantime, you have two visitors who've been waiting most of the night. I'll be back in a few minutes."

Jesse and Annie walked into the room. Annie's eyes were red. Jesse looked terrible.

"You both look worse than me," I said, trying to smile. Jesse took my hand and held it. Annie held my other hand.

"I should have seen the knife. I was too slow," I said in a weak voice.

"Did you see his face before he attacked you?" Jesse said.

"It was dark out. I think he was wearing a hooded sweatshirt covering part of his face and he was looking down. This wasn't random. I know it had something to do with Ben Bradley. His father threatened me and now that Heather went to the police, it's going to get really ugly for Ben."

"Excuse me," Nurse Margie said, when she came back into the room. "It's time for my patient to get some rest. You can come back later."

"I'll be back soon. I love you," Jesse said.

"I see that look in your eyes. Don't do anything stupid. I'll handle it in my own way," I said to Jesse as he was leaving.

"See ya later, sweetie," Annie said, kissing my cheek.

Nurse Margie told me they couldn't increase the dosage of morphine until later. I could hardly move and Jason needed me.

"I need my phone. It's in my backpack. Can you please get it for me."

"You shouldn't be moving around so much. You'll tear the stitches."

"When do you think I can leave? I need to get out of here."

"The doctor will be in later. He'll explain everything. What you need is to get plenty of rest."

"As soon as I make one phone call, I'll sleep."

The nurse left and I called Nina Demsky. My voice was weak and Nina was having a hard time hearing me. I gave her the contact information for the guy who was interested in hiring Jason. Though she asked why I was whispering, I told her I was in a bad location since I didn't want her to worry. She thanked me profusely for helping Jason.

I slept for a while. When I woke, the pain wasn't as bad. The morphine was doing its job and I was grateful. I was still having trouble moving around. Two police detectives came into my room. One looked like the character Munch on the Law & Order SVU show and his sidekick was a Jennifer Aniston look-alike.

"Hello, Maddy. I'm Detective Olsen and this is Detective Green. Can you tell me what happened?"

I told them the little I knew but left out who I thought might be behind the stabbing. I wasn't sure why. They took down a few notes, asked me if anyone had a beef against me, and did I get a look at the person. They left with not much to go on. I had a feeling I might not hear from them for a while. As they were leaving, Jesse walked in.

"How are you feeling?"

"Great. I'm ready for a jog around the park."

"Well, how about instead a nice relaxing weekend at my place. All expenses paid."

"It's hard to pass that offer up, but I really need to stick around in case something happens with the case."

"I don't think you'll be in any condition to do anything for at least a few days, if not more."

At that point, Dr. Greenberg came in. Jesse introduced himself.

"Your girlfriend is very lucky. If she was stabbed any lower, she might have bled out."

"I need to leave here as soon as possible."

"I'll come back tomorrow morning and we'll see how you're doing. Even if I release you, you're going to need plenty of bed rest or else you'll find yourself back in here and I don't think you'll want that."

Jesse left the room while the doctor examined me and then came back in when the doctor left.

"You know I'm going to have a pretty nasty scar from this."

"Nobody wants someone who's perfect," he said, giving me a gentle kiss on my lips.

"Don't get me excited. It's not good for my health." Jesse gave me a big smile.

"I have to go back this afternoon. Annie will be here later, but I need you to promise me you won't get into any trouble till I see you tomorrow. Hopefully, you'll be able to go home after the doctor sees you. We'll figure everything out then."

I felt a hand touching me. When I opened my eyes, it was Annie. I must have slept after Jesse left.

"Hey," Annie said. "Doug sends his love. How are you feeling?"

"I realized I left my Thai food in the alley."

"Well, that answers my question," she said grinning. "I stopped by the apartment and got you some fresh clothes and underwear."

"Thanks. Listen, I think I know who attacked me. I'm pretty sure it was Ben Bradley, but I can't prove it. I think he's also been harassing me on the phone, leaving threatening messages."

"Did you tell the police?"

"No, I can't prove any of it. I need to stay at my place. If I go up to Jesse's, he'll keep me there indefinitely. I have to try to speak with Mia."

"You sound as if he's kidnapping you. Tomorrow is Thursday. You were going up to his place on Friday anyway. And we don't even know if Mia is home yet, and if she is, she's probably going to be recuperating just like you should be."

"Well, if you put it that way." The telephone rang in the room. *Who would be calling me?* I thought to myself.

"Hello. Hello, anyone there?" I didn't want to scare Annie, but I was thinking it might be Bradley. "It was probably for someone who was in the room before me," I said to Annie when I hung up.

"I'm not buying it, Landon."

"What am I supposed to do, lock myself up and never go out?"

"That sounds like a plan."

"Don't mention any of this to Jesse."

"I gotta go. If you need anything, let me know. I love you."

"Love you."

When Annie left, I was thinking about both Ben and Jonathan Bradley, and whether I should have told the police about my suspicions and Jonathan Bradley's threat.

CHAPTER 66

The following morning, Dr. Greenberg came in and said I could leave the hospital but gave me a strong warning that what I needed was plenty of bed rest. I was listening with one ear. All I could think about was getting out of there and getting Mia to confess that she lied about Jason.

Though I was exhausted, I didn't let on to Jesse when he picked me up. I hated the idea of being wheeled out of the hospital in a wheelchair, but the thought of walking out on my own two feet was even more repugnant.

Getting into Jesse's car was no minor matter. Once settled in, I wasn't looking forward to getting out. When we arrived at my building, I was happy to see my doorman, Louis. I was trying to hide my pain from him as I was exiting the car.

"Are you alright Miss Maddie?"

"No worries, Louis. You should see the other guy." My attempt at humor. "Can we leave the car here while we get some stuff from my apartment? I'm going up to Jesse's place for the weekend."

"Of course. When you get back, if you need anything, just let me know."

"Thanks, Louis."

"I just want you to know I'm going under duress," I said to Jesse. "I can take care of myself, and I should be here just in case something breaks in the case."

"Duly noted. Now tell me what you want packed."

On the way up to Jesse's, I was quiet. Where was Mia now? Was she home or still in the hospital?

"Jesse, what if whoever it was that tried to kill me tries to go after Mia? It would make sense if they thought she would talk."

"Whoever it was would have to be pretty desperate to try to kill Mia."

"I think Ben's father is ruthless enough to try anything to help his son. He could have hired someone to kill me."

"I hope you're wrong."

"Me too."

When we finally arrived at Jesse's place, I was tired and took a nap. When I woke up, I called to him.

"Hey, babe. Are you hungry at all?" he said when he came upstairs.

"Not really." I heard my phone ringing. "Hello, hello. Piss off whoever you are," I said.

"What was that about?" Jesse said.

"Probably a wrong number or one of those unsolicited calls trying to sell me something."

"From your language on the phone, I'm guessing this isn't the first one. What's going on?"

"I don't know. Could be, and it's just a wild guess, related to my attack."

"So you think these people know you're alive and now they're trying to scare you?"

"Do I look like I'm scared?"

"This isn't funny. They tried to kill you once. They might try again. Did you tell the police your suspicions when they spoke to you at the hospital?"

"Not exactly. I can handle it. I don't need the police meddling in my case."

"You are the most stubborn person I have ever met."

"One of my endearing qualities, wouldn't you say?"

"This isn't funny. If someone wants to kill you, they'll keep trying until they do."

"Well, I doubt if they know where I am now, so there's nothing to worry about at the moment. Remember what you said, you have to take me in sickness and in health." Jesse walked out of the room shaking his head.

***

The weekend went by without incident. I did think about what Jesse said and I was on the fence about whether I should inform the police when I got back. On Monday evening, Jesse brought me home and stayed over till the morning. From the look on his face as he was leaving, I knew he was concerned about my safety but didn't say anything. On Tuesday, Annie came over with Chinese food.

"I contacted the detective investigating Mia's shooting," I said to Annie as she was rationing out the food. "He informed me that Mia has been recuperating at home for the past few days. I need to try to convince Mrs. Franklin to let me speak to her daughter," I said as I picked up a piece of broccoli with my chopsticks.

"Let's say her mother gives you her blessing to talk with Mia. And let's say Mia confesses everything. Then what? You think Ben is going to admit that he raped Mia?"

"No, but maybe there's another way."

"How? You're not going to do anything stupid, are you?"

"No, of course not. Don't worry."

"You know you could leave it up to the police."

"By the time they investigate the charge, that could take months, and Jason doesn't have months before his trial."

"Why do you have to solve everything by yourself? Why can't you let anyone help you? Don't you care about the people who love you?"

"That's not fair. That's like saying I should never have been on the police force. At any moment I could have been killed. It was my job then and it's my job now."

"I understand, but I think you're taking unnecessary risks."

"I'll be careful. I promise. Did you get to work on making that baby yet?"

"You're a laugh a minute."

We agreed to disagree and changed the subject. After Annie left, I suddenly felt very tired and was down for the count by 9:00 p.m.

**

On Friday, I felt well enough to take a crack at Mrs. Franklin. I had a feeling if I could just see Mia, I could get her to talk, but I had no illusions that it would be easy.

CHAPTER 67

By mid-morning, after taking two Advil, I called an Uber to take me to Mia's house. My finger was shaking as I rang the buzzer of their brownstone. When the door opened, Mrs. Franklin was standing in front of me. She looked older than the last time I saw her. Maybe the stress of what happened to her daughter finally caught up with her.

"What are you doing here?" Melissa Franklin said in almost a whisper.

"Please, I know I'm the last person you want showing up at your door, but it's important that you hear me out." She opened the door wider to let me in but only as far as the entrance hallway.

"The woman who I told you about that accused Ben of raping her recently filed a complaint with the police. Last week, I was stabbed in the stomach and almost bled out. I believe Ben and his father are afraid I'm getting too close to the truth. If Ben is desperate, he may come after Mia if he can't get to me. I'm guessing you know by now Mia is frightened. I need to talk with her. I promise I'll tread lightly." I could see Mrs. Franklin was relenting.

"I'll give you five minutes with Mia, but I need to be present."

"Thank you."

I walked up the stairs slowly following Melissa Franklin. All I could think of was how I was going to get Mia to admit she lied about Jason. Mrs. Franklin opened Mia's bedroom door.

"Hi, Mia, I'm Maddie Landon. Remember me? How are you feeling?" She looked so fragile under the covers.

"What do you want?"

"I need to tell you a few things about Ben."

"Mom, please get her to leave. I don't want to talk to her," she said as she pulled the covers closely around her neck.

"I think you need to listen to what she has to say."

"I know you've been through a lot but there are things you need to know about Ben. Two women at his school filed complaints against him. One was a rape charge and the other was an attempted rape, but fortunately she was able to get away before anything happened. The young woman who was raped recently went to the police and they're going to be calling Ben in for questioning. I know Ben threatened you and that's why you accused Jason. I know you didn't mean to. You were scared. What did Ben say to you?"

"I don't know what you're talking about," she said, looking away.

"I think you do. I know you didn't mean to accuse Jason, but when Ben threatened you, you didn't know what to do."

At this point, Mia started crying. Her mother took Mia's hand and told her that everything was going to be alright.

"I'm so sorry. I was scared and I panicked. Jason's name just popped into my head when I told Tiffany. You have to believe me," Mia said, sobbing.

"Can you tell me what happened?" I said after Mia calmed down.

"Ben just showed up after Jason left."

"Did he say why he came in through the side door?"

"No. I was just happy that he came over and wanted to see me. I really liked him. I had always thought he looked at me like his kid sister, so I was so excited when he showed up."

"How did he know your parents weren't going to be home?"

"I had spoken to him the day before and I must have mentioned that they were going out for the evening."

"What happened next?"

"At first, he was sweet and started kissing me. It was like a dream. I couldn't believe he liked me that way. Then all of a sudden he got aggressive. I didn't understand what was going on. And then he started pulling at my clothes. I screamed but he put his hand over my mouth and then he pushed my skirt up and raped me." Mia started crying again.

"Why didn't you tell the police it was Ben?"

"He said if I ever told anyone, his father could have my father fired. He also knew that I was selling drugs. I didn't know what to do. I was so frightened. I wasn't going to report it, but someone told the school headmaster, and they called my mother. My mother kept badgering me. I had to tell her it was Jason since I had already lied to my friend."

"If you didn't want anyone to know, why did you tell your friend in the first place?"

"I told her in confidence that night because I was so upset after Ben left that I needed to tell someone. What's going to happen to me?" *Unfortunately, probably nothing*, I thought to myself.

"Don't worry about that now."

"Mommy, I'm so sorry. Please forgive me."

"It's alright, baby. I know you didn't mean to get Jason in trouble."

Though I felt sorry for her, I was so angry. It was hard for me to forgive her for what she had done to Jason.

"Thank you for finally telling the truth," I said, smiling through my teeth.

When I was walking out the door, Mrs. Franklin said: "What's going to happen now?"

"Mia will have to go to the police to tell them what really happened. Then they'll bring Ben in for questioning. Your daughter's been through a lot, and now that the police are going to be asking questions about her involvement in selling drugs, she's going to need you and your husband's support. And for what it's worth, I would seek counseling for her."

"What will happen to Jason?"

"I'm not sure. Ben, of course, will deny he had anything to do with raping Mia. She's already lied once and without any physical evidence against Ben, Jason will still have to face a trial."

"Isn't there anything you can do?"

"I don't know."

"If there is any way we can help Jason, please let us know. I feel awful."

When I left, instead of taking an Uber home, I decided to walk for a little bit. After a few blocks, I was running out of gas. Thankfully, I found a coffee shop and sat at a booth in the back far right-hand corner. When the waitress came over, I ordered eggs and toast. I hadn't decided what I was going to tell Nina Demsky yet. Instead, I took out my phone and called Jesse.

"I have some news. Call me back."

As I was drinking some water, my phone rang.

"Hey there."

"What's the news?" Jesse said.

"I finally spoke to Mia after convincing her mother to let me talk with her. Mia broke down and told me what happened. She told me that Ben had threatened to have her father fired if she told anyone what happened. If it wasn't for the fact that her friend Sandra blabbed to the headmaster, her mother may not have found out. Seeing Mia's face after she told me, I think she was relieved to finally tell the truth."

"What did the mother have to say?"

"It's her daughter, what would you expect. She said if there was anything she and her husband could do for Jason to let her know. I thought of a few things but didn't say them out loud."

"At this point what can they do?"

"How about getting Jason back in school; how about paying a good lawyer to defend Jason. The problem is there's no evidence linking Ben to the rape. And Mia has already lied once. Short of getting Ben to confess, I don't see how this doesn't go to trial."

"How are you feeling?"

"I have my moments but I'm getting around."

"It sounds like it."

"Don't worry, I'm going home to rest."

After hanging up, I called Nina Demsky.

"Hi, Ms. Landon. I'm glad you called. Jason got in contact with that person about the job and he starts working for him on Monday. He seemed really excited."

"That's great. Listen, I have some news but I don't want you to get your hopes up yet. I finally convinced Mia's mother to let me speak to her. Mia confessed that it wasn't Jason who raped her. I don't want to go into everything now, but I know who is responsible and unless I can prove it, Jason will still have to stand trial."

"I don't understand. Why isn't that girl's word good enough?"

"First, she already lied once, and second, there's no actual physical proof that this person did it. It becomes a he said, she said."

"Is there anything you can do?" Nothing like more pressure than I already have imposed upon myself.

"I don't know." I didn't want to give Nina any false hope.

"Jason told me he's gay."

"I'm glad that he finally unburdened himself."

"I have to tell you something."

"What is it?"

"For a long time, I was pretty sure Jason was gay. I keep thinking if only I had told him sooner he would have known it didn't matter to me."

I didn't know what to say so I kept quiet.

"Thank you for everything you've done. I don't know how we would have gotten this far without you."

"I wish I could do more for Jason. He deserves to have a bright future. Don't give up hope yet."

My next call was to Paul Greer, Jason's public defender. I hadn't heard from him in a while. "Mr. Greer, it's Maddie Landon. I have some news on the case. Please call me back as soon as possible."

I took an Uber back to my place, undressed, and was fast asleep as soon as my head hit the pillow. When I woke up, it was after 6:00 p.m. As I was warming up the leftover Chinese food that Annie had brought over, my phone rang.

"Ms. Landon, it's Paul Greer. What's going on?"

I went on to explain what Mia told me. "Is there anything we can do for Jason?"

"Right now there isn't. Even if the police believe Mia and they look into it, short of a confession from Ben Bradley, the charges against Jason will stand. And as we know, there is no physical evidence against Bradley."

"There has to be something we can do."

"Get a confession."

After hanging up, I turned on the TV. I was watching an old Friends episode trying to lighten my mood but was quickly distracted thinking about how I could get Ben to admit to raping Mia. At the moment, nothing was coming to me.

CHAPTER 68

When I woke up in the morning, I was trying to recall the dream I had last night. I remembered being followed by Ben Bradley and running into an alley waiting for him. When I heard footsteps coming, I called out to him and when he showed his face, I shot him twice in the chest. Though the thought of shooting Ben would give me great pleasure, I knew that wouldn't help Jason. I was pretty sure it was Ben who stabbed me in the alley. I just didn't know how I was going to prove it.

While I was on the police force, we had a case where we had a suspect we knew was guilty, but we needed a confession or had to catch this person in the act. The guy had raped two women but there was no DNA. Since the suspect had never seen me, I offered myself up as bait. We knew the subject frequented a hotel bar downtown. I dressed for the part in a black low-cut dress and sat at the bar waiting for this guy to make a move. When he did, he was very smooth and charming. He bought me a drink and we made small talk. About forty-five minutes later, he told me he had a room at the hotel and asked me if I wanted to continue our night upstairs. As soon as we got into the room, he offered me a drink. We were sitting on the bed and he started kissing me before I even had a chance to take a sip of my wine. I asked him to slow down, but he just got more aggressive. It wasn't till he tried putting his hand under my dress that I started fighting him off. At that point, he punched me in the face and I began screaming. I knew my partner and another detective were on the other side of the door, ready to pounce.

I speculated on how I could get Ben Bradley to confess. I didn't think if I asked politely he would comply.

***

The weekend went quickly. Jesse came down to my place and we spent a fairly low-key weekend since I still tired easily. We did manage to go to a Chagall exhibit at the Metropolitan Museum of Art.

Jesse left early Monday morning and I went into the office later in the day. I had ignored a couple of emails from attorneys who needed my assistance. One was a background check on an individual where the attorney's client wanted to invest in a new start-up business. The other was a locate search for someone who was named in a will, therefore, since it's required by New York State that we show due diligence, I had to try to track this person down.

After working on the two cases, I was interested in finding out more about Jonathan Bradley. I believe he knew what his son was up to and turned a blind eye to his behavior. When I looked at my watch, it was 7:00 p.m. I went into the hallway to see if either Cousin Will or the attorney, Larry Banks, were still around, but they appeared to be gone for the day.

I did a few quick searches, seeing what I could find out on Jonathan Bradley. Nothing of significance popped up. Until I did a further background investigation, I was limited to basic searches. I then looked for information on his company. After scrutinizing the internet, I found a small article that said the SEC (the Securities and Exchange Commission) was looking into the firm. That might or might not mean anything. I'd have to delve further into it. It was almost 9:00 p.m. the next time I looked at my watch.

I was packing up my computer, getting ready to leave, when my office went completely dark. I quickly fumbled for my cell phone, switching on the little light in the back of the phone. It was at that moment that I saw the shadow of Ben Bradley and a gun pointing in my direction.

"You couldn't keep your nose where it didn't belong." My heart started racing and my mouth went dry.

"What are you talking about?" I said, trying to keep calm.

"Do you think I'm stupid?"

"No, of course not." This was someone who was young, probably felt cornered, and maybe thought he had nothing to lose. Not the person you want holding a gun on you. I quickly assessed my surroundings and the only way out was through Ben. I could try to reach for my gun in the drawer but I was afraid he would react without thinking and start shooting.

"Listen, Ben. At this point, there's no evidence against you for either the rape of Heather Paxton or Mia Franklin. It's your word against theirs. Don't do anything crazy." I noticed his finger was pressed against the trigger. "Ben, why don't you put the gun down and we'll talk about it. You're not thinking straight."

"Stop telling me what to do," Ben yelled.

"Okay, just relax. What I don't understand is why you had to rape Mia. She would have welcomed your advances since she had a big crush on you."

"You don't get it. I like seeing the fear in their eyes, just like the fear that's in your eyes now. When they scream and beg me not to it's such a high, better than drugs. I did everything to stop you from investigating. My warnings weren't enough for you. Why didn't you just die when I stabbed you? Everything would have worked out perfectly." A cruel smile played on his lips. This guy is really sick. Every part of me was sweating. I needed to act quickly since I knew there was no way I was going to talk him down.

I grabbed the giant paperweight from my desk and threw it at him, hoping I didn't miss. A wild gunshot went off and I quickly ran and lunged at Ben, his gun flying out of his hand. Ben was stronger than I thought, and my breath was coming quickly. He was able to pin me to the ground and grabbed me around my neck. I was having trouble breathing. I was trying to loosen his grip but he held on tight. For a moment, I thought I was going to pass out, but I knew that wasn't an option. With the little strength I had left in my body, I pushed with my legs. Ben loosened his grip for a second, which allowed me to shove him off of me, but he was quick and was on his feet before I had a chance to even get up. He pointed his gun at me and put his foot right where he stabbed me. I was in excruciating pain. Ben was staring down at me, his face contorted with rage. He started to unzip his pants. I tried not to panic, but I knew I didn't have the strength to fight him off.

"Bitch, now you're going to pay."

I had to think quick. With one swift motion, I grabbed his foot and he fell backward. I saw his gun on the floor out of the corner of my eye. I tried to reach for it but Ben was faster.

"Ben, if you walk away now, I promise this never happened." It was my last desperate attempt. Just as he was about to pull the trigger, there was a loud commotion in the hallway outside my office door. For a split second, Ben was distracted. I saw the paperweight on the floor out of the corner of my eye. I grabbed it and threw it at him as hard as I could. He went down and I was able to grab the gun. It took every ounce in me not to pull the trigger.

As I was calling 911, I was trying to get my breathing under control. I sat in my chair, holding my stomach, my body giving out, unable to move.

When the police came, Ben said I had threatened and attacked him. Since I was holding the gun on Ben, the police didn't know who to believe. They brought us both down to the station. After playing the tape recording on my phone of Ben admitting to raping both Heather and Mia and the police verifying that it was not my gun, they released me, but only after they took my statement.

I was barely able to walk as I was leaving the station. The thought of how close I almost came to getting killed sent chills throughout my body. I had no idea who caused the commotion in the hallway. Maybe the people who lived in one of the apartments on the second floor, but I was eternally grateful to whoever they were.

CHAPTER 69

A week later, I was sitting in Jesse's kitchen sipping a glass of wine while Jesse was preparing lunch. I decided to take a few days off to help my body recuperate from all it had been through. I slept through the first day I was here. On the following day, Leo's mother was dropping him off to spend a few hours with Jesse. I was nervous since I wasn't used to being around children. With my cousin Noah it was different since I knew him from the day he was born and what does a baby know anyway. It was easy to make Noah laugh. Leo is already a little person and not easy to fool. I had no idea what to even say to him.

Jesse thinks I'm making too much of it, and that I should just be myself. Leo is going to be a big presence in my life. Was I scared that I wasn't up for the task or was I scared it was more than I bargained for?

"So what are you making for the three of us?" I said, trying to lighten my own mood.

"I thought grilled cheese sandwiches and tomato soup. That will get your arteries flowing."

"It certainly will. Yummy."

"What's going to happen to Mia now that she's admitted to what she did?" Jesse said, as he was busy grilling the sandwiches.

"I heard the school isn't going to let her come back, not after she lied about Jason and was selling drugs to high school kids. I have a feeling she'll probably get probation and court-appointed therapy, but that's just a guess on my part. The good news is the charges against Jason were dropped. According to his mother, Jason is doing a lot better, though she regrets she hadn't told him sooner that she thought he was gay. Maybe if she had, it would have eased his burden. Jason still has to finish his senior year, but I think the school is going to allow him to take online courses so he can graduate on time."

"And what about Ben Bradley?"

"He's out on bail, but hopefully, all the money his father has for a good defense attorney won't keep him out of prison. When his trial comes up for the attempted murder on my life, I'll have to testify. It's a good thing my father taught me how to throw a baseball. It came in handy as I was aiming the paperweight at Ben."

The doorbell rang. A few seconds later, I overheard Jesse talking to Leo's mother in the hallway. Leo walked into the kitchen and approached me.

"Hi, I'm Leo. Are you Maddie?"

"I am. Your dad has told me a lot about you." Though Leo had lighter coloring than Jesse, you couldn't mistake the eyes. They were dark and penetrating, just like Jesse's.

"You do what my dad does," he said.

"Yes, except I work in New York and he works here." Jesse was right. Leo was a very bright, inquisitive kid and seemed to speak his mind.

Jesse came back into the kitchen and Leo went to him. Jesse winked at me, and for the moment, I was willing to put all my fears aside.

THE END

Thank you for reading my novel. As an author your feedback is invaluable. I would appreciate your taking time to leave a review wherever you purchase your books.

ACKNOWLEDGMENTS

First and foremost, I want to thank all my readers. Without you my books would have no voice.

Thirty years ago, I started writing my first novel in a notebook. At that time my career as a private investigator was just beginning and I put my writing aside to concentrate on developing my business. Twenty-five years later, I reached into my closet and grabbed that notebook and realized how much I wanted to continue writing. Little did I know at that time how much joy writing would bring into my life. Now seven books later the love I feel every time I sit down to write inspires me.

My heartfelt gratitude to my wonderful friends for their love and support. Their continued encouragement gets me through the rough patches. A special thanks to the beautiful Scarsdale Library where I came everyday to write this novel.

Thank you to everyone who has helped with the completion of this book: The team at BooksGoSocial for their assistance with the editing and cover; IndiesUnitedPublishing for their help in publishing and marketing my book; and to Alexa Recio and Siobhan Mitchell for their valuable input even when I didn't want to hear it, thank you.

Also, to my dear friend, Ann Spadafora, who took on the task of reading my manuscript to check for any mistakes I may have missed.

And finally, to my daughter, Carrie Lozo, my biggest supporter and fan, whose insights have contributed to the writing of my book. With my love and deepest gratitude for always being there for me.

ABOUT THE AUTHOR

As a private investigator with more than thirty years of experience, Ellen Shapiro's professional expertise has brought an authenticity to her characters and the storylines she has created for her novels. Acting on her passion for writing, she enrolled in the Sarah Lawrence Writing Institute where she took courses in creative writing.

Ellen has written articles in her field for both local and nationwide newspapers and is the author of seven mystery novels. Ellen is a member of Mystery Writers of America and resides in Scarsdale, New York.

Author website: eshapiropi9.wixsite.com/ellen-shapiro
Facebook: @facebook.com/ellen.shapiro.948
Twitter: @twitter.com/EllenShapiro10
Instagram: @instagram.com/eshapiroauthor